STATE OF THE UNION

STATE OF THE ONION

JULIE HYZY

WHEELER
CHIVERS

This Large Print edition is published by Wheeler Publishing, Waterville, Maine, USA and by BBC Audiobooks Ltd, Bath, England.
Wheeler Publishing, a part of Gale, Cengage Learning.
Copyright © 2008 by Tekno Books.
The moral right of the author has been asserted.
A White House Chef Mystery.

The text of this Large Print edition is unabridged.
Other aspects of the book may vary from the original edition.
Set in 16 pt. Plantin.
Printed on permanent paper.

LIBRARY OF CONGRESS CATALOGING-IN-PUBLICATION DATA

Hyzy, Julie A.
   State of the onion / by Julie Hyzy.
     p. cm. — (A White House chef mystery)
     ISBN-13: 978-1-59722-725-4 (alk. paper)
     ISBN-10: 1-59722-725-0 (alk. paper)
     1. White House (Washington, D.C.) — Fiction. 2. Cooks — Fiction. 3. Washington (D.C.) — Fiction. 4. Large type books. I. Title.
PS3608.Y98S73 2008
813'.6—dc22   2008000324

BRITISH LIBRARY CATALOGUING-IN-PUBLICATION DATA AVAILABLE

Published in 2008 in the U.S. by arrangement with The Berkley Publishing Group, a division of Penguin Group (USA) Inc.
Published in 2008 in the U.K. by arrangement with The Berkley Publishing Group, a division of Penguin Group (USA) Inc.

U.K. Hardcover: 978 1 405 64520 1 (Chivers Large Print)
U.K. Softcover: 978 1 405 64521 8 (Camden Large Print)

Printed in the United States of America
1 2 3 4 5 6 7 12 11 10 09 08

For Mike . . .
Thanks

ACKNOWLEDGMENTS

What wouldn't I give to be invited to dinner at the White House! Better yet, to spend just one day in the White House kitchen. I'd love to work alongside the women and men there who personify excellence. Just one day. It would be a dream come true.

While no one actually said they'd have to kill me if they told me the truth, researching this novel has presented some interesting challenges. I'd like to thank all the Secret Service personnel and staff at the White House who answered my peculiar questions about how Ollie might "do this or that" as best they could. And I'd like to thank the Department of Homeland Security for not breaking down my door after my many Internet searches of "Camp David," "terrorist," "assassin," "White House floor plan," and the like.

So many wonderful people have helped me to the extent they could without compromising security. Any and all errors with regard to the White House and its protocols are mine.

A sincere thank you to those who helped me with firsthand information: Karna Small Bodman, Tony Burton, and Chris Grabenstein. Thanks also to Paul Garbarczyk, Mitch Bramstaedt, and Marla Garbarczyk, who provided me with a plethora of valuable resources. And to Congresswoman Judy Biggert, whose office arranged for my White House tour.

Enormous thanks to Marty Greenberg of Tekno Books for allowing me to create Olivia and her pals — a true thrill. Thanks also to John Helfers from Tekno for his editing expertise and unflagging good cheer. Also from Tekno, many thanks to Denise Little, who put me on the right path to learn White House lore and whose innovative recipes keep Ollie cooking.

I also wish to express my gratitude to my editor, Natalee Rosenstein, at Berkley Prime Crime, for having faith in me, and for taking time out at Bouchercon to meet and talk. I truly appreciated the welcome.

If it weren't for the Second Amendment Foundation and the Tartaro family, Ollie wouldn't have a clue about firearms. Of course, she's still learning . . . and she needs lots more practice.

My dear friend Ken Rand inspires me every day. And he'd be the first to remind me that Max Ehrmann does, too.

From the moment this project began, my writing partner, Michael A. Black, offered support, advice, and unfailing encouragement. I wouldn't be here without him.

I am exceptionally blessed with a wonderful family and great friends who encourage me to follow my dreams. Thank you to Curt, Robyn, Sara, and Biz. You guys are my life.

Finally, special thanks to the Southland Scribes, Sisters in Crime, Mystery Writers of America, and to the entire writing community. What a privilege it is to belong to such an interesting and generous group.

CHAPTER 1

I slid my employee pass into the card reader at the Northeast gate of the White House, and waited for verification — a long, shrill chirp that always made me wince. The pedestrian gate unlocked with a *click* and one of the guards, Freddie, emerged from the checkpoint to meet me. Like all of the staff here, he was fit, smart, and imposing. But he had a soft spot for those of us in the kitchen. We gave the guys cookies when we had time to make an extra batch.

"Hey, Ollie," he said, looking at the bulky parcel in my hand, "What's that?"

I pulled the commemorative silver frying pan out from its bag and smiled as I ran my fingers over the words engraved on its base. "Henry's retirement gift," I said. "Think he'll like it?" Henry Cooley, the White House executive chef, was formally retiring after many years of dedicated service. All of us who worked in the White House kitchen

11

had chipped in to give him something to remember us by.

"It's cool," Freddie said. "He'll love it."

"I hope so." I eased the pan back into its bag just as the sky rumbled and a crack of lightning zinged from the direction of the Washington Memorial. I grimaced. "I practically ran from the Metro to beat the storm. Looks like I just made it."

"Like the Prez says, 'You're helping conserve energy and battle traffic congestion,'" he said, jotting notes on his clipboard. "Be proud of it, Ollie. Or should I start calling you Executive Chef Paras?"

"I am proud. I'm also getting wet," I said. My stomach did its customary flip-flop when Freddie mentioned the executive chef position, and I struggled to quell the excitement that rose every time I thought about being appointed to succeed Henry. "Besides, I don't have the job yet. Nobody knows who'll end up running the kitchen."

A grin split Freddie's dark face. "Well . . . I know who I'm rooting for. Just don't forget us uniformed guys when you get that promotion. We get hungry, too."

"I'll bake a batch of celebration goodies just for you."

Freddie stepped back out of the morning rain and into the well-lit guard post. Shoul-

12

dering my purse, I gripped the bag to my chest and headed up the walk to the East Appointment Gate, hunching my shoulders against the growing storm. Like many White House employees, I commuted to work via the Metro, but it only took me so far. And in the rain, a three-block walk from the station to the check-in seemed to take forever. Thank goodness I was almost there.

The sky was overcast and the weather wet and cold for mid-May — a perfect day to spend cooking. But I'd snuck out to pick up Henry's gift, and I needed to get back before tonight's dinner preparations began.

Just as I passed the first tri-flagged lamppost, a commotion up on the North Lawn caught my attention. There were no White House tours scheduled today — no one should have been in that area. I turned and watched in disbelief as a man raced between trees from the direction of the north fountain toward the East Wing of the White House, two Secret Service men in furious pursuit.

My breath caught as the intruder pounded across the high-ground lawn. Although my view was skewed — the North Lawn was elevated a good four feet from the east walkway where I stood — I could see that this guy was long-legged and moving fast.

13

He was clearly in excellent physical shape, but I knew he'd never make it. Our Secret Service personnel are the most dedicated and best trained in the world. If he didn't surrender soon, they'd quit yelling at him to stop and would start shooting. But right now the runner, one arm pumping, the other wrapped around a black portfolio, was outpacing the agents by at least two strides.

The guy had to be nuts. Ever since 9/11, anyone with common sense knew better than to try to circumvent the enhanced White House security. A threat to our president's safety meant getting shot almost on sight.

I crouched, scanning upward to see the ever present snipers posted atop the White House roof, their dark silhouettes menacing against the gray sky. They jockeyed for position, taking aim. But the profusion of trees on the North Lawn, in full bloom, apparently provided too much cover.

The man didn't look back, not even when the Secret Service guys bellowed at him to stop. He sprinted faster than I've ever seen a person run before. He zigzagged, staying beneath the cover of the trees, as if he knew exactly what he was doing.

My heart pounded and my limbs tingled as I stared. It was like watching a terrifying

14

movie. But this was real. It was happening right in front of me.

Then the requisite emergency training kicked in.

Don't panic. Think.

I stepped off the pavement and ducked behind one of the tall trees lining the walkway. Digging out my cell phone, I dialed the White House security number, even as I kept an eye on what was going on. Remembering to breathe, I also reminded myself that the best thing to do was to stay out of the professionals' way. They'd have this guy caught in no time. If he didn't slow down, he was in for a nasty tumble down the east embankment. And that would get him nowhere except jammed between the ground's gentle slope and the iron fence that surrounded it.

I could see that he had Middle Eastern features: a dark complexion, full mustache and beard, and shoulder-length black hair, which trailed after him like a short cape. His expression — white teeth gritted in a tight grimace — made him look like a snarling Doberman.

A flat-voiced woman answered the phone. "State the nature of the emergency."

"A man," I said. I told myself to stay calm, but my body rebelled, making my voice tremble. "On the North Lawn. There are two Secret Service agents chasing him."

"Yes," she said. "We are aware." I heard clicking in the background. "Your name?"

"Olivia Paras, I'm one of the assistant chefs."

Another click. "Where are you, Ms. Paras?"

I was about to tell her when the man threw the thick folder to his left. Both agents' eyes followed the item's movement. The man stopped, spun, and launched himself at them. He used his split-second advantage to grab one agent's right arm, twisting it around in some kind of martial arts move — and effectively using the man's body as a shield from the other agent. Cracking his elbow into the captured agent's temple, he knocked the man out cold and snatched his pistol from a suddenly limp hand.

Now he had a gun.

I was frozen in place.

"Ms. Paras?"

I almost couldn't speak.

"He . . ."

The second agent dropped into a shooting stance, his firearm extended. The intruder gripped the first agent and whirled, releasing the unconscious figure like an

Olympian throwing a hammer. The second agent fired, but missed. His colleague's body slammed into him before he could get another shot off, knocking them both to the ground.

"The agents are down — he's got a gun!" I said.

The intruder didn't wait to see if either agent would get up. He retrieved his package and sprinted away.

As he ran, he lifted the firearm, pointed it at the sky, and thumbed its side. The magazine fell out of the pistol, tumbling behind him. A second later, the gun followed.

"He just tossed the gun," I said, my words sounding slow and stupid. Not surprising, since my mind was shouting that this couldn't be happening. "He's running again. But . . ."

"Where are you, Ms. Paras?"

I wondered how the woman on the other end of the phone could stay so calm at a time like this. I was having a hard time sorting through the flood of stimuli to give her crucial information. I swallowed hard.

"He's headed toward the East Wing," I finally managed. Then, remembering to answer her question, I added, "I'm on the walkway, just north of the East Appointment Gate. Behind a tree."

17

"Stay there." I heard her address someone else before she returned to me. "Stay out of the way."

I didn't say anything; I was in perfect agreement with that command.

I peeked around the other side of the tree, going up on my toes to see better, just as more Secret Service agents appeared: Five sentries snapping into action, positioning themselves like the pillars of the North Portico. They stood along the East Wing, firearms drawn. They aimed for the man, who was now close enough for me to hear the wet *splat* of his footfalls in the grass.

The intruder spotted the guards and altered his trajectory, veering in my direction.

Then shots sounded.

And I was in the line of fire.

I dropped to the ground, staying low even as I watched. I told myself that being behind a tree could save me from getting nailed as an innocent bystander.

I hoped to God that was true.

Transfixed by terror, I was powerless to move. The sounds of shouting agents and popping gunfire washed over me like some video game sound track.

But this was real.

The man did a skip-step.

He must have gotten hit.

Then, unbelievably, he doubled his speed, heading right for the sudden embankment decline. He was sure in for a surprise when the ground dropped out from under him.

"Stay where you are, Ms. Paras," the woman said into my ear. "And don't hang up."

The intruder was bent in half and weaving from side to side as he ran, trying to avoid the bullets of the sentries and the snipers. Secret Service agents were racing this way now. But they were so far behind that I worried the guy might get away after all.

A sudden sprint. And then, as if he knew precisely where the embankment declined, he leaped into the air, clearing the ground-drop and the iron fence that surrounded it. It looked like slow motion, though it was anything but. Pedaling madly as he soared above the fence, he landed in a thumping skid, rolling onto the pavement less than fifty feet from my position. He boosted himself upright, and in a couple of hops, cleared two small decorative fences that kept people from walking on the grass. He was headed right for me. As if he knew I was there.

I should have shouted into the phone. I

should have screamed.

But I didn't. I realized that I was here, at this moment, with an opportunity. I was the one person in the perfect place to do something just right. I knew he couldn't have seen me. He was too focused on getting away.

I dropped the phone. I looked around. But Henry's retirement gift was all I had.

The man closed the distance between us in a heartbeat.

I grabbed the skillet with both hands and jumped to my feet. As he ran past I slammed him with it, right in the stomach. I heard his grunt of pain, and an exclamation in a language I didn't understand. He sank to the ground.

"Ms. Paras?" a tinny voice called from my discarded phone.

I shouted to the agents, "Here! Over here!" I jumped, hoping they could see it was me — hoping they wouldn't open fire again. "Don't shoot!"

The man's expression, though suffused with pain, softened when he looked up at me. Dark brown eyes met mine. "Please," he said.

As he spoke, he scuttled to his feet faster than I would have thought possible. Not dazed or weak at all.

I didn't think. There wasn't time to think.

I whacked him upside the head with the frying pan — the impact reverberated up my arm and sounded like a melon being dropped into a stainless steel sink. He fell to his knees, grunted an expletive.

After a hit like that, I figured he'd be out cold for sure.

But he turned to face me. Still conscious.

I took a step forward, ready to smack him again.

"Over here," I screamed, panic making my voice shake.

The intruder tumbled sideways, cradling his head in one hand, blood dripping from the top of his scalp. His legs worked like he was trying to ride a bicycle, and this time his words were labored. "Please," he said, "must warn . . . president. Danger."

I stood openmouthed, heart pounding, wielding the pan like a tennis racket, when the man's foot gained purchase and he started to pull himself up again.

"Please," he said. "I . . . must . . . warn . . ."

I cracked him again, this time slamming his shoulder.

From behind me, I heard the welcome sound of running feet.

"Ollie, get back," Agent Craig Sanderson said as they surrounded us in a half circle.

"Quick. We've got him covered."

They didn't have to tell me twice.

I had a good view of the man from the side, but he kept his face down. His eyes were clenched shut, and he looked awful. Blood dripped from the gash in his head, pooling in the grass below him. He held his hands out, open and empty, shouting to the agents, "I am unarmed."

I noticed now that he wore shabby clothing, but brand-new, high-end athletic shoes and what looked like body armor. No wonder the shots hadn't stopped him. This intruder had come prepared.

The portfolio he carried was tucked under his leg.

I backed up farther as fast as I could, praying I wouldn't trip.

As I cleared their established perimeter, the Secret Service closed in on the intruder, bending his arms behind his back. With a circle of .357 semiautomatics trained on the guy, two agents stepped in to put some kind of plastic zip-tie thing on his wrists. Lots more operatives gathered, and Agent Thomas MacKenzie broke away from the group to gently remove the skillet from my white-knuckled fist. "You okay?"

I nodded. But I wasn't. All of a sudden my knees went weak; my hands started shaking. I steadied myself by grabbing his shoulder.

"Better get out of the way." He gestured toward a bench across the walk. He held my arm as we made our way over. "Sit down." In a low voice, he asked, "What the hell are you doing here?"

I knew his irritation had nothing to do with me. He was worried about the president and this situation. "I was picking up Henry's gift," I said. "The skillet." I pointed to it in Tom's hand.

Back in the knot of Secret Service personnel, Agent Sanderson lifted the intruder to his feet. Then Sanderson gave an exclamation of surprise, and I heard the sound of a body hitting the ground. I craned my neck to see better.

The intruder lay flat on his back, his bound hands behind him. He stared upward, his gaze still radiating fierce energy, but his voice was strangely conversational.

"It's good to see you again, Craig," he said. "How is Kate? And the children?"

CHAPTER 2

Tom's hand dropped from its protective perch on my shoulder and he stared, as we all did, at the bloody man on the grass.

Agent Sanderson said, "Naveen?" then glanced up, saw me and Tom and the skillet. "Oh, Christ. Gentlemen, let's get him out of here."

Brusquely, Tom took me by the elbow, stood me up and steered me toward the East Appointment Gate. "Let's get you out of here, too."

He handed Henry's dented and bloodied skillet to another agent, who carried it gingerly, held away from his body.

"Hey, I just bought that," I said. "It's a gift."

"Sorry, ma'am," the agent said as he placed the abused frying pan into a large, clear plastic bag, "It's evidence now."

"But . . ." I said, uselessly.

I could feel Tom's arm pressuring me to

move on. "Henry's not retiring for a couple of weeks yet," he said, "you'll probably have it back before then."

"Probably?"

He didn't answer. Just kept us walking. Tom was six-foot-four, 238 pounds of muscled Secret Service agent. I'm five-foot-two, 110 pounds of busy chef. I'm very strong for my size — handling industrial-sized pots full of boiling water all day will do that for a lady. But I wasn't anywhere near strong enough to resist Tom. It was no contest.

Twisting, I wriggled around in his grip, trying to watch what was going on inside the tight circle of agents. Although there were women in the Secret Service, there apparently weren't any on duty this morning. All I could see were strong, broad shoulders clad in business suits, forming a cage that the intruder could not possibly escape. Between the agents' legs, I could see the man being pulled from the ground. I heard him talking with Agent Sanderson, but I couldn't make out what was being said.

"Naveen, huh?" I asked. Sanderson had called him by name.

"Come on," Tom said with impatience.

I planted my feet. The hundred tasks I'd been prioritizing as I walked back to work could wait. Even I knew that this morning's excitement would throw the First Family's schedule into a tizzy. "I want to see how this ends, since I was in on the start of it," I said.

"This is a crime scene. You don't belong here."

I put my hands on my hips and stared up at him. The flat, expressionless look was gone from Tom's eyes. He was mad. At me. For what, I had no idea.

"But I'm a material witness."

His lips compressed. "Don't you have work to do in the kitchen?"

"Yes. I do. It'll keep. Craig knows that guy," I said. "It sounded like they were friends."

The storm had passed and the sun was making a welcome appearance — but I could see doubt clouding Tom's blue eyes. He glanced over to the cluster of activity around the intruder and I realized why he was so ticked off with me. He wanted to be part of that group, not the bodyguard who made sure the assistant chef made it to the kitchen safely.

"He's bluffing," Tom said. "Guys like that are pretty resourceful. He must have studied Craig's dossier."

"No." I shook my head. "Craig recognized him."

When Tom took my arm again, I let him lead me the rest of the way. "I'm fine," I said, when we reached the staff entrance. "Go on back. I don't need an escort from here."

He didn't need telling twice.

Before I was through security, he was lost in the sea of agents bustling along the walkway.

Although the number of staff often mushroomed to twenty for state dinners, the permanent White House kitchen staff numbered only five. Marcel, the executive pastry chef, had agreed to cover for me while I was out picking up Henry's gift. In repose, Marcel's black, aristocratic face could have graced the cover of any men's magazine, but when he was worked up, his large eyes popped, making him look like an alert, dark-skinned Muppet.

"Olivia! *Qu'est-ce que* . . ." he said as I shed my jacket and opened the linen cabinet. "What happened?" Whenever Marcel got agitated or upset, he forgot himself and dropped into his native language for some colorful invective. I'd picked up a lot of French when I studied in Paris, but my vocabulary had more to do with cooking than with street patois. I didn't understand Marcel very well when he really got on a tear, but I sure loved to hear him talk. One of these days I needed to look up the words he yelled so fast. I didn't want to use them in public until I was sure they weren't unforgivable.

Marcel finally wound down enough to lapse back into English. "They have shut down the building," he said.

"I know." I sat. "Secret Service told me."

"What?" he asked. "And you, *mon petit chou* . . . How you say . . . ? You look like three-week-old escarole."

"Thanks a lot." I blew out a long breath. My little adventure had taken a toll on me. Now that I was safe, back in the haven of the kitchen, I could feel cracks working their way through my usually calm veneer. Forcing a smile as I looked up into his worried face, I lied. "I'm fine."

"*Oui,* and I am the pope," he said.

I stood up, but my hands shook so much as I pulled out my white tunic and tall toque that I wondered if I could put my uniform on.

My hesitation to talk wasn't just nerves. I wondered how much I was allowed to say about what had just happened. The less I said, the better, I imagined. But since the attack had happened outside on the North Lawn, where tourist video cameras were always running, I figured the whole thing would be on CNN or FOX News any minute now. Plus, Tom hadn't told me to keep my mouth shut.

Thinking about it, I was pretty sure I didn't need to maintain total secrecy. There were always newscopters hovering around. We lived in an up-to-the-minute world. The incident was probably already on the wires.

"The Secret Service caught some guy trying to get in."

"Merde." Marcel strode over to the corridor that connected our busy kitchen with the rest of the lower level, and peered out. "I saw agents running by earlier, but it is quiet now. Where did this happen? Did you see him?"

"I saw him," I said, hoping that would be enough to keep Marcel happy. "And Agent MacKenzie made sure I got back here safely. So, everything's good."

"Yes," Marcel said, with a wry pull to his lips. "If the oh-so-handsome Thomas escorted you up here, then I'm certain everything is quite good. For you."

I ignored his comment. Striding back into the heart of the kitchen, I was all business.

"Anything else going on?"

"Quiet as, how you say, a grave."

"I think you mean *tomb*."

Marcel shrugged. "Henry is still at the White House Mess." He made a face. Marcel hated the term we used for the other kitchen, the one run by the navy that serviced the round-the-clock staff. "He will be back shortly. But where is Henry's gift? Was it not ready?"

Shoot, in all the excitement I had already forgotten what I supposed to be carrying. I was about to answer when the chief usher, Paul Vasquez, came into the kitchen. As head of the executive residence staff, Paul dropped by occasionally, usually to confer with Henry over menu decisions. Today his handsome features were strained, and he ran a hand through his salt-and-pepper hair, a gesture I'd seen him use only during periods of stress. "Olivia, may I have a word with you?"

Uh-oh.

I followed him through the corridor and into the China Room. It was one of my favorite rooms, and I couldn't wait until the day my mother finally made the trip out here to visit me. She'd be captivated, as I was, by the gorgeous display — and the wealth of American history it represented.

When I was first hired at the White House, I'd poked my nose in here fairly often, determined to memorize which china pattern belonged to which First Family. I'd gotten pretty good at it.

As Paul gestured me into one of the two chairs flanking the room's fireplace — the one with its back to the door — I reviewed the china patterns to myself in an effort to calm my nerves. Whatever Paul wanted probably had something to do with my being outside when I shouldn't have been. News traveled fast around here.

He ran his hand through his hair again before meeting my eyes. "I've just been notified about the disturbance outside. The Secret Service has characterized your involvement in the incident as . . . reckless."

I opened my mouth to protest, but he stopped me with a look.

"You got in the middle of a firefight," he said.

"How was I supposed to know I was walking into it? I was just heading back to work from —"

"I know all about your important errand."

That didn't surprise me. Paul knew everything that went on in the White House.

He sat all the way back in his chair — I sat at the edge of mine, with my hands

31

folded in my lap like a schoolgirl's. I didn't think whacking an intruder with a pan was cause for White House dismissal, but I was pretty sure that interfering with official Secret Service business was.

I kept silent, uncomfortably aware of each inhalation in the quiet room.

"Where is Henry's gift now?" Paul asked.

That surprised me. Paul didn't know? "One of the agents took it."

He nodded; undoubtedly some loose end was tied up for him. "Agent Sanderson is on his way to debrief you. He's understandably . . . upset . . . by the breach in security." Paul stared at one of the bas-relief figures carved into the fireplace surround, but I could tell he wasn't seeing it. "Your actions today will have serious repercussions for all of us. We can't ever afford to do anything that might put ourselves at risk, because to do so puts the White House — and everyone in it — at risk." When he met my eyes again, his expression softened. "But I have to tell you, Ollie, I personally think it was a damn brave thing you did."

When he glanced over my shoulder, I turned. Craig Sanderson crossed the threshold, a dour look on his face.

As he left, Paul patted my shoulder and leaned down to whisper in my ear, "You'll be okay."

Craig strode across the carpeting, emanating anger with every step. He sat and stared at me, waiting a long time before he spoke. The tension in the room grew so tight that the china on display almost seemed to hum.

"Ms. Paras."

Craig and I were on a first-name basis and for the first time, his gentle Kentucky drawl took on a menacing air. The fact that he wasn't calling me Ollie made me feel nervous and small. I didn't like it. "Yes, Agent Sanderson?"

His eyes snapped up, warning me to not take this lightly. I wasn't, but if he had a problem with what I'd done this morning, I wished he would just say so. At least then I'd have a chance to explain what happened.

"We have a tape of your call to the emergency operator."

I waited.

"She instructed you to stay low and get out of the way."

"I did."

His eyebrows rose and he continued, enunciating each word with slow precision. "Then how do you explain the fact that when we reached you, you were attacking an armed intruder with a frying pan?"

"He ran right by where I was hiding. I was

the only person in place to stop him. So I stopped him. But you're wrong — he wasn't armed."

"You don't know that."

"Yes, I do. I saw him drop the agent's gun as he ran. I was just inches away from him when I hit him." I thought about the black portfolio the guy had been carrying, and I suddenly realized that I truly had no idea as to whether he'd been armed or not. So, I took a different approach with Craig. "You know, I heard him ask you about your family. Is he a friend of yours?"

For the first time since he'd come into the room, Craig's face registered emotion — I'd surprised him. Before he could answer, I touched his arm. "He really *was* trying to warn the president about something, wasn't he?"

Craig's muscles were taut beneath my hand. I pulled away.

"No," he said. "He was not. He was an unauthorized intruder and he is being dealt with even as we speak. As for you," he said, glaring, "in the future, when you are given a direct order by *any* of the security staff — and that includes uniformed guards as well as the emergency operators — you will follow that order without deviation. Is that clear?"

There was so much more I wanted to say, but this was not the time. "Yes. Very clear."

Nodding as though granting absolution, he continued in a gentler tone, "Now, tell me what happened, from your perspective, and let me know exactly what he said to you."

I went through everything, including my fears and my puzzlement at the running man's quiet demeanor when he tried to talk to me. I tried to read Craig, tried to see behind his blank, professional expression, but I got nothing.

When I finished, Craig stood. "I will direct Chief Usher Vasquez to eliminate all mention of this incident from your personnel files. It will not appear on your permanent record. But don't let it happen again." He fixed me with a look that was anything but friendly, and left.

I wasn't fooled. The only reason my involvement in the skirmish wasn't going on my record was because of how bad it looked to have a little lady assistant chef stop the bad guy that the big macho Secret Service couldn't catch.

I resisted the urge to make a face at Craig's retreating back.

To keep my hands busy, I chopped fresh

tomatoes and onions for use later in the day. We always needed things chopped. When one of the other assistants, Cyan, came in a few minutes later, she shrugged out of her jacket and donned an outfit similar to mine, jabbering all the while.

"You should see all the network crews out around the perimeter. Lafayette Park is a mob scene. What's going on? I thought the president's news conference was scheduled for tomorrow. Wasn't it? I didn't think it was today — he's not back in residence till this afternoon, right? Did Marcel make coffee?"

"Over there," I said. The coffee carafe sat where it did every day, but Cyan had a powerful need to keep conversation going. She was a few years younger than I. Taller, too, but then again, almost everyone was. Her red hair was pulled back into a half pony, which bounced as she made her way to the carafe.

I thought about what she'd said. The president wasn't due back to the White House till later. The determined trespasser, Naveen, had obviously gotten some bad intelligence if he'd come to warn the president on a day when he wasn't even in the country.

"Where's Marcel?" she asked.

"He went over to the White House Mess to meet Henry."

"Did you pick up the gift? Can I see it before they get back?"

The awareness that I'd lost the commemorative pan during this morning's encounter hit me hard — like I'd been the one slammed in the head. "I don't have it here," I said, not wanting to explain further. Not now, at least.

I bit my lip and kept working. I always chopped onions next to an empty stove burner, with the flame turned high. Cyan, used to my habits, ignored me as she stood before the computer monitor to study the day's schedule. Late last night, Henry and I had updated it.

"What's next?" she asked, clicking ahead on the calendar.

"Getting ready for India's prime minister," I said. "He's arriving this afternoon, and meeting with the president this evening. Remember that menu we worked up a while back?"

"Oh, yeah," Cyan said. "The one you came up with when Henry was on vacation. I hate working so far in advance."

I laughed. "And so you're working here — why?" The meals we designed were so scrupulously planned that we always started weeks in advance, to be certain to get everything just right.

"I'm just saying I like spontaneity."

"Speaking of spontaneity," I said, looking up, "what color today?"

"Emerald green." She blinked wide eyes at me so I could appreciate her contact lenses.

Returning to my chopping, I shook my head. "You change so often that I've forgotten what your real eye color is."

"Blue." She grinned. "Just like my name."

"Good morning," the president said, striding into the kitchen's work area.

My hands stopped mid chop.

President Harrison R. Campbell had a boyish face, but a statesman's bearing. He'd taken office in January, upsetting the incumbent by a wide margin, his victory due in no small part to his platform of unity.

"I thought you were in Reykjavik, sir," I said before I could keep the words from tumbling out.

Two Secret Service men in dark suits followed him in. The White House kitchen has relatively narrow aisles running between cabinets, countertops, and our center work area. Although Cyan and I were small, the president's imposing authority and the two giants behind him made for some cramped quarters.

"Nope," he answered — casually, like I had any right to question his whereabouts. "I got in late last night." He pointed to the pile of minced onions on the far end of my cutting board and then to the flame flicking upward from the range's burner. "Cuts the crying, doesn't it?" he asked.

Startled that he noticed, I stammered. "Yes . . . yes. It does."

"My mother used to do the same thing."

I smiled. "Mine, too."

The fact that he'd been in residence last night made me remember my musings about the intruder's erroneous intelligence. The man had been right after all. He'd claimed to want to warn the president — who shouldn't have been here this morning, but was. I tucked away that little tidbit as I shut off the stove and wiped my hands.

President Campbell towered over me, but smiled as he made a small gesture to the two agents behind him. "May I have a word with you, Olivia?"

Like I would say no.

"Sure," I said, then winced at my flip-sounding response. "I mean, yes, of course, sir." I turned to look for a quiet corner, but the two agents had already directed Cyan out of the room.

The moment it was quiet, the president fixed his bright blue stare on me. "I want to thank you for what you did this morning."

Surprised, all I could manage was, "Oh." And despite the worry that I'd say something stupid if I continued talking, I plunged on. "It was an honor. Sir."

Wearing the same expression he did during difficult press briefings, he nodded. "The Secret Service is handling the incident in cooperation with other agencies, and the man has been taken into custody. I just wanted to let you know so that you don't worry about your safety here at the White House."

My safety?

"I wasn't worried." Words raced through my mind, all out of order. I'd never had so much difficulty putting sentences together. "That is . . . not for myself. The man was trying to get to you, sir. He said he needed to warn you."

"You spoke with him?"

"No," I said. I pictured myself standing over the guy, skillet in hand. "It was more like he tried to talk to me."

The president waited.

"He . . . he said you were in danger."

The president's face was grim. "As are we all, in times like these." We both felt the weight of his words. "The security staff might have a few more questions for you. Don't be alarmed if they call you in again."

He must have caught my quick glance at the clock.

"I didn't have a chance to eat breakfast this morning," he said. "Scrambled eggs and toast will be enough for now." He smiled at me. "And Mrs. Campbell informs me that tonight's menu for India's prime minister is your creation."

I nodded.

"Then I'm very much looking forward to dinner."

"Thank you, sir. I hope everyone enjoys it."

"I'm sure we all will."

He stretched out his hand. It was only the second time I'd shaken the president's hand, but this time was just as thrilling as the first. "And, Ollie, one more thing." He fixed me with those intense blues again. "Other than Secret Service personnel, I would appreciate it if you don't speak of this morning's events with anyone else."

CHAPTER 3

"Ollie, are you okay? What's happening?" Henry walked in moments later, talking up a storm. "I just passed the president in the corridor. Was he in here with you?"

I opened my mouth to speak, but stopped myself as Cyan and Marcel appeared behind Henry. Not thirty seconds before, the president of the United States of America had asked me not to discuss this with anyone, and here I was about to spill the spaghetti with my coworkers.

"Yeah," I said, "he'd like scrambled eggs for breakfast."

Henry glanced in the direction the president had exited and gave me a thoughtful look. "He came down here to tell you that in person?"

I nodded.

Although he was set to retire on his sixty-seventh birthday, Henry was still one of the most vibrant and quick-witted people I knew. He was also the most talented chef I'd ever worked under. It was just in the past couple of years that I'd noticed him taste-testing more often, as evidenced by his expanding waistline, and delegating the more physically demanding tasks to us. His light brown hair had started to thin and go gray at the temples, but his voice was just as resonant as it had been when I'd joined his staff during the administration immediately prior to this one.

Cyan's eyes widened. "That's all he said? Why did he have to talk with you in person, then? Alone? I bet it had something to do with all the commotion outside this morning. Did it? Hey, you must have been outside when it happened, weren't you?"

Henry picked up on Cyan's comment, but she didn't seem to notice her gaffe. "What commotion? You were outside, Ollie?"

I shook my head, "I forgot my keys down by the staff entrance." I hated lying to Henry, but between the president's words and the need to keep my errand secret if we were to pull off our surprise, I didn't think I had much choice.

He smiled. "Maybe you should tie those keys around your neck." He let out a satisfied sigh. "As for the commotion, I'm sure we'll hear more about it later."

Cyan moved closer. "So, what did the president really say?"

"Not much." I pointed to the computer monitor. "President Campbell said he was looking forward to the big dinner tonight. And that he hadn't had breakfast and he's hungry. We should probably get those scrambled eggs started."

"Oh, come on. He must have wanted something. What was it?" Cyan took a deep breath which, I knew, heralded another slew of questions.

Henry raised his hand, silencing her. "Less talk, more work." To me, he said, "Say no more, Ollie. The president's meals are our first responsibility. Scrambled eggs it is."

We set to work on a second breakfast. The timing was tough because of the official dinner tonight, but it wasn't anything we couldn't handle.

In addition to the scrambled eggs, we prepared bacon — crisp — wheat and rye toast, fruit, coffee, orange juice, and Henry's Famous Hash Browns. More than just pan-fried potatoes, Henry used his own combination of seasonings that made my mouth water every time he prepared the dish. The president and First Lady were so impressed with the recipe that they insisted we serve them at every official breakfast function.

Henry wielded the frying pan with authority, flipping his special ingredients so they danced like popcorn, sizzling as bits landed back in the searing hot oil. "Work fast, my friends. A hungry president is bad for the country!"

After the meal was plated and sent to the family quarters, we cleaned up the kitchen and began preparations for lunch. Then it was time to pull out the stops as we got the official dinner together for India's prime minister. This wasn't as significant an event as a state dinner, where guest lists often topped one hundred, and we were required to pull in a couple dozen temporary assistants to help. This was a more sedate affair; it required a great deal of effort, but it was certainly manageable for a staff of five.

I'd designed a flavorful menu, and the First Lady, after tasting the samples we provided, had approved. We'd feature some of the best we had to offer: chilled asparagus soup; halibut and basmati rice with pistachio nuts and currants; bibb lettuce and citrus vinaigrette; and one of Marcel's show-stopping desserts. We'd done as much as we could in advance without sacrificing freshness or quality, but the time had come to marshal the troops and get everything in the pipeline for the big dinner.

Talk among us turned, as it inevitably did, to the subject nearest to our hearts — the First Lady's choice for Henry's successor.

After months of interviews and auditions, the field had been narrowed down to two: Laurel Anne Braun and me. Laurel Anne was a former White House sous-chef, and host of the wildly popular television show *Cooking for the Best.* She and I had worked together at a top restaurant when I'd just graduated from school, long before my White House days. I'd been promoted over her. She'd never forgiven me. And she made it a point to make sure I knew that. I was hoping to avoid her, if I could, when she came in to prepare her audition meals at the White House.

"She does not have a chance against you," Marcel said, his "chance" sounding like "shantz." He deftly arranged chocolate petals to form lotus blossoms. Tonight's dessert of mangoes with chocolate-cardamom and cashew ice cream, would be the crowning glory of the evening's meal. He'd worked late for several nights to create the fragile chocolate pieces, and I held my breath as he assembled them. The gorgeous centerpieces came together like magic, without his breaking even one of the delicate petals. "Henry recommended you, *n'est-ce pas?*

This is the most important consideration."

Cyan had removed the asparagus from the boiling water after its four-minute bath then waited for it to cool slightly before beginning to slice the blanched stalks for the soup. "Really, Ollie, I don't think you have a thing to worry about —"

She was interrupted by Bucky's arrival. The final member of our permanent staff, he didn't socialize much with the rest of us. That was fine by me. Bucky and Laurel Anne had worked together in the White House kitchen under the previous administration. Henry had never told me the entire story of why she left. All I knew was that my subsequent hiring after Laurel Anne's departure had won me a prime spot on Bucky's hit list.

The four of us stopped talking the minute Bucky walked in. But it bothered me that we did.

I shrugged. What did it matter if Bucky heard us? We all knew that Laurel Anne was the lead contender for the executive chef position. Catching Cyan's eye, I said, "Thanks, but come on." I cut into a segment of grapefruit and expressed its juice into a bowl. "The First Lady's been Laurel Anne's guest on the show . . . what? twice? . . . in the past *four* months. That wins her big brownie points." I diced the remaining fruit, grimacing at nothing in particular. "I don't even know why Laurel Anne needs to audition. The prior First Family ate her meals for years. For crying out loud, Mrs. Campbell's probably already made up her mind. And this is all just wait-and-see . . . for show."

Next to me, Henry prepared the entrée. Since halibut is a lean fish easily susceptible to over- or undercooking, I'd decided on a simple pan-frying method. We'd had the fish flown in from Alaska waters, vacuum-sealed in manageable-sized pieces and kept on ice to maintain freshness, but no flesh ever touched ice directly. Later, we'd brown them on one side in olive oil, then bake them in flavored butter. Henry shook his head as he expertly sliced the flatfish into steaks. "Don't be so down on yourself, Ollie. Mrs. Campbell knows you, too." He graced me with one of his fatherly smiles, the kind I couldn't resist. "And I know you."

"Thanks," I said, smiling back.

Cyan piped in again. "And you know, the TV show might just work against her. The White House doesn't allow that sort of distraction among the staff. Knowing her, she'd never give up the glamour."

Bucky spoke up from his quiet corner.

"Laurel Anne gave an interview about her upcoming audition. I saw it on a local channel last night."

I stopped what I was doing. We all did.

"She's from Idaho, you know. The First Lady's home state." Bucky raised his eyes to ensure we were paying attention. We were. "If Laurel Anne gets the executive chef position, she says she'd happily give up *Cooking for the Best* because her new vocation will be 'Cooking for the Prez.' "

When Bucky returned to shelling pistachio nuts, I made a gagging motion for Cyan and Henry to see.

Like he had eyes in the back of his head, Bucky addressed me again. "Just think, Ollie, if Laurel Anne gets the nod, you'll be reporting to her."

"Maybe, maybe not." I bit the insides of my cheeks to keep my voice level. "If she's in charge, I don't see myself sticking around here very long."

Henry gave me an avuncular pat on the back. "Then it would be the White House's loss."

Before the guests arrived, I stole over to the State Dining Room to have a quick look. As always, the sheer grandeur took my breath away. The staff bustled about, making last-

49

minute adjustments to the placement of water glasses and candles on round tables covered in saffron-colored silk. Our floral designer, Kendra, and her staff snipped and pruned and made tiny changes to the green mums and hot pink roses she'd shaped to resemble elephants in honor of India's prime minister. The entire room, with its magnificent attention to detail, suffused me with pride. I glanced up at George P. A. Healy's portrait of Abraham Lincoln. It hung above the fireplace, and I got the distinct feeling that our sixteenth president was watching over us as we strove to make our current president proud.

What thrilled me most was that I'd designed tonight's menu — the centerpiece of the evening. I'd done it. Me. The lowly assistant chef.

A smile tugged at my lips. The lowly assistant chef with her eye on the executive chef's position. I stood over one of the place settings and ran my finger along the rim of the dinner plate. This was the Clinton china collection, with architectural designs from the State Dining Room, the East Room, and the Diplomatic Reception Room incorporated in its gold band. The north face of the White House graced the plate's center — a first for presidential china. It was one gorgeous design.

I'd worked hard to make tonight's menu sparkle, and with a small sigh of pride, I realized I couldn't ask for a more perfect setting to showcase it.

Just as I made my way out, Craig Sanderson appeared in the doorway with another agent. Though I recognized him as Secret Service, he was not part of the usual Presidential Protection Detail, or PPD, as we liked to call them.

"Agent Sanderson," I said, not sure if he and I were back to first-name friendliness. "I'm surprised you're still here."

Without missing a beat, he turned to his companion. "This is the assistant chef I told you about. Olivia Paras. Olivia, this is the assistant deputy of the Secret Service, Jack Brewster."

The man, a taller, older fellow with a wide-set nose and ruddy complexion, raised an eyebrow as he gave me the once-over. "You were the young woman involved in the altercation this morning?"

"Yes," I answered, suddenly ill at ease.

"And you are employed here as an assistant chef?"

"Yes."

He stared a long moment. Nodded. "We may have more questions for you later."

I scooted away before he decided to question me right then and there.

At home that night, I turned on CNN, snuggled into my comfortable red pajamas, brushed my teeth, and spent a few important moments at the mirror fixing my hair. I poured a glass of wine for myself, and made sure I had a chilled mug in my freezer and a supply of Samuel Adams in the fridge.

The official dinner for India's prime minister had gone so well that the White House social secretary, Marguerite Schumacher, had made a special effort to visit the kitchen and let us know what a success tonight's event had turned out to be.

I sighed, contented.

It still amazed me that I was here, in Washington, D.C., working in the most important kitchen in the world. A far cry from life back in the Chicago two-flat with my mom and Nana.

The sun had gone down two hours ago, and I couldn't believe it'd been just this morning that the Secret Service had carted away the man . . . Naveen . . . the guy I'd knocked to the ground. It felt more like a year ago.

I caught a glimpse of the clear, starry night above my balcony, and I wondered if Mom and Nana stared up at the stars and thought of me, as I thought of them. I would love to have them both relocate here, but Nana was set in her ways, and my mom would never abandon her. Not even to live near me.

I'd made noises today about leaving the White House if Laurel Anne got the executive chef position, but I wasn't kidding anyone, least of all myself. This was my dream job, and I'd fight with everything I had before I'd give it up to the likes of Laurel Anne.

On a whim, I popped a blank tape into my VCR and started recording the news. As I expected, they were still running the story. I wanted to know more about this Naveen. And what danger he had talked about. And how he knew Craig Sanderson.

Mostly, though, I just hoped to catch myself on screen. Vanity maybe, but someday I'd be able to pull out the tape and brag about my participation to my grandkids.

I settled into my leather sofa and took a long sip of Gewürztraminer. The German wine fluttered down my throat, filling me with quick warmth.

Tonight's handsome anchorman kept a studious look on his face as he reported the headline news: A change of regime in the Middle East. Prince Mohammed of Alkumstan had been overthrown by his brother Sameer, who immediately assumed total control of the country. Sameer claimed to stand for peace.

I sighed. Yet another tale of Middle East unrest and more empty promises. I waited for the juicy stuff. Finally, the anchor introduced the clip. "From Washington, D.C., dramatic footage shows an intruder apparently attempting to gain access to the White House."

The recording showed the man running toward the building. This was a completely different perspective — a view from behind. It looked like it'd been shot from along the front fence. Somewhere in D.C., a lucky tourist was probably counting his windfall tonight. In the tape, the intruder ran away from the camera, dodging the two men in pursuit. Ahead of him, I saw the five agents waiting, guns at the ready.

But something looked off in the picture. Something not quite right.

I brushed the thought away. It had all happened so fast, and I'd been much closer to the action than the camera was. Frightened, too. The scene was bound to look a lot different from that viewpoint.

The running man's figure was small and grainy in the wide-angle shot, and I watched

54

as he threw his package off to his left and turned to face the two agents chasing him. They cut the playback there, and resumed the clip with the man being led away in handcuffs. They shoved him into an unmarked vehicle, his face turned from the camera's prying lens.

The anchorman continued to narrate. "The man, who officials refused to identify, is thought to be Farzad Al-Ja'fari. He threw an object the Secret Service initially believed might have contained a bomb."

Blood rushed from my face. My limbs went weak. A bomb? And he'd picked it back up. He'd had it when I whacked him. What if I'd whacked the bomb instead?

I felt the room grow small as I focused on the television.

"Al-Ja'fari, who is wanted for questioning in connection with several recent bombings in Europe, was apprehended without incident. There is no word yet on whether he actually carried a bomb, or what he intended to do if he had reached the White House."

Nothing about my involvement. I wasn't entirely surprised. How would it look if the intruder evaded our Secret Service only to be smacked on the skull by the mighty chef and her silver skillet? In a way, I was relieved. It looked like I still maintained possession of my anonymity.

I took another sip of wine and half-listened to the remaining commentary. When it finished I stopped the VCR, then changed channels. It was just about time for me to tune in Laurel Anne Braun, master chef and host of *Cooking for the Best.*

Maybe it was masochism on my part, but curiosity compelled me to watch my competition. Just before Henry had publicly announced his impending retirement, he'd told me in private that he'd recommended me to succeed him. I was flattered, honored, and just a little bit starstruck. If named executive chef for the White House, I would be the first female in history to hold the position.

I paid close attention as Laurel Anne canted her head at the camera. It responded by zooming in on her expressive face.

"Welcome again to *Cooking for the Best,* where I always cook for the best. Because I cook for you!" She pointed to the camera and gave a winsome smile.

While the woman was no raving beauty, she certainly had presence. Like an over-the-hill Julia Roberts, she wore a constant little smirk — as if sharing a private joke with her beloved audience — yet always radiating confidence.

By comparison, I was tiny. Short, with dark hair and brown eyes. She had me by half a foot, at least. And even I could see how her height helped maintain an air of power. Still, having worked with the woman, I knew that in real life her mask of self-assurance often dropped, and she became manic at the very times she should've maintained her cool. Mishaps were common in any kitchen. Keeping a level head made all the difference in the success or utter failure of an important meal. Laurel Anne was a control freak who shattered when things skidded out of control.

Watching her depressed me, so I switched it off. Instead of turning CNN on again, I rewound and replayed my tape of the news. My disappointment that I hadn't made it to the small screen had faded. Now I wanted to figure out what was bugging me about that clip. A little voice in the back of my head insisted it was important.

There he was. Again, the long-distance view. But again, something struck me as being not right.

Three replays later I started to catch subtle details. Although the recording was grainy and I couldn't see the man's features on the screen because he faced away from

57

the camera, he had the same flowing dark hair I'd noticed this morning. He seemed shorter, but that could've been due to the camera's angle. He rapidly outdistanced the two agents.

I stopped the playback just as he lofted his package to the left. The purported bomb. As I stared at the screen I tried replaying the real scene in my mind, and all I could recall was that he was getting *away* from the agents. That he'd *chosen* to turn and confront them. Why?

The scene on the screen, frozen before me, mocked my memory: the man's arm held high; the black portfolio spinning, airborne; the two agents running behind him.

The intruder's head had twisted toward the camera as the package flew into the air. On my prior viewings, I'd watched the package. This time I took a look at the man.

I inched closer to the TV screen.

Too close. At this foreshortened distance everything turned into wiggly patches of light.

Backing up, I squinted.

"It's the nose!" I said aloud.

I moved forward and backed up a few more times to get the best angle I could. The tape was fairly clear, but the runner's profile took up only a very small portion of the screen. It was hard to be sure, but the man's nose and chin were all wrong.

I stood two feet from my screen and shook my head. This wasn't the man I whacked.

Despite my panic as he tried stumbling to his feet, I knew I remembered his profile perfectly. I always remembered faces.

And this face was not his face.

I perched on the edge of my couch and stared at the frozen screen, my hands running through my hair, as though my fingers might unearth answers there. This didn't make sense. How could a tourist have the wrong man in the film? It made no sense at all.

Wait a minute.

I rewound the tape and replayed.

The anchorman said that the recording came from an "undisclosed source."

An undisclosed source?

Something was rotten as week-old stew meat.

I wanted to shout, to tell someone. To report it. But there was no one I could talk to.

That is, not until the doorbell rang.

CHAPTER 4

I flung open the door, expecting to usher Tom straight to the sofa where I could replay the tape for him. But before I could utter a word, he surprised me by thrusting forth a tissue-wrapped bouquet of flowers. This wasn't a generic pick-'em-up-at-the-grocery-store arrangement, either. This weighty bundle had all sorts of exotic blooms mixed in with the requisite profusion of roses, daisies, and greenery.

"They're beautiful," I said, touching a delicate snapdragon and taking a deep sniff of the fresh-cut scent as he came in and shut the door. Puzzled by the unexpected gift, I opened my mouth to ask what the occasion was, but he interrupted.

"Happy anniversary."

"Anniversary?" We'd been dating for more than a year, and we'd gone out for a special dinner to celebrate that momentous occasion in April. I knew he hadn't forgotten that, which made me feel like a very bad girlfriend for asking, "But, it's been —"

"Thirteen months."

This was not at all like the Tom I knew. While he was always a gentleman, his thoughtfulness generally revealed itself in unusual ways, like the time I mentioned some of my favorite old-time movie stars. That same day, he went out and bought me *Captains Courageous, Roman Holiday,* and *Mr. Smith Goes to Washington.* We snuggled in for the first of many black-and-white movie nights. He could be incredibly sweet. He was always thoughtful. But Tom was not a flowery kind of guy.

"Well, technically," I said, still perplexed, and hoping for a little more clarification, because I sensed that something was up, "it'll be thirteen months tomorrow."

He grinned, stepping forward to snake an arm around my waist. I looked up into those blue eyes twinkling down at me. "True," he said, "but I didn't think it would be very romantic for me to run out on you after midnight to go pick these up."

"Oh," I said, stringing the word out, "so you expect to be staying overnight?"

His arm snugged me in tighter. "That's the basic idea."

I loved being close to Tom. I loved pressing myself against him, feeling those taut muscles, the power in his arms. As one of the Secret Service, and a member of the elite PPD, he was charged with protecting the president of the United States — often referred to as POTUS — the White House, and everyone associated with it. He was a formidable guy and I had to admit, I felt protected when I was with him. Still, I inched away. "We're crushing the flowers," I said.

He let loose, a little. "Got anything to eat?"

I smirked. "What do you think?"

As he rummaged through my refrigerator, I put the flowers in water, thinking about the evening that lay ahead. "There's a mug in the freezer," I said.

"Don't need it."

"Hey!" I snapped my fingers, and spun to face him. "There's something you have to see."

He'd opened a can of Pepsi. Taking a long drink, he gave me a once-over from head to toe and back up again. "Something I haven't already seen?"

I slapped his arm in a playful gesture. "No, really. I taped the news and there's something wrong with what happened this morning." I canted my head. "What's with the Pepsi?"

"I'm on call."

That took me by surprise. "How come?"

Tom shrugged, not looking my direction. "Did you know that *Inherit the Wind* is on tonight? The Spencer Tracy version." He grabbed the clicker and changed channels. Fredric March's face took up the small screen as Tom lowered himself into the sofa's center cushion and placed his Pepsi on the coffee table. He patted the area next to him. "Hurry up. It's one of your favorites."

"Actually, I have to show you this tape of the news," I said. The president had explicitly asked me not to discuss this morning with anyone but the Secret Service. How convenient it was for me to have a Secret Service boyfriend. I couldn't wait to show him the news program I'd taped. More than that, I wanted him to be as intrigued and excited about the inconsistency as I was.

I reached to take the clicker, but Tom didn't let go.

"Come on," I said, laughing. "We usually fight because neither of us *wants* to hold the clicker. This time I'm willing to take it from you." I tugged again.

Tom tugged back, grabbing me with both hands as he reclined on the couch. He

63

pulled me on top of him and nuzzled my neck. "God, you smell good," he said.

I was a sucker for neck-nuzzling, and I felt my body tingle itself into readiness for what it hoped was to come.

But the discrepancy in the news tape nagged at my brain even as Tom's lips sought mine. Try as I might, I couldn't put the morning's events out of my head until we talked.

I pulled away. "Tom," I said, just a little bit out of breath, "Can I just show you something I taped on TV first?"

"You want to stop now?" he asked, snuffing a laugh against my face so that his warm breath tickled my ear. "You sure?" He pulled me tighter against him and I fought the urge to ravish him right there.

"It's really bothering me."

He took me by the shoulders and pushed us apart, staring up at me. I watched disappointment cloud his eyes. "What's so important?"

The tone of his voice made me hesitate, but I knew this couldn't wait. I slid off him and headed to the VCR. "I taped the news."

"You said that already."

"Yeah, but you have to see this. I think somebody faked the released tape."

I turned to catch his reaction to my

pronouncement, but he'd already boosted himself off the couch and was heading back to the kitchen. "I'm hungry," he said.

The tape was all set to play. "Give me five minutes and I'll fix you something."

I heard the sound of the fridge opening. His voice was muffled. "You watch it," he said.

"I've seen it." I raised my voice so he could hear me, but I knew I sounded strained. To keep from shouting to him, I made my way to the kitchen. "What is with you?" I asked.

He stood, shutting the fridge, holding a plate of bacon-wrapped olives speared with little wooden skewers that prevented them from unrolling. Shrugging, he turned to the countertop, his back to me, while he removed the Saran Wrap cover and downed two of the appetizers.

"Those are better warmed up," I said.

He shrugged again. "Guess I better get used to things being cold."

"What is that supposed to mean?"

He still didn't turn, so I got next to him, real close. He popped two more in his mouth and chewed, not making eye contact.

I touched his arm, keeping my voice low. "Tom, what's wrong?"

He took one of the small wooden skewers

and stabbed at a wayward olive. "I brought you flowers. It's our anniversary. And all you want to do is watch some news program? I might get called in any time tonight for a big debrief."

My eyebrows raised and he graced me with a glance.

"No, nothing I can talk about," he said, then continued. "But instead of relaxing, you want me to watch some news program that you think is faked."

This took me aback. Tom was never a whiner. In fact, he was one of the most even-tempered souls I'd ever encountered. That's what drew me to him in the first place. The fact that he was complaining like this made my antennae go up. I wondered about this debrief that he mentioned. It must be something big to be working on his emotions like this. "Okay," I said, squeezing his arm. "I didn't mean to ruin the moment. I guess I didn't realize that you really might get called in tonight. But, this isn't a fake news program."

"Oh yeah?" He turned to me now, pointing another little skewer. "What is it then, a scene from one of those silly 'reality' shows you like to watch?"

The jibe against my guilty pleasures bothered me. But what bothered me more was the fact that it seemed he hadn't been listening at all.

"Tom," I said, and this time I waited till he actually looked at me. "Something is wrong, okay? Can you give me that much? I want to get your opinion on something."

"I brought you flowers," he said again.

"And they're beautiful." I was getting angry. What was this? Bribe time? Give the girl flowers and have your way with her? This wasn't the relationship I'd signed on for. "But if you care for me at all, you'll sit on the couch for five minutes and watch something. All I want is your opinion. Okay?"

I couldn't believe it. He actually had to think about it. I watched him slowly come to a decision, even as his eyes slid toward my front door. He was truly considering leaving.

I planted my feet. "Tom?"

His expression shifted. To me it looked like he winced before saying, "Okay. Five minutes."

I sat next to him on the sofa, and pointed the clicker to start the tape. There was Naveen, running. As he prepared to throw his portfolio, I paused. "See? Right there."

Tom ate a couple more appetizers.

Getting up, I stood next to the television,

indicating the key spot on the screen, like a teacher with a PowerPoint presentation. "Look," I said with a triumphant smile. "That's not him."

"What are you talking about?"

I fought my exasperation. "That's not the same guy from this morning."

"Sure it is." Shaking his head, Tom returned his attention to the food and Pepsi on the table before him. "Who else would it be?" he asked. "If they caught some other guy running across the White House lawn this morning, somebody forgot to tell me about it."

"Tom," I said, and I waited till he dragged his gaze from the table to meet mine. "Look close. This isn't the guy from this morning. Whoever sent this tape to the networks changed the guy's face."

His blue eyes didn't waver, but I caught the set of his jaw. Something was up.

I set my hands at my hips. "Why would they do that?"

"You're seeing things." He stood, carrying the half-finished plate back to the kitchen. "Quit worrying about stuff that doesn't concern you." When he turned to me again, his expressions crinkled into that skeptical look he often wore when we watched the news. "You know how these media people

68

are. They don't get the footage they want, they create it."

I pointed to the drama still frozen on my screen. "I was there this morning. This footage is real. It's just the face that's fake."

"Give me a break. You're seeing things."

I didn't have an answer to that, and I said so. I hadn't been expecting him to laud my observational skills, but I did expect something more than this abject lack of interest. The derision in his tone hurt.

"But . . ." I persisted, staring at him in disbelief. How he could not be as blown away by this as I was mystified me. My voice went limp. "But I was there."

And then, it hit me. Tom *knew* why the news stations were playing this fake tape because he was in on it. He'd known about it from the start. Hence, the disinterest. Hence, the reluctance to watch the tape.

I stared at the flowers. Hence, the "Happy Anniversary" distraction. Damn it, how could I be so dense sometimes?

"There is no Farzad Al-Ja'fari, is there?" I asked, butchering the name from the newscast. "The guy this morning really is called Naveen, and he really is a friend of Craig's, isn't he?"

Tom rolled his eyes, licked his lips, and otherwise tried to avoid answering me.

69

"Just tell me why they faked this news coverage," I said. "That doesn't make any sense."

"Nobody faked any news coverage."

That was an out-and-out lie and we both knew it. A swift anger washed over me. I knew there were a lot of things Tom couldn't tell me, but I never expected him to deliver a blatant lie and expect me to swallow it.

"Fine," I said. "Have it your way. Just tell me one thing. Is he okay?"

"Who?"

"Naveen. I hit him pretty hard. I feel bad about that."

"Don't. He was just another loony trying to get close to the president. Maybe he should thank you because you knocked some sense into him."

"Do you guys have him in custody?"

"We turned him over to the Metropolitan Police. He's their problem now."

That very moment, Tom's pager went off. After checking the numbers he glanced up, met my furious glare, and gave a weak smile. "Duty calls."

I kept silent as he kissed me on the forehead and turned to leave.

"I'll call you."

I nodded and followed him, not wanting this argument to end here — not wanting him to leave while I was angry. Mostly just wanting him to stay to work this out. "Be safe," I said.

He raised a hand in acknowledgment.

Two seconds later the door shut and my gaze drifted to the vase of flowers. I didn't understand. I didn't understand at all.

CHAPTER 5

We all applauded as Paul Vasquez concluded the morning's surprise announcement. Thanking us for our time, he turned away from the lectern to let the buzz begin. Now that the official presentation was over, everyone relaxed and a few of us stepped forward to meet the most recent addition to our White House staff family.

Head of the newly created cultural- and faith-based Etiquette Affairs department, Peter Everett Sargeant III wore pride in his position like the perfectly pressed, bright red pocket handkerchief that contrasted against his dark Armani suit. Though not especially tall, Sargeant cut an impressive figure. He was just as polished and dignified as Paul, but Sargeant's deepened crow's feet and line-bracketed mouth made me believe he had at least ten years on our chief usher.

Shaking hands with Henry, the new guy

raked his gaze over all of us kitchen personnel, and with patent curiosity, we watched him right back.

"Actually," Sargeant said, responding to Henry's greeting, "I would prefer being addressed as the 'sensitivity director.' " He drew out his syllables in such careful, round tones that I was reminded of that elocution scene from *Singin' in the Rain.* Giving a self-deprecating smile, he added. "It's so much less cumbersome when addressing me. Don't you agree?"

Cyan glanced over, lifting her eyebrows and elongating her nose in a hoity-toity expression. I shot her a reproving look. I knew Sargeant had to be nervous and I didn't want him to catch Cyan's little joke. I remembered when I'd been presented to the staff. My debut was done with a lot less fanfare — after all I was an assistant chef, not the head of a department — but I'd been awestruck, eager, and hopeful that everyone would like me. I was sure Sargeant felt the same way.

Henry shifted to the side and I thrust my hand forward. "I'm Olivia Paras," I began.

Sargeant cocked his head to one side. "How tall are you?"

Puzzled, I answered, "Five foot two."

He turned to Henry. "Isn't such slight

73

stature a hindrance to keeping the kitchen running efficiently?"

Henry took a moment before answering. His usually jovial face now mirrored the confusion I was feeling, but his cheery demeanor returned in half a beat. He laid a hand onto my shoulder. "When it comes to the kitchen," he said, beaming, "Ollie here outclasses anyone. And I'm talking even the great chefs of Europe. Ollie may be tiny, but she's got what it takes."

Sargeant licked his lips. It was the only movement in his otherwise rigid body. As though he tasted my name and found it bitter, he said, "Ollie."

My hand still hanging out there, I looked to Henry for guidance, but his pointed glance seemed to warn me that I was on my own. I could almost hear him lecture me that if I were fortunate enough to become the next executive chef, I'd be handling much more prickly situations than this one.

"Right . . . Ollie," I said, my voice a little too high, a little too animated. "That's what everyone calls me." With the high-voltage confidence I displayed, I decided Mary Poppins couldn't have done better. And, since Sargeant didn't look like he was about to shake my still-outstretched hand, I took the initiative and grabbed his. "It's a pleasure to meet you."

We shook briefly. He grimaced and dismissed us with a nod.

On the way back to the kitchen, I shook my head. "What were they thinking when they hired this guy?"

"Let's not be too harsh, Ollie," Henry said, but when he glanced back at the gathering, he wore the same expression he had the time we realized we'd accidentally left Limburger cheese out all night. "He's probably just nervous."

"Maybe," I conceded.

Cyan rolled her eyes — violet, today. "Look at the guy. He walks like he's got a pole stuck up his —"

"Cyan!"

She shot Henry an abashed smile. "I'm just glad he doesn't oversee the kitchen." She gave a mock shudder. "Can you imagine having to report to someone that stuffy?"

Marcel wasn't scheduled to come in until the afternoon. I wondered what his take on the new man would be. I suspected I would never get the warm and fuzzies from Peter Everett Sargeant III.

Bucky, trailing behind us, spoke up. "Nothing wrong with running a tight ship."

Henry's neck flushed red.

"Of course . . ." Bucky continued, picking

75

up his pace to make it to the kitchen first, "I'm not saying you don't." He cast a benevolent smile over his shoulder, but his eyes remained expressionless.

I patted Henry's back. "He's just jealous," I whispered. "That Sargeant guy completely ignored Bucky when he went up to say hello. At least I got an insult out of the deal."

Henry winked at me. "That you did."

The president's lunch today was a special affair. He had morning and afternoon meetings scheduled in-house, so he'd opted for a low-key meal with Mrs. Campbell in the residence. With the limited time the couple spent together alone, we knew we wanted to serve up something memorable.

I drew one of my trusty American-made Mac knives from its holder and went to work. As I chopped crabmeat for the first course, a crab-spinach appetizer served with crostini, Bucky stewed cherry tomatoes for garnish, and Henry and Cyan prepared risotto. I had a supply of truffle oil on hand. I'd add that, and a tiny bit of shaved truffle into the risotto just before serving. A little truffle goes a long way, and we knew that this extravagant addition would be just the right touch for today's meal.

A sharp rap pulled our attention to a visitor in the doorway.

Peter Everett Sargeant III reminded me of a grouchy squirrel. With his hands positioned as though he were cradling a precious nut, he canted his head three different ways in the space of two seconds. Alert, wary, eager.

"Welcome to our kitchen," Henry said.

Henry placed emphasis on the word *our.* I liked that.

"Yes," Sargeant said. He smiled, looking as though the effort caused him pain. "I'm availing myself of the opportunity to familiarize myself with the layout of the property." He seemed to take in everything in quick snippets — a tendency that contrasted with the careful cadence of his speech. "And the organizational structure."

His smile faded when it rested on me.

What had I done to incur this man's immediate distaste? His disapproval radiated toward me just like that Limburger cheese aroma.

Henry washed his hands in the sink, raising his voice to be heard over the rushing water. "It's a little tight in here for a tour, but we'd be happy to answer any questions you have about food preparation."

Sargeant scratched the side of his nose. "No tour. I'm here to explain some procedural changes."

Henry shut the water off, dried his hands. "Such as?"

"Effective immediately, all official dinner menus will be vetted through my office."

"But we —" I took a step toward him.

"Ah-ah-ah," he said, holding up the same index finger he'd used to scratch his nose. "I'm not finished."

Cyan and I exchanged a look. Had Paul Vasquez approved this change in the chain of command?

As though he'd heard my thoughts, Sargeant continued. "The chief usher and I have discussed this at length. In view of the administration's commitment to supporting diversity, we've decided that I shall have final say on all menu offerings."

I couldn't stop myself. "*You're* doing the taste-testing?"

He nodded.

Henry stared up at something near the ceiling for a couple of beats before he took a position next to the diminutive Sargeant. Looking down, he addressed him by his first name. "Peter," he began, squaring his shoulders and scratching at his wide neck, "I can't say I'm happy to hear this." Sargeant fidgeted. "We always defer to the First Lady's preferences. It's not only tradition. It's *our* policy. Perhaps I should have a talk with Paul."

Sliding sideways, Sargeant raised both squirrelly hands. "No, you misunderstand."

"Oh?"

"When I said that I had final say, I meant only that I will decide along with the First Lady." He shrugged his shoulders three times as he talked. "That's all."

Henry glanced back at us. It was difficult enough to come up with varied and exciting menus for visiting dignitaries that met their dining requirements while pleasing our decision maker, Mrs. Campbell. She wasn't fussy, but she certainly had her own tastes. We were still in the process of learning them. To also have to clear all choices through Sargeant would make the task arduous at best. I didn't understand why the change had to be made, and said so.

Sargeant graced me with another derisive stare, but didn't answer. "And," he continued, "when you draw up the menus, and provide me with samples, I will want to know which of you" — he allowed his glance to fall on each of us in turn, avoiding Henry's glare — "is responsible for which course."

"What is your reason for that?" Henry asked.

"In addition to being the sensitivity director, I like to think of myself as a mentor." Stepping backward, he nudged his way toward the door. "In time, I'll know which of you are contributing to the kitchen's success — and which of you are simply dead weight." His hand reached up, holding the jamb as though for support. "I enjoy helping people grow."

Then it hit me. I was shorter than he was. I was, in fact, the only one of the chefs whose stature didn't compete with his. It dawned on me at that moment, that Peter Everett Sargeant III had singled me out to pick on — because he thought he could. Because he perceived me as weak.

The man was no better than a playground bully.

Once he was gone, I sidled over to Henry at the computer screen. Unruffled, he clicked to open up a new document. I watched him for a long moment, as I thought about Sargeant's new directive, thinking about all the changes that had taken place since our new president took the oath of office in January. We'd seen a whirlwind of activity in the past few months. This was just one small part of it.

"What's that?"

Henry's large shoulder lifted. "If we are to have a new procedure, I need to set it up."

"How do you do it?" I asked.

He twisted his head to look at me. "You've set up dozens of spreadsheets and documents before. What are you talking about?"

"No, I mean, how do you cope with all the changes? All the time? With each new administration, there are adjustments. I know that. But how do you keep from questioning the wisdom of the decisions?" I glanced at the doorway. "If they're choosing a man like Peter Everett Sargeant III to run an entire department —"

"Ollie," he said, now turning his entire body my direction, giving me his undivided attention, "we are the chefs for the most important home in the world."

"I know that."

"Our country depends on our president. And he depends on us. When we step through the White House gates, we become more than just ordinary citizens." He stared north, as if seeing the endless stream of protestors standing sentry in Lafayette Park. "We leave behind the controversy, the rancor, the turmoil."

His voice rumbled to the crescendo I knew was coming. "We are our country's decision makers when we cast our votes on Election Day. But when we leave the polling place, when we enter our world *here*," he jammed a finger onto the countertop, "we must be focused on the part *we* play in keeping our country great. We are not here to change policy, but in a way, to help promote it. And we must be vigilant to discourage dissension." He lifted his chubby index finger, pointing skyward. "We are here to cook for President Campbell, the most powerful man in the world, and for his guests. If these heads of state are well-fed and content, they will be cooperative. They will make wise decisions."

He broke into a wide smile. "What power we hold, Ollie."

I'd heard his lecture before. I earned a recitation each time I questioned anything, from the president's decision to open trade negotiations with a former enemy country, to what color tie he chose to wear for a press conference. Although Henry and I differed on *how* to put aside our beliefs and convictions, we both did it. We all did. As far as I knew, all White House staff members set aside politics to serve our country in the best way we knew how. For me, and for most of us, it was a point of pride.

Bucky interrupted the sudden quiet with slow applause. "Nice speech, Henry. Do you practice that in front of a mirror?"

Throwing Bucky a look of disgust, I

returned to my chopping board, hands on hips. Hiring him was another decision I questioned.

Henry must have sensed my thoughts, because he drew up next to me and whispered in my ear, "A White House chef must be less concerned with the state of the union, and more concerned with the state of the *onion.*"

That made me giggle.

He was right, though. Since George Washington's time, when the building of the "President's House" was first commissioned, this center for democracy has held immense stature in the world. The building, designed by James Hoban, was finally completed in 1800, too late for George Washington's use, and almost too late for John and Abigail Adams. They took occupancy shortly before Jefferson's inauguration.

History lived in these walls. And as a member of the staff, it was my duty to ensure the level of grandeur never diminished.

Just then, Peter Everett Sargeant III reappeared in the doorway. "One more thing," he said, his voice ringing high above the kitchen noises. We stopped our activity to hear him better. "I need a curriculum vitae from each of you. Today, if possible. Tomorrow at the latest." Again, he fixed only me with a look of contempt. "I need to know what I'm dealing with."

Bucky snorted as Sargeant left. "What a pompous ass."

Henry looked ready to admonish Bucky, but stopped himself.

"Since when do we report to him?" I asked.

"I'll make an appointment to talk with Paul," Henry said. "We'll get this settled."

I picked up a plate, hefted it in my hands, and eyed the doorway. "I think I'd like to settle this myself," I said, "with a well-aimed smash over the man's head."

"Relax, my dear," Henry said. "With a disposition like that of Peter Everett Sargeant *III,* it is doubtful there will ever be a *Fourth.*"

CHAPTER 6

Naveen's name simmered on the back burner of my brain, bubbling around and keeping me from devoting my complete attention to the tasks at hand. After we finished lunch preparations and the waitstaff served it, we started in on the thousand other items that required attention. I went to the computer screen, knowing I needed to put the finishing touches on the ladies-only luncheon Mrs. Campbell would host the following week.

My alert program reminded me to contact our sommelier. He was prepared for tonight, but he and I needed to chat further about the upcoming luncheon.

Next week we'd be serving prosciutto and melon, followed by Chicken Maryland. Mrs. Campbell had requested a menu similar to one Mrs. Johnson had served during her tenure as First Lady. I thought about that now as I stared at the screen.

Security had changed a lot over the years. Before I was born, visitors lined up outside for White House tours, and they were granted free access most mornings each week. Today visitors were required to plan in advance. Submit official requests, provide social security numbers.

I sighed.

Naveen was an example of why the rules had changed. And I'd been the one to stop his unauthorized intrusion. Why didn't I feel better about that?

Henry meandered by to assure me that he'd look into Peter Everett Sargeant's dictum. Little did he know that it wasn't the supercilious little man who'd set me off-kilter — well, not entirely — but the dark intruder from yesterday's skirmish. I wished I could confide in Henry, but he'd be the first to remind me that my top duty was to the president.

Tonight, one of the Campbells' adult children would be present at dinner, and we'd already planned the family favorite — ultra thin-crust pizza. Loaded with artichoke hearts, sun-dried tomatoes, and Italian sausage delivered from Chicago, it was one of our specialties. Cyan was kneading dough even as I tapped at the keyboard.

Pizza was easy. But planning the next

several weeks was more of a challenge. It took the remainder of the day to work out logistics for seven "intimate" dinners of less than ten guests each, four larger affairs with guest lists topping twenty, and three luncheons of varying sizes. I studied diet dossiers, made notes on allergies, and juggled entrée, accompaniment, and dessert choices, until the arrangements lined up perfectly like a culinary version of a Rubik's cube.

Twilight kept me company after work as I trudged three blocks to the McPherson Square Metro station. I used the time to check my voice mail. Hearing Tom's voice cheered me at first, but his message — he'd be tied up but would try to call later — chased away my hopes for a cozy evening. He and I hadn't parted on the most upbeat of terms last night and I was eager to see him so that we could make things right.

The stations and the trains themselves were lonely at night. We pulled into Farragut West and I stared out the window — this time of day I rarely had trouble getting a window seat. At the stop, my attention was captured by two Metro Transit Police officers talking with a Middle Eastern man on the platform. He resembled Naveen. Not enough for me to believe it was the same man, of course, but enough for yesterday's incident to jump once again to the forefront of my thoughts.

The transit cops seemed to be unruffled, in control, and even as I wondered what their conversation was about, we pulled out of the station, one stop closer to home.

But . . . the scene jogged my memory. Tom had said that Naveen was the Metropolitan Police's problem now. Which meant there must be a record of his incarceration.

The world whispered by as I put together what I knew.

A man had been apprehended, running across the White House lawn.

This same man was apparently on a first-name basis with one of our Secret Service PPD agents.

The videotape of the man's transgression, however, hadn't made it to the news. Not really. What had been offered for the viewing public's pleasure was a snippet of the scene. Carefully faked. Though obvious to anyone who'd been there.

I made an unladylike snort, which caused the old man sitting across the aisle to glance over. With a smile to convince him I wasn't a commuter loony, I continued my musings.

The Secret Service had been there.

I'd been there.

For some reason, the Secret Service didn't want Naveen's face broadcast across the country. Why not?

The people who usually jumped the White House fence were either mentally unstable or on a mission. Naveen struck me as one of the latter. When an intruder was caught inside the perimeter on an unauthorized jaunt, the incident generally ensured him a few minutes of fame wherein he (and it was almost always a male) used his screen time wisely to shout his vital message to a national audience.

But . . .

Naveen hadn't shouted.

My cell phone buzzed from the recesses of my purse. A quick glance at the number and I knew Tom had managed a little free time. I was still amazed that I could get service belowground.

"Hey," he said when I answered.

"Hey, yourself. Where are you?"

"Driving," he said. A second later I was able to make out the fast-moving car noises in the background. I also heard another voice.

"You alone?"

"Nope."

I guessed. "With Craig?"

"You should have been a detective."

I laughed at that. Tom and I hadn't exactly "come out" with our relationship to our colleagues, although a few of the kitchen folks weren't fooled. I knew Tom's end of the conversation would be as devoid of identifying characteristics as he could make it.

"You're still on duty?" I asked.

"Yep."

"And so you just called to tell me how much you missed me."

"Uh-huh."

"Because I'm the light of your life and you don't know what you'd do without me."

I could almost see him roll his eyes at that. He didn't answer as much as grunt.

"And because you're so crazy about me," I continued in a chipper voice, trying to keep the tone light, but determined to press my point, knowing he'd be forced to respond agreeably because Craig was right there, "you'll tell me more about that faked news broadcast later, right?"

Dead silence.

"I'll call you back later," he said. And the phone went dead.

Damn. Sometimes when I pushed my luck it snapped back to bite me.

I knew there were things Tom couldn't tell me, and I was okay with that. Keeping things classified was part of his job, after all. Part of his sworn duty. But I also knew that Tom often chose to keep things from me when there was nothing classified about them. He didn't appreciate the way I analyzed and picked at things until I understood them. I found the process fascinating. He found my doing so annoying.

Tom was just trying to protect me from too much knowledge, and from knowing things I shouldn't know. I understood that. But this time it felt different.

I watched out the window as the train emerged into the evening light at Arlington cemetery. I thought about my dad, and how I hadn't been out to his grave in a long while. The world was a dangerous place for heroes.

And then, another thought began to grow and take hold.

Maybe Naveen really did have an important message for President Campbell.

Blood rushed from my feet to my face and back down again, heralding a moment of absolute clarity. The look in the man's eyes when he'd stared up at me hadn't been the unfocused, crazed look of a lost soul. He wanted to tell me something. He'd said that the president was in danger.

But Tom hadn't taken Naveen's warning seriously. No one had, apparently. The man had been sent to the D.C. Jail.

My arm reclined against the train's window frame. Not particularly comfortable, but it gave me the chance to tap my fingers against the glass as I pondered all this.

Naveen had been willing to talk with me. He'd been about to tell me of the danger when I'd whacked him in the head.

I grimaced.

The train pulled into my station just as I pulled myself out of my musings.

By the time I made it to my apartment, I knew exactly what I had to do.

CHAPTER 7

"I'm trying to get in touch with one of your inmates," I said, wondering if that was the politically correct way to phrase it. I held my cell phone in a grip so tight I thought the plastic casing might crack. "I'd like to talk with him."

The woman's flat, capable tone — uncannily similar to that of the dispatcher who'd warned me to stay out of the way yesterday morning — made me wonder if there was some moonlighting going on here. "I'll need his name," she said.

"He was caught running across the White House lawn. Yesterday."

"I need a name," she repeated.

"Naveen."

"First or last?"

I guessed. "First."

"I need the inmate's last name." This time the tone wasn't so flat. I caught a hint of her impatience.

"It's . . ." Shoot. I had no clue. "Well, you see," I said, "I — he —" My heart raced, making clackety pounds against my ribcage. I knew I was overstepping my boundaries here, knew I had no right to make this phone call. When I first picked up the phone, I'd been nervous. Now I was near panic. I'd foolishly expected my description of "White House Intruder" to be enough to identify him. After all, how many fence-leaping Naveens could there be?

"Ma'am?"

"I'm his girlfriend," I said in a rush.

Where did that come from?

"And you don't know his last name?"

Thinking fast, I decided to go for ditsy bimbo. "Well —" I began, trying to buy time as I came up with a logical explanation that would still provide the information I needed, "— we haven't been together very long, and he has a hard name to pronounce. I'd never be able to spell it."

The woman's irritated sigh *whoosh*ed over the phone line. It gave me hope. "Naveen," she repeated, then spelled it.

"That's right," I said, hoping it was.

With the memory of Craig's anger crawling along my insides, I paced. I crossed my fingers as I listened, hearing the woman tap computer keys. I sure hoped repercussions of this phone call didn't blow up on me like yesterday's call to the dispatcher had. That's why I'd taken the precaution of the cell phone. The jail's caller ID, if they had it, would just show up as numbers, and wouldn't include my name. I was sure the D.C. Jail got hundreds of phone calls for inmates each day. No one would bother to find out who was looking for Naveen. At least I hoped they wouldn't.

Another sigh. More clicks.

"I'm sorry," the woman finally said. "We have no one in our system by that name."

"But, they told me . . ."

"I'm sorry. Whoever gave you that information was incorrect. We have no one incarcerated for trespassing on the White House grounds."

"I —"

"Is there anything else?"

My fingers now uncrossed, I dropped my shoulders. Stopped the anxious pacing. "No. Thank you very much for your time."

The logical portion of my brain, which I occasionally suspected occupied less than its allotted half, ridiculed my efforts. What was I hoping to accomplish by talking with Naveen?

I didn't know, exactly. I just couldn't shake the sense that I'd screwed up somehow and I needed to make things right. I certainly didn't regret playing a part in Naveen's apprehension, but I did regret cracking him in the head with the commemorative pan. He hadn't threatened me in any way — in fact, it had been more like he'd been asking for help.

Resting my butt against my kitchen countertop, I rubbed my eyes. I should just let this go. I knew that.

But.

Just a quick Internet search, I told myself. Real quick. If I didn't come up with anything, I vowed to let it go.

After inputting countless different combinations of "Naveen," "White House," "trespass," "Secret Service," "D.C. Jail," and "Farzad Al-Ja'fari" — the intruder's name from the newscast — I came up with nothing beyond the broadcast pabulum from the night before. I was just about to try a Google image search when the phone rang.

"I was just thinking about you," I said as I picked it up.

Tom made a noise that was half rumble, half laugh. "Good. I was afraid you'd be sleeping."

"But it's not that —" I glanced at the tiny clock at the bottom of my screen. "Holy geez, it's almost two."

"Yeah, I'm finally off for the night." He didn't yawn, but I could hear the weariness in his voice. "Heading home."

"I should probably get some sleep, too," I said. "I have to be up in a couple of hours."

"What're you doing up so late, anyway?"

I opened my mouth, with no idea how to answer. What could I say? Oh, I've been conducting my own investigation — because you won't tell me anything.

I hesitated. And, despite being wiped out from his extended shift, Tom unfortunately picked up on it.

"Ollie?"

"Just surfing the 'Net. You know how I get sometimes."

"What were you looking up?"

A clock-tick went by.

"Just . . . stuff."

He made a noise. Frustration, agitation; I couldn't tell. He knew I was hiding something. That drove me nuts. The few times I'd tried to surprise him — either with a special date or a gift — he always had an inkling of what was coming. Some people might call it a sixth sense, but I knew that Tom was just that good of an agent. He'd been trained to pick up on clues others might miss. Trying to put one over on him was an exercise in futility.

"What were you looking up?"

I pushed out a laugh and said, "You caught me." Using what Tom always told me was the most effective way to lie — the best spies in the world did it — I kept my answer as close to the truth as possible. "I was searching online for news about the guy who jumped the fence." I left out the little tidbit about calling the D.C. Jail.

"For crying out loud, Ollie." A slight scratchy noise over the phone line told me Tom was rubbing his face in frustration. "That's done. Over with. Case closed."

"Did you ever find out what the guy wanted to warn the president about?"

"We found out everything we needed to know."

"What does that mean?"

"It means that the guy was a loony who jumped the fence just like a dozen loonies do every year. We sent him to the D.C. Jail where he belongs. End of story."

I started to protest that Naveen wasn't in the D.C. Jail, but Tom would want to know how I knew that. I took a different tactic. "What's his last name?"

"Why?"

"Because I'm not finding a whole lot on-line under the name 'Naveen.'"

"Good," he said. "Let's keep it that way.

98

Listen, the Secret Service already handled this. That's what we're here for. We've got lots of experience and we know what we're doing. It was just bad luck that you happened to be there when the intruder got past security. But . . ." He slowed his next words down, emphasizing each syllable. "We have taken care of this. We have handled incidents like this in the past. We don't need help from a White House chef. Understand?"

I wrinkled my nose at the phone.

Perhaps sensing that he had come down too hard on me, he added, "Come on, you wouldn't want me to tell you how to fry a chocolate mousse, would you?"

In spite of myself, I laughed. "You don't fry a mousse, silly."

"See what I mean?"

I knew I should just give it up. Heck, I'd done all the investigation I could. I'd attempted far more than I should have and I'd come up empty. Agreeing to let it go kept Tom happy and made me look good, so I had nothing to lose. "Okay," I said. "I'll drop it. On one condition."

"And what's that?"

"That if any of this gets resolved, you let me know." I added, quickly, "Only if it's declassified, I mean."

I heard Tom yawn and stretch. "You got yourself a deal, little Miss Detective. Now, why don't you get some sleep and I'll see you tomorrow — er — later today sometime."

With a smile, I nodded into the phone. "Can't wait."

When pounding noises roused me from sleep at four fifteen, I jerked into that startled state of alertness that everyone dreads. It took me several seconds to realize that someone was at my door, and my bleary mind couldn't fathom the reason for the insistent thumping even as habit sent me scurrying to answer it.

I had a moment of awareness before throwing open the deadbolt and I remembered to check the peephole first. Tom and Craig stood in the hallway. Craig's hands were at his side in classic alert stance, his gaze moving back and forth, taking in the length of the short corridor.

"Ollie, wake up. Open the door."

I blinked and looked out the peephole again. "Tom?"

My voice croaked, but both of them snapped to attention at the sound.

Tom wore an expression I'd never seen on him before. Well, at least not directed toward me. "Let us in."

Fairly confident they weren't here to shoot me, I swung open the door just as Mrs. Wentworth across the hall swung open hers. Her arthritic hand clawed at the doorjamb as though to steady herself and as Tom and Craig pushed past me, she asked, "Want me to call the police, honey?"

The two men spun to face my elderly neighbor. She didn't flinch.

"No, thanks," I said, trying to force a smile. "These are friends of mine."

They both turned to stare at me, frowning with such obvious effort that for a moment I doubted my own words. My skin sizzled. Could something have happened to Henry?

"Well, if I find out in the morning that you're dead, I'm going to give the police their full descriptions." She brushed at her wispy white hair as she backed into her apartment, raising her voice. "You hear that, you two goons?"

"Good night, Mrs. Wentworth," I said. Then, shutting the door, I rested my butt against it. "She looks out for me."

The angry frowns hadn't disappeared. If anything, they'd gotten more intense. Tom paced my small living room as Craig stood before me, hands at his sides, eyes glued to mine.

"What's wrong?" I asked. "What's happened?"

"Have a seat, Ms. Paras," Craig began, gesturing toward my kitchen. Behind him, Tom's hands worked themselves into fists.

Despite the fact that I'm short and relatively petite — and I'll stay that way as long as I keep from ingesting large doses of carbs — I don't back down easily. But I knew these two — one of them intimately — and until I knew what was up, it probably wasn't a good idea to provoke a confrontation.

I sat at my kitchen table.

Craig took the chair opposite mine. Tom continued to pace, staring down at my linoleum as though he were trying to memorize it.

"Are either of you going to tell me what this is about?"

"Jesus Christ, Ollie," Tom said. He stopped moving long enough to flash a look of fire my way.

"What?" I asked, flaying my hands out. But I fought a sinking feeling in my gut. I had a feeling I knew exactly "what."

"Where is your cell phone?" Craig asked.

They had me.

"Shoot," I said. Then, attempting an extremely feeble joke, I added, "I don't mean that literally, of course."

Craig's words were precise, his drawl more intense than ever. "Do I take your reaction to indicate that you comprehend the reason for our visit here at this godless hour?"

Craig talking to me in Secret Service-speak was more frightening than Naveen's performance had been.

Tom kept pacing.

I decided that the old adage about the best defense wasn't applicable only to football. "Have you been tapping my calls? That isn't right. That isn't even legal." A moment's doubt as I turned to Tom. "Is it?"

He stopped pacing. "You ever hear of caller ID?"

"Well, yeah," I began to say, the way some people say "duh," "but how the heck could you guys have done it?" As I spoke, I tried putting the pieces together in my head, but the picture wasn't coming clear. "You have some sort of alert put on all White House employee phone numbers? So no matter where I call, you can tag me?"

Craig's lips moved. But not much else did. "You overestimate your importance, Ms. Paras."

That was a slam. It got my back up. "Apparently," I said, "I'm more important than I thought if you've got nothing better to do than pay me a visit because I happened to dial the D.C. Jail tonight."

"Happened to dial?" Craig repeated. "Are you claiming that you reached the D.C. Jail's number in error?"

My brain finally defuzzed enough to grab hold of the facts and make sense of them. Tom and Craig weren't here because my phone number raised an alert — they were here because they'd been instructed to follow up with anyone who tried to contact Naveen at the jail. Because they were watching the guy for suspicious activity.

When my cell phone number popped up on the jail's caller ID, Craig probably assumed it belonged to another conspirator. Finding out that it was one of the assistant chefs calling on a whim probably made the two men in my kitchen want to throttle me.

"I'm sorry," I said.

"Sorry?" Tom asked. "Didn't I tell you that we were handling this?"

Craig's head perked up. "Agent MacKenzie? Have you been in conversation with Ms. Paras about this subject prior to this visit?"

The last thing I wanted was for Tom to get into more trouble than I'd already put him in. "Craig," I said, pulling his attention to me again. "I'm Ollie, remember? We're friends. Or we were before that Naveen guy ran at me."

To my surprise, he didn't interrupt. So I continued. "*Of course* Tom talked with me about this." Tom squeezed his eyes shut, but I ignored it. "He walked me up to the gate after it happened and he took the pan I had engraved for Henry, too. He said it was evidence." I raised my voice as though addressing Tom, who resumed his pacing. "I haven't gotten that back yet either, you know."

"Why did you call the D.C. Jail?" Craig asked.

Tough question. I worked hard not to look over to Tom as I spoke. "I hit the guy pretty hard," I said. "And then, when he called you by name . . ."

Craig's expression didn't change but for a tiny flinch that deepened the tiny lines bracketing his eyes.

". . . I thought that I might've been wrong to have hit him. And he seemed so sincere when he told me the president was in danger." My words came out in a rush now. "I knew that if he was a bad guy he probably got taken to the D.C. Jail, so that's why I tried to call there. But the woman said he wasn't locked up there, that there wasn't even a record of him being arrested. And so

I'm wondering now — did I hurt him? Is he okay?"

Tom and Craig exchanged a look that, to me, appeared to be Tom saying, "Isn't that what we figured she was doing?"

Craig worked his tongue around the inside of his mouth. When he finally spoke, his Kentucky drawl was soft. "Ollie," he began. I felt my shoulders relax at the nickname. "We understand that you have a soft heart. We understand that you found yourself in a situation that you were not trained to handle. But I must take this opportunity to remind you that you cannot involve yourself any further in this matter."

"I didn't mean to —"

He held up a hand. "Tom and I have taken it upon ourselves to talk with you. We are not bound to report your actions, nor take this matter any higher than our conversation here tonight. But I caution you that the jail is under orders to let us know when anyone tries to contact yesterday's uninvited guest. I suggest that you do not try to contact him again."

"So he is at the jail, but they just couldn't tell me?" I asked.

Exasperation crossed Craig's face. "I am not at liberty to disclose that information."

My apartment faced east, and I caught a

106

glimpse of the sunrise, just at that point where the sky is pink and full of promise. Its hopeful brightness helped convince me that tonight's crisis was over.

"I'm sorry to have caused you any problems," I said.

Craig stood, nodded to Tom.

As they prepared to leave, I realized I'd have to hustle to get myself to the White House by my regular time. At the door, Craig turned to me. "No more secret investigations. Are we clear on that?"

"Cross my heart," I said, gesturing across my chest. But I didn't add, "Hope to die."

CHAPTER 8

"Don't you sleep anymore?" I asked Tom.

He shrugged.

We'd agreed to meet at one of the many hot dog stands interspersed between souvenir vendors along 17th Street NW. Tom ordered a Polish with sauerkraut and I got my usual hot dog with mustard and tomato. If I'd been by myself, I'd have taken onions, too.

As I ducked under a tree to get out of the unseasonably hot sun, Tom gave our snacks a frown. "With all the amazing food you create, how come we eat this junk?"

"A taste of home. For me, at least." I thought about Chicago-style hot dogs, the stuff of which legends are made. "But you're avoiding my question."

He shrugged again.

"You've got some nasty dark circles there," I said. "And you look like you're ready to drop."

"Gee, thanks," he said, rolling his eyes.

"Come on." I touched his arm. "You know I'm just worried about you."

There was a long moment of silence. I took a bite of my hot dog, and Tom stared out to some middle distance. I tried to figure out what he was looking at, but there was nothing unusual out there. I waited. I knew what was coming.

"Just what the hell did you think you were doing?"

A bench opened up and I motioned toward it, buying time. "Let's sit."

Tom grumbled, but complied.

Once settled, he started in again, keeping his voice low enough to prevent strangers from eavesdropping, but yelling at me all the same. "Do you have any idea how much trouble you caused me last night? When the number turned out to be yours, I thought Craig would explode. What would've happened if he decided to then look at all your calls? Huh? Then he would've found my number on your recent call list — and we would've had a lot more questions to answer."

"I thought you said that there's nothing wrong with us going out together. I thought you said that it isn't against any regulation."

He frowned again, looking away, his Pol-

109

ish tight in his hands, still wrapped, apparently forgotten. I glanced down at my hot dog. I was starving, and I could've wolfed it down in three bites, but it felt somehow impolite to eat while I was being chastised.

"That's not the point."

"Then what is the point?"

He turned to me, staring with such intensity that I leaned back. "I told you we were handling this. I know you were involved. It's unfortunate that you were there. But now your only job is to get uninvolved. Do you understand that?"

I nodded.

"Good."

Tom unwrapped his Polish and started in.

I took a big bite of my hot dog. Chewed, swallowed, and then said, "There's just one thing —"

His expression dropped. "What?"

"I just wanted to find out if I'd screwed up or not. And — okay — I was worried about the president. Naveen said —"

"Quit calling him Naveen."

"That's his name, isn't it?"

"Just quit it, okay? It makes it sound like you know the guy. You don't. And you won't."

I decided to take a different approach. "You know how nosy I can be sometimes."

"That's an understatement."

I ignored the dig, and took another bite before continuing. "I caught the guy," I said, allowing just a bit of wheedling to creep into my voice. "I think I'm owed a little explanation."

Tom ate more of his food.

I waited. Sometimes that's all it takes.

"You know I can't tell you anything that's classified."

"And you know I would never want you to."

He nodded. "Craig and I discussed this before we went to see you. We disagreed. I wanted to lay out the information for you, because I know how you can be. How you pick, pick, pick at things till you figure them out." From the look on Tom's face, I gathered that this wasn't one of my more endearing traits. "Craig didn't appreciate that idea at all. He decided to take the hard-ass approach. Figured it would be more effective with a timid assistant chef." For the first time that afternoon, Tom smiled. "Little does he know."

I felt the ice begin to crack. I smiled, too.

Tom continued. "I couldn't very well tell him that I knew how to handle you, so we did it his way."

I tried to disguise my eagerness, but the

hopeful lilt to my tone gave me away. "You're saying that the matter has been declassified?"

He glared, but I could tell that his anger was long gone. "Some of it. Only some."

"And are you willing to share that 'some' with me?"

With a twist, he shifted his body to face me. "I'll tell you what I can — it's the same information we would give any White House staffer who asked. But." He held up a finger. "I first need you to agree that you'll drop this little investigation of yours."

I finished off my hot dog. It was better than biting my tongue. If I'd have spoken, I'd have blown it by protesting his exaggeration. I was about to get answers. Arguing now could only hurt me.

"I have no intention of calling the jail again. I swear."

He cocked an eyebrow and waited.

"And I promise not to try to find Navee— I mean, the guy who you guys caught yesterday."

I meant it. I really did.

Tom's fears apparently assuaged, he continued. "I can't tell you where he is right now, but I can tell you that his name *is* Naveen." He held up his hand. "No last name, okay?"

I nodded.

"Naveen is one of ours. Different agency."

I was about to ask if he was CIA, but Tom's look stopped me.

He continued. "And yes, he does know Craig. That's not classified. Neither is the fact that he's uncovered some information that suggests President Campbell may be in danger."

"You mean he thinks someone's planning an assassination?"

"Ollie," Tom said in a voice just shy of warning, "there are always threats against the president. If I knew about a planned assassination attempt, I couldn't tell you. What I can tell you is that the matter is sufficiently grave that we're following up on every possible front."

"If this Naveen fellow is one of the good guys," I said, trying to reason it out, "why was he running across the White House lawn?"

Tom sighed. "He's a talented agent — one of the best — and he's uncovered a lot that other guys might've missed, but he's fanatical. Naveen is always seeing conspiracies. Everywhere." Tom rolled his eyes. "He claims that there are higher-ups in the Secret Service who have been compromised."

"Do you believe him?"

"Right now, we have to believe him. We can't afford not to."

I considered this.

Tom stared off into some middle distance again, then seemed to come to a decision. "There's more," he said, "and this is off the record."

"Gotcha."

"We're eventually sharing this information with everyone on staff, but I figured it won't hurt to bring you up to speed early."

I wadded the hot dog's wrapper into a ball, itching to egg Tom on, wanting him to hurry up and tell me whatever this big thing was. But he was not a man to be rushed. I gripped the little paper ball tighter.

"Information will be disseminated. Soon." He licked his lips, the last bite of his Polish still in his hand. He took a deep breath. Blew it out. "Naveen told us that the Chameleon has targeted someone at the White House."

Targeted. The way Tom looked at me when he said it gave me shivers.

"The Chameleon?"

Almost whispering now, Tom continued. "You know there are paid assassins out there who'll go after anyone if the price is right?"

I nodded.

"The Chameleon is as ruthless, as mercenary as they come. I don't know of a single one of our allies who wouldn't celebrate if the bastard was caught."

"Why is he called the Chameleon? Because of his slimy activities?"

"No." Tom stood up. "Let's walk."

We tossed our trash and headed north up 17th Street. Tom kept watch as we strolled past the Eisenhower Old Executive Office Building, fondly known as the OEOB. We crossed to the west side of the street because of construction. Whenever anyone came too close, or someone passed us, he stopped talking entirely.

"The guy is called the Chameleon because he blends in, no matter what the circumstance. No one has been able to spot him yet. We don't know his name, what he really looks like, or even where his allegiance lies. If he has any." Tom snorted. As we waited for the light to cross back east at Pennsylvania Avenue, he looked down at me. The smile in his eyes was back. I'd been forgiven for my phone call fiasco. "That's it, okay? Right now you don't need to know anything else."

"I understand."

"And until we bring the rest of the staff

up to speed, keep this to yourself, okay?"

"I will."

We started walking again. "But," he said, "I wanted you to know because it'll help us to have another set of eyes. You see anything unusual . . . you get a new delivery boy . . . or anything seems amiss, you let us know."

One thing was bothering me. "If the guy — Naveen — wasn't arrested, and he isn't at the jail, then where is he?"

"We've got him somewhere safe."

I pointed north. "Blair House?"

"No way," Tom said. "Too high-profile. We want to keep this all very quiet. If the Chameleon knows Naveen's been talking with us, then we've got a whole 'nother set of problems to worry about. Right now we've got Naveen covered. We were afraid that his little stunt the other day might've alerted the Chameleon that he's here."

"So that's why you guys faked the news coverage!"

"Shhh."

"I wasn't that loud," I said, but I lowered my voice. "Sorry."

Tom glanced around. Nobody. "It's okay. Just trust me, all right? We agents are trained for this stuff, just like you're trained. We're both working to be the best in the world." He stopped. "We better split up."

"Yeah," I said. Although a few coworkers probably suspected there was more to our relationship than agent and chef, we both felt more comfortable keeping things under wraps for now.

"I guess I better see if there's any trouble brewing across the street." He turned toward Lafayette Park, then stopped. "Hey. When are you going to find out about the executive chef position?"

My stomach flipped at the question. I wished I knew. "The other woman — Laurel Anne Braun — hasn't had her audition yet."

"That the woman with the TV show?"

"Yeah."

Tom grimaced.

Great. Everyone thought that Laurel Anne was the shoo-in. Even my boyfriend. "You'll knock 'em dead," he said, but I wondered if he meant it. "Speaking of knocking 'em dead — you think you'll have any time this weekend to head out to the range? I need to get some practice in." I knew that. Secret Service agents needed to qualify at the range two weeks out of every eight. Before his turn came up for qualification, he always spent time practicing on his own.

"I'd love to."

He gave a quick wave and was gone.

Just as I cleared the northeast gate and

passed its accommodating chirp, my cell phone rang. I pulled it out of my purse, smiling because I knew it had to be Tom, calling from across the street. But when I glanced at the number, I didn't recognize it.

"Hello?"

"Ms. Olivia Paras?"

The voice was familiar, but it held an accent I couldn't place. "Yes."

"My name is Naveen Tirdad. I believe you have been looking for me?"

CHAPTER 9

"What?" I spun, then ran to the massive black gate. "How did you find me?" I looked out across Pennsylvania, trying to catch a glimpse of Tom in the park. Or of Naveen. For some reason I thought he might be watching me. After all, I was in almost the exact same spot I'd been when he ran past. "Where are you?"

"Before I answer your question, I must know why you attempted to locate me."

"I wasn't. That is, I mean . . ."

"Did you not try to reach me yesterday by telephoning the jail?"

Holy geez. How could he know that? I considered lying, but all of a sudden I was afraid to. Craig and Tom knew I'd made the call. And Naveen was one of ours — so it followed that he knew, too. "Yes," I said, my voice coming out as sheepish as I felt. "I did. But . . ."

But . . . what? I had no explanation

beyond my own foolish inquisitiveness. Not for the first time, I thanked God I wasn't born a cat. My curiosity would've killed me years ago.

"You are the young woman whom I encountered near the northeast gate, yes?"

That was a polite way of putting it. I relaxed a little and stopped searching the passing pedestrians. Freddie stepped out of his security booth, looking concerned.

"Hang on," I said into the phone.

Freddie checked me in, still looking puzzled. I faked a smile, and mouthed, "I'm okay," before hurrying toward the East Appointment Gate. To Naveen, I said, "I'm sorry for hitting you with the frying pan."

"Is that what it was? It felt like a sledgehammer."

"It was a gift," I said and realized how silly that must sound. I'd been about to ramble on further about Henry, but I stopped myself. "I hit you too hard. You were bleeding," I said. "I'm very sorry."

"Your apology is unnecessary," he said. "Your actions were precisely right. Your goal was to protect the president — and for that I commend you."

"That's very gracious of you. I know that . . . that . . ." For the life of me, I couldn't figure out how to politely say ". . .

that you're a bit of a fanatic." So, I stumbled. "That your intentions were good."

"Ah, so the Service has spoken with you."

All of a sudden it dawned on me that I'd promised Tom not to involve myself further in this affair. Now, here I was, on the phone with the very subject of our most recent conversation. Tom would kill me if he knew I was talking with Naveen.

But I hadn't initiated the phone call. Not that that little fact would make a difference with Tom.

"I can't talk to you."

"Why not?"

"I . . . they . . . I shouldn't have tried to contact you. I'm going to hang up now."

"Wait." He made a thoughtful-sounding noise. "Have they told you about the communiqué I intercepted?"

"No," I said. "Really. I have to go."

"Then why did you attempt to contact me?"

I made it to the East Gate, but I couldn't very well continue this conversation as I cleared security, so I paced in circles outside, talking fast, as though that made my conversation less of a transgression. "I was afraid I had hurt you and I just wanted to make sure you were okay."

121

He seemed to consider this. "That is what I thought."

"Well, it's been nice talking with you," I said. Lame, very lame. "I'm glad you're all right . . ."

"Wait, do not hang up. I must speak with you."

"I have to get back to work. I'm late as it is."

"Then meet me."

"No!" Tom's angry face loomed in my mind's eye, and my answer came out fast and loud. But then my curiosity reared its quizzical head. "Why?"

"I have information about an —"

He stopped himself. I was sure he was about to say "assassin."

"About?"

"The communiqué I intercepted has vital information that must be conveyed to the president."

"You should tell the Secret Service."

"I believe they have been compromised."

"No way."

"It is true."

I shook my head.

"May I call you Olivia?"

I answered automatically, "Sure," then frowned.

"Olivia, think about it. What if I am right?

What if there has been a breach in the Service? Do you really wish to take the risk of not listening to what I have to say?"

This was getting weird. And I needed to get back to the kitchen.

"Listen," I said, beginning to understand Tom's insistence that this guy was a conspiracy freak, "I'm just an assistant chef. I don't have anything to do with this. You should talk with one of the agents you trust."

"I cannot."

"I really have to get going."

"Please," he said.

I heard the word and it was déjà vu. When I'd whacked him he'd said "Please." And then I whacked him again. But Tom said Naveen was one of the good guys. I hadn't listened to him then, but I had the opportunity to listen now. Didn't I owe him that much?

"Okay, what's so important?"

"Not over the phone. We must meet in person."

This was beginning to sound like a bad Internet chat hookup. "No."

"You must. Your actions proved to me that you are trustworthy. After you risked your life to stop me, I knew then that you value the president's life very much. I need to convey a message to someone who is not part of the security contingent. It is imperative that I do so. And right now you are the only person I trust who has the ability to deliver this message."

I opened my mouth, but he interrupted.

"I promise I will not hit *you* with a frying pan."

That made me smile. "I don't know," I said. I knew my resolve was wavering. And I think he knew it, too.

"Tomorrow. Somewhere very public, so you need not be afraid of me."

I was surprised to realize that I wasn't afraid of him. Naiveté or stupidity — I wasn't sure which it was. "Where?" I waved to the guard at the East Gate. "Hurry. I really have to get back."

"At the bench next to the merry-go-round."

I knew where that was. Everyone in D.C. knew the merry-go-round on the Mall just outside the Smithsonian Castle. "What time?"

"Twelve o'clock."

"Midnight?"

I thought I heard him laugh. "Certainly not, Olivia. Noon. Will this work for you?"

"I don't think —"

"Please."

He just had to say that again, didn't he?
I sighed. "I'll be there."

CHAPTER 10

I thought if I cooked up something familiar I'd be able to get my mind off my troubles. I planned to start a batch of Crisp Triple Chocolate Chip cookies. My comfort food. But there were more surprises in store for me when I got back.

Peter Everett Sargeant — his back to the door as he addressed our group — prevented my surreptitious return to the sanctuary of the kitchen.

I tapped his shoulder to ease past him. "Excuse me," I said.

He drew back as though slapped. "It's about time you showed up. Where were you?"

I didn't think it would behoove me to tell him I'd been on the telephone with the White House fence-hopper from the other morning, so I said, "Lunch."

Sargeant made a dramatic show of looking at his watch. He still hadn't moved enough out of the way to let me pass and join the rest of the kitchen team. "And how much time is allotted for 'lunch'?"

The way he said it made my skin crawl. As though he somehow knew where I'd been.

Henry answered before I could retort. "If Ollie would have known about this impromptu meeting, I'm sure she would have been here earlier." He waved me forward and Sargeant was obliged to allow me by. "Ollie, Peter here has just informed us about an upcoming state dinner."

Peter. I loved the fact that Henry called this guy by his first name.

"If you'd been here," Sargeant began, as I took a position between Marcel and Cyan, "you would know how important it is for us to make this dinner a success."

I couldn't stop myself. "I think we all realize how important it is to make *every* dinner a success."

Sargeant looked taken aback. He sniffed, settled himself, and continued. "Which brings me to the next item on my agenda: Laurel Anne Braun's audition."

My stomach squeezed, and I felt blood rush up from my chest to flush across my face. As though Sargeant knew exactly how Laurel Anne's name affected me, he took that moment to laser his gaze my direction. My face grew hotter.

"It is my understanding," the little man said, "that up until now, this kitchen has been unable to schedule Ms. Braun's audition. I know that everyone here is very busy. And that there may be some misguided loyalty afoot" — he made another point of looking at me — "but perhaps, instead of taking extended lunch breaks, we should consider putting the White House's needs first."

Behind me, Henry made a sound that could have been muted anger or a warning for me to keep my cool.

I sucked my lips in and bit down to keep from saying something I might regret later. We'd been in touch with Laurel Anne's people almost every day for the past several weeks. Since she was a television star, with appearance commitments and filming deadlines, we worked through her representatives rather than with Laurel Anne directly.

Twice she'd been scheduled for her audition and twice she'd cancelled out on us at the last minute.

"So," Sargeant continued, "I have taken it upon myself to see that Ms. Braun is provided the opportunity she deserves. She will be here two weeks from tomorrow and I trust that you will all work with her to ensure that her audition goes smoothly."

I was about to protest that, as her primary competitor, it would be a conflict of interest for me to assist her, but apparently Sargeant wasn't finished with his announcement.

"I am particularly pleased to tell you that not only will Ms. Braun bring her *Cooking for the Best* talents to share with us" — Sargeant beamed — "but she will bring a cameraman along as well. Her producers have agreed to film her audition for broadcast purposes."

Henry and I exchanged worried glances. "No one is allowed to film at the White House," he said. "It's not done."

Sargeant shook his head as though he'd expected Henry's protest. "We will make an exception for this. I'll take care of it."

"Have you cleared this with Paul Vasquez?" I asked.

His lips barely moved as he repeated, "I'll take care of it." Without missing a beat, he turned. "If there are no other questions, I'm off to my next meeting." As he left, he tossed us a dismissive wave. "Carry on."

Henry pinched the bridge of his nose. "Just when you think you've seen it all."

Cyan and Marcel made supportive noises as they moved back to the tasks Sargeant had interrupted. Bucky wasn't in today, and I wasn't sure if that was a good thing or not. I patted Henry's back. "So when is this state dinner and who is it for?"

He raised his big head, as though grateful to me for bringing up a topic he could relate to. "It's next Wednesday," he said. "We will host the heads of state from two countries."

"Next Wednesday?" I was aghast. We usually had months to prepare for state dinners. And then the rest of the message made it through to my brain. "And we're hosting two countries? How? Which ones?"

Henry rolled his eyes. His bushy eyebrows arched upward melodramatically. "Peter Everett Sargeant III hasn't deemed it appropriate to provide those specifics just yet."

"What? We have a state dinner to prepare for in just over a week and he won't tell us who the guests are?"

"That's what he says." Henry lowered himself onto the stool near the computer. The way he sat made me believe he carried the weight of the world across those broad shoulders.

"How can we plan a menu that way?"

"A week," he said. "I have prepared state dinners in less than that. But I've always known who the guests are." He shook his big head. "And I also haven't ever had to deal with a prima donna television star and her entourage before."

This was a double bomb. We would be scrambling to get as much prep work done as possible over the next few days. We usually had at least two months' notice before anything this big. I could only imagine the anxiety in the social secretary's office today. This was madness. It ordinarily took weeks to compile a guest list, and even with three calligraphers on staff, they'd be working 'round the clock to get invitations out. I'd heard of these last-minute official events, a rarity around here. The staff still talked about Prime Minister Ehud Barak of Israel's visit in 1999 when a working lunch for eighteen people was transformed into a dinner for five hundred over a matter of five days. Successfully.

If that team could do it, so could we.

But with two heads of state and a "secret" guest list, deciding on a menu would be close to impossible. There was almost no time to schedule a taste-test. "Have you talked with Paul?" I asked. "About the reporting structure, I mean?"

"We're stuck with Sargeant. He's apparently golden. I have no idea why."

That was the worst news yet. "What are we going to do?"

For the first time since I came back from lunch, the sparkle returned to Henry's eyes. "Yes, Ollie. What are we going to do? You want the executive chef position, don't you?"

I bit my lip. Nodded.

"Then this is your project as much as it is mine. The executive chef position is a job like any other. There are ups and downs. You may get this appointment and not like it at all."

"With the way they're rolling out the red carpet for Laurel Anne, there's no danger of that."

"Don't be so sure." He clapped his hands together and stood. "No time like the present. Let's see what menu items we can come up with to submit to the First Lady for taste-testing." He pursed his mouth. "And to our good friend Peter as well."

I stole out of the kitchen to find Paul Vasquez. Fortunately, he was in his office and not overseeing the million other duties that were carried out by White House staffers on a daily basis.

"Paul, do you have a minute?"

He gestured me in as his desk phone rang.

Thirty seconds later he'd responded in the affirmative twice, the negative once, and he thanked whoever was on the other end before he clamped the receiver back in place and turned his full attention to me.

"How are things in the kitchen?" he asked. The tone was amiable, but the eyes were questioning. We both knew I would never come visit this office unless I had something important to talk about, so I spared him the extraneous chitchat and dove right in.

"I'd rather not be here when Laurel Anne Braun auditions."

His expression tightened. Creases appeared between his dark eyebrows as he consulted some papers on his desk. "She's not due here for two weeks."

"I know, but what with this surprise state dinner, I didn't want to lose sight of the audition issues."

He nodded, as though he'd expected me to say that. "I understand your frustration," he said, "but as soon as we get a menu settled the kitchen should be in good shape." Shaking his head he squinted, as though a thought just caused him pain. "But I have to tell you, our director of logistics is pulling her hair out tonight to get everything arranged in this short time frame."

"Why so little forewarning?"

Paul gave me a cryptic smile. "Circumstances presented themselves. And our president is taking advantage of a unique situation. It's a good move." His index finger traced information on the page as he spoke. "But, back to your request. Why don't you want to be here with Laurel Anne?"

I shifted. "From what I understand, she and I are the final two contenders for the executive chef position."

Paul's silence kept me talking.

"Don't you think it would be a conflict of interest for me to be here during her audition?"

He smiled, a bright flash of white. "You mean like you may be tempted to sabotage her efforts?" The smile widened. "Come on, Ollie, we know you better than that."

"I know," I said, my face blushing to acknowledge his comment. "But for appearances' sake, I thought it might be best — and besides, the kitchen isn't that big," I said. It was stating the obvious, but I desperately wanted out of the place when Laurel Anne and friends showed up. "Especially if she's bringing her television crew."

Paul laughed. "Why on earth would you think she'd do that?"

"Sargeant . . . er . . . Peter Everett Sargeant said so."

Paul sat back, blinking as he digested my

134

statement. No question, that little bomb had come as a surprise. "I will look into that."

It was a crack — an opening. I decided to push my luck. "Chief Sargeant won't tell us who the guests are for the state dinner."

Got him again. This time Paul sat up. "You must be mistaken."

I shook my head. "Henry and I have no idea what to plan for, what to stock. I mean, if we had an idea of even the region they come from —"

"They're from the Middle East," he said sharply. "The prime minister of Salomia and the prince of Alkumstan. I will see to it that the kitchen gets the complete dietary dossier on all our guests by this afternoon."

"Thanks."

Paul looked as though he wanted to grab the phone and get things in motion, so I stood. "One last thing," I said.

He glanced up and I knew I had to take my best shot, one more time.

"I'd be happy to work ahead, as much as possible, for all our commitments. I'll put in as many hours as needed. You know I will." Paul nodded and I could see him waiting for the other shoe to drop. "But I'd really appreciate it if I could be excused when Laurel Anne arrives for her audition."

I could tell I'd won this one. He gave a

brief nod. "I'll mention it to the First Lady. She has the final say on these decisions."

"Thanks, Paul."

As I exited his office, I heard him punching numbers into his phone.

I suppressed a smile. Something was finally going my way.

CHAPTER 11

The next day Henry finally received the dietary dossiers. "Salomia and Alkumstan," I said. "I couldn't believe it when Paul told me." Prime Minister Jaron Jaffe of Salomia was a sworn enemy of Prince Sameer bin Khalifah of Alkumstan. The two countries had been at war for decades. Ill-will didn't begin to describe the horrors these two populations inflicted on one another. "I'm surprised Prince Sameer is coming here now. Isn't he the guy who just overthrew his brother?"

"One and the same," Henry said. "And he did it without bloodshed."

We went over the dossiers, and read the hastily prepared summary of the purpose of this joint visit. During recent talks, the president had detected an opportunity for truce between the two countries, at least as far as trade agreements were concerned. Logic followed that if they could find common ground in business, perhaps eventually both countries could envision peace between their peoples as well.

"I guess Sameer really meant what he said when he took over Alkumstan," I said finally. "He claims to want peace in the Middle East. This would be a logical first step."

"Apparently so. His brother, Mohammed, and Prime Minister Jaffe haven't ever shared the same soil. This is a major coup. They will be creating history here. And whether or not a final trade agreement is achieved, it is a step in the right direction."

Working in the White House was big. Not just big; huge. I knew it and I remembered it every single day, but the truth was, after being on staff for this long, I'd gotten used to hearing the names of powerful individuals. After all, I'd discussed their preferences for meals, made myself aware of their dietary quirks and eccentricities. I'd gotten to know VIPs in my own way and slowly I'd become used to the idea of playing a part in the big world that was the White House.

But the upcoming state dinner exceeded all. This summit to discuss trade agreements could herald the beginning of a new era.

Delighted by the plethora of information provided about our guests and their nutritional needs, Henry was eager to design a menu that would wow and delight all those present. Immediately after breakfast preparations, he urged me to join him at the computer.

I eased onto the stool next to him, my voice nonchalant. "Oh, by the way, I'm going out for lunch today."

He cocked his head. "I thought we would work through lunch."

"Oh," I said, not knowing what to say. "Um . . . something came up."

"What is it?"

I hated lying to Henry. But I couldn't very well tell him that I was meeting Naveen.

When I hesitated, he asked, "A date?"

"No." Then I thought about it. "Well, kinda."

He rubbed his chin as he stared up at the clock. "Okay, then we'll just move a little faster this morning." His thick finger pointed to the first name on the list, Prime Minister Jaffe's. "I know how much you enjoy bringing the flavors of the visiting dignitary's culture into our American fare. Any ideas for an entrée that will please this man . . ." he moved his finger to the next two names, "as well as these two?"

He indicated Prince Sameer and his wife, Princess Hessa. Again, I realized how significant this was. Almost as momentous as Jimmy Carter's Camp David Accords. I stared at the computer screen, where we always recorded our meal plans, and tapped my lips with my finger. "No," I said honestly. "The two cultures, while close in proximity, are far apart in what they prefer to dine on. This might take some research."

Henry nodded. "Where are you going for lunch?"

The question took me aback. "Um," I said, stalling, "up near the Mall."

He gave me a funny look. "Really? Where do you plan to eat?"

I opened my mouth, but he interrupted.

"None of my business, I know. But I assume you're heading into the commercial area, if you have lunch plans. Can you pick something up for me?" He leaned sideways to write out the name of a book. "Here," he said. "If you don't mind. I ordered this from the bookstore on Thirteenth. They're holding it."

Great. I shouldn't have opened my mouth. I'd planned to zip out to the Mall and back. This detour would cost at least fifteen minutes and we were already pressed for time in the kitchen. Still, Henry rarely asked for favors, so I smiled and said it'd be no problem at all.

"Good," he said. "There are a number of innovative ideas in that book. I've been meaning to get it for months. It will come in handy for this event."

With Henry's note in my capacious purse, I struck out for my meeting with Naveen, just about ten minutes before noon. I could've taken the Metro, but I knew I could walk the distance faster. I wore my new Jackie O sunglasses — purchased specifically for today's meeting — and just as I veered off of Pennsylvania, taking a right on 12th Street NW, I pulled the rest of my disguise out from the recesses of my purse.

No one paid any attention to me as I twisted my hair and shoved it beneath a Chicago Bears baseball cap. Still walking, I tugged the cap's brim low so that it almost touched the top of my sunglasses. Within minutes I had the National Mall in sight. I stepped up my pace, pulling out the final items from my stash — a dark blue, very wrinkled windbreaker, and my old 35mm camera. When I pulled the strap over my head and settled the camera into place, I knew I looked like your average eager tourist on a jaunt to the Capitol. The one thing I couldn't do much about was my height. Belatedly, I realized I should've worn some-

141

thing with a heel. Darn.

It was a meager disguise, but a necessary one. I wanted to get this meeting with Naveen over with as quickly as possible — give him the chance to impart his vital piece of information and then get myself out — but I didn't want the Secret Service detail shadowing Naveen to recognize me. Without this disguise, I hadn't a prayer.

I'd done the best I could, under the circumstances, to blend into the sightseer background. I was still afraid of one thing — Tom. Even with my oh-so-clever appearance manipulations, Tom would know me in a heartbeat. I sure hoped he was on a different detail today.

As the merry-go-round came into view, I slowed my pace. A tourist wouldn't rush to the side of a carousel. Not without a little kid in tow. Plus, the windbreaker's added layer on this unseasonably warm day was making me hot. I drew a finger across my brow between the hat and sunglasses, and came away with a load of perspiration.

Never let 'em see you sweat.

I almost laughed.

Right about now, sweat was the least of my worries.

The sun overhead, the hat, the sticky windbreaker, and my own nerves were working overtime to produce a different kind of heat — that of real fear. But I couldn't stop now. Not until I knew what Naveen wanted to tell me.

Circus music drew me closer. I saw small children on brightly colored, rhythmically rising and falling horses, attentive parents with protective arms around their backsides. Just a normal, pleasant day in our nation's capital.

For me, however, it was anything but.

My feet continued forward, each step bringing me closer to the spinning ride even as my brain argued that this was one of the most foolish things I'd ever done.

I checked my watch. Noon.

Naveen had to be here somewhere. There was an elderly couple on a park bench near the ice cream vendor's cart. They wore matching red shorts, wraparound sun-glasses, and white visors. Three people stood in line for ride tickets, but all three had small children with them. There were about a half-dozen other adults surrounding the merry-go-round, pointing cameras or wav-ing at the riders. Not one of them looked like my memory of Naveen.

The carousel began to slow, but it wasn't until its shrill bell rang, signaling the end of the ride, that the passengers were able to get off their horses and make their way to the exit.

I scanned the riders as they filed past me. I checked my watch again. I was certain he'd said noon.

There seemed to be nothing to do but wait. I worried, briefly, about the Secret Service guys noticing my loitering, so I lifted the camera and took a couple of shots of the ride, the Capitol, and the Washington Monument, all of which would've made great pictures if I had any film in the camera. Bringing it along had been a last-minute inspiration but I hadn't had time to pick film up on the way.

Yep, I'd make a great spy, wouldn't I?

I wandered toward the ice cream cart, and eyed the chocolate bar with almond crust. It might be the only lunch I got today, I reasoned, and reached into my purse for some money.

A tap on my shoulder.

"Excuse me, ma'am, but I believe you dropped this."

I turned. Naveen was there, smiling, handing me something. A piece of paper. Folded. Like a note kids would pass in grammar school.

Automatically I took it, thanked him, and felt my mood shift from startled to puzzled when he walked away again.

The red-shorted elderly couple had vacated the bench next to me, and Naveen took a seat there, opening up a newspaper to read. Ignoring me completely. I took my cue from him and walked a few feet away.

Ice cream novelty forgotten, I opened the note, bracing myself for the big important information that Naveen needed to give me.

Purchase a ticket to ride the carousel. Choose the ride's bench seat. I will join you there.

Not what I'd been expecting. And I was beginning to feel prickly annoyance. The sooner I got what I came for, the sooner I could rush over to the bookstore and pick up the cookbook Henry wanted. Then, I could get back to my normal life and not have to worry about the Secret Service, and more important, Tom, who would be furious with me because of this little adventure.

I decided to cut the silliness right here. I turned, prepared to confront Naveen, prepared to ask him straight out to tell me what was on his mind.

But he was gone.

Maybe the guy was a nutcase. But then again, maybe he was the smart one, here.

145

Secret Service personnel were shadowing him, and the last thing I needed to do was to have one of them scrutinize me too closely.

Fine. I'd play along.

Another carousel ride was ending. I hurried over to the ticket booth.

In my haste, I bumped into a man rushing the other way.

"Sorry," I said.

He locked eyes with me — shooting me a look of such instant, violent disdain, that I was taken aback. The man was blond enough to be mistaken for an albino, but his eyes were a luminescent blue. He shoved me out of his way with the back end of his arm — like an old-time villain clearing a table of debris — and pushed past without a word.

"Well, excuse me," I shouted after him as I regained my footing. Some people were just born rude. I thrust my two dollars into the booth's window and remembered to thank the woman behind the glass as I claimed my ticket.

Last in line, I stood behind a man holding two kids' hands. I tried not to be conspicuous about looking around — looking for Naveen — but I couldn't help myself. What was I doing here but playing a part in someone else's conspiracy fantasy?

I'd gone this far. I'd take my seat on the bright red bench and see what happened.

Just as the ride operator opened the gate for the next set of riders, I felt a soft poke in my back.

"Do not turn around," he said. "I believe we are being watched. I will not join you on this ride."

I started to move away, but his fingers grasped the back of my windbreaker, stopping me. In a voice so low that the shuffling man in front of me wouldn't have been able to hear, Naveen said, "You must ride. I will wait. If it is clear, I will join you on the next ride." He let go and whispered, "Do you understand?"

I nodded, and walked forward, clearing the gate as Naveen took off.

This was getting to be too much.

Faced with the prospect of riding the merry-go-round alone, I made my way toward the miniature bench amid the painted horses. Wouldn't you know, it was already occupied by the red-shorted old folks. Completely annoyed at this point, I made my way to the outer perimeter, and grimaced when a ten-year-old beat me to the bright turquoise serpent. I chose one of the last empty critters, a white horse with a patriotic red, white, and blue saddle.

The ride's shrieking bell sounded the moment we were all in place, and the merry-go-round began its never-ending path to nowhere with me bobbing up and down, feeling more than just a little bit foolish.

I caught sight of Naveen in snippets as the ride turned. He had on sports sunglasses and navy blue running pants. His gray sweatshirt, with cutoff sleeves, revealed very impressive biceps. Looking like every other runner in the area, he wore nonchalance like a second skin. If I hadn't been attuned to his concerns, I wouldn't have given him a second glance.

He pulled his newspaper up, made his way to the bench near the ice cream vendor, sat, and began to read.

There were two round mirrors placed just outside the merry-go-round's fence. Sitting atop tall metal poles, they were placed strategically at about one-third and two-thirds around the perimeter. Their large convex surfaces gave the ride operator a constant view of the entire mechanism.

I tried to catch Naveen's reflection in the westernmost mirror every time my horse turned its back on the bench.

Nothing out of place.

He sat there and continued to read the paper.

Was this all just a hoax? Let's see how far the silly assistant chef will go? Was there a hidden camera somewhere, and a grinning television host ready to leap out and tell me this was all one big joke?

I came around again. Up and down, up and down. Without being too obvious, I watched Naveen as I circled past. No, this was no joke. His body was tense, and his dark eyebrows arched over the black lenses. He'd seen something, or thought he had.

We were slowing. Naveen hadn't yet gotten up to buy a ticket and I wondered if I should ride alone again. It'd be just my luck for some paranoid parent to call security and have me detained for suspicious behavior. Or a kid complain that I was hogging a horse.

The music continued as I whirled past again, but this time I felt a subtle change in speed.

The slowing went on for another several turns. I decided that as soon as I got off, I'd march over to Naveen, sit next to him, and force him to cough up this "vital information." If he wouldn't, I'd leave. Simple as that. I needed to take charge here.

Coupling this ridiculous errand with a trip

to the bookstore meant I'd probably be late getting back. I hated to be late.

We were almost stopped now.

Naveen sat up straighter, suddenly alert.

A man approached him. The same man who'd pushed me aside. He was moving too quickly. Oddly fast.

Naveen recognized the guy. Jerked away.

But the guy came in close.

Too close.

This was no Secret Service agent. Even I knew that.

My horse finally stopped, and as I rose in the stirrups to get off, the shrill bell announced the ride's end.

But this time, the bell sounded different — with a cracking background noise.

Naveen toppled off the bench onto the ground.

The blond man stood and began strolling away.

"Naveen!" I screamed.

Facedown in the dirt, Naveen didn't move.

I leaped off the horse and made my way to the exit, realizing belatedly that my shout had attracted the blond man's attention. He turned around. For the second time, we locked eyes. And I read in them a coldness I'd never experienced before.

He changed his direction and came after

me. Not strolling anymore.
I had no other option.
I ran.

CHAPTER 12

My short legs wouldn't win me this race. I needed help and I needed it now.

I took off as fast as I could, my feet straining for purchase on the gravelly path. With nothing in my mind beyond escape from whoever this creep was, I skidded around the front of a bright orange stroller, its front wheel catching the edge of my foot. I almost fell, but my arms windmilled like a vaudeville comic's, and the sunglasses flew off my face. I forced myself to move forward, to run, the camera bouncing against my chest in a rhythm that mimicked my pace.

I looked back long enough to ease my conscience. Thankfully, the stroller hadn't fallen — its occupant was unaffected.

But the white-blond man was gaining on me.

I shot forward, heading for the blue-and-white tour bus kiosk. They had phones in there. They could call security. "Help," I screamed, banging flat-handed against the Plexiglas windows as I raced around the kiosk's left side. The woman inside the booth recoiled in alarm. "Call the police," I shouted. "There's a killer after me."

As the words escaped my lips, I realized they were true.

Naveen was dead.

I couldn't wait.

The world froze and narrowed. There was only me — my shouts ringing hollowly in my ears — and the man close behind. His face wore anger like a grotesque mask.

I read his expression — there was no doubt that he would catch me. And soon I would be just as dead as Naveen.

I concentrated on putting one foot in front of the other.

Weren't there people around? As though standing at the mouth of a bright tunnel, I couldn't see anything beyond ten feet in front of me. Colors meshed, shapeless forms surrounded me. I heard nothing but the *whoosh*ing blood in my brain and the echo of my gasps as I skipped the curb, vaguely aware that I was supposed to check for cars.

Let the damn car hit me. Then maybe the assassin behind me wouldn't.

Horns blared.

I didn't stop. Didn't turn.

Just across the street was the welcoming red brick of the Arts and Industries Building. A haven. There would be security inside. I tripped up the steps and yanked at the door.

It didn't budge.

Horns blared again.

Brakes screeched.

"Help me!" I screamed. My voice, raw with emotion, pierced my consciousness enough to let me read the sign: CLOSED FOR RENOVATIONS.

I spun.

The blond man was on the ground in the middle of the street. Rolling. A taxi had hit him. People called for help.

My breath caught. Thank God.

And then — unbelievably — he righted himself. Back on his feet, he slammed both hands on the hood of the taxi and started to push his way past the bystanders who'd stopped to stare.

Where were the gapers when I needed them?

I took off to my left. To the Castle. There had to be someone there.

"Help!"

But I'd hesitated too long. The blond man was almost on top of me. His footfalls echoed my own on the short run across the

154

brick walkway that separated the two buildings.

He snatched the neckstrap of my camera, yanking me to a halt. The camera slammed into my face. I saw sparkles before my eyes. He seized my arm and turned me to face him.

All my self-defense practice with Tom paid off in that moment. Muscle memory, he'd called it. With an instinct borne of many hours of repetition, I slammed the heel of my hand against my attacker's temple. Then I sent a knee to his groin.

The man hadn't expected me to fight. His fingers loosened just enough for me to wiggle away.

I turned away, screaming again for help. Where was everyone? How could they just ignore me?

Still hampered by tunnel vision, I strove for focus. I ran past the flowered fountain. Purple flowers glowed in the sunlight.

Why on earth was I noticing flowers?

I heard scrambling behind me and I knew the killer had gotten up.

Three white-shirted security men came running around the front of the Castle, just as I was about to turn the corner. One grabbed me by the forearms.

I pointed behind me. "Get him!"

155

The black man holding me kept a tight grip. "Get who?"

I turned, still pointing.

The assassin was gone.

"He . . . he . . ." Safe now, in the presence of Smithsonian Security, I tried to pull away, looking for the white-blond man. But the guard held tight.

"You're not going anywhere, lady."

High-pitched wheezing shot out of me as I gasped for breath. "But he killed a man. He killed . . ." What was I supposed to say? That the guy who'd jumped the White House fence a couple days ago had been killed? And I didn't even know that it was true. Maybe Naveen had fainted.

I hoped.

But I knew better.

"Have you been drinking, miss?" one of the other guards asked.

I shook my head. "Follow me," I said, still trying to catch my breath. "I'll show you."

The black man holding me exchanged glances with the other two guards. They were all about my age, and their looks seemed to suggest that they were unwilling to humor me. "I think we better call for some help."

They started to walk me toward the Castle's front doors. "No," I said. "I have to get back to the bench."

For the first time I noticed I was shaking. Not chilly-outside-shaking, but whole-body trembling. All that had just happened, and my narrow escape from what I imagined could have happened was affecting me physically. I wanted to sit, but I couldn't. Not with Naveen lying alone by that bench. Please let someone have called for help.

An answering siren sounded nearby. "Thank God," I said, "maybe they can save him."

"Are you on medication?" my guard asked.

"Would you stop with the accusatory tone?" I'd been polite long enough. "There's a man over there who needs help. I saw him get . . . get . . ."

"Get what?"

"He slumped over. I think he's dead."

One of the other guards grabbed at his radio. "I'll call it in," he said, but the siren's wails were close now.

I shot my captor a look that said, "See?"

CHAPTER 13

The paramedics arrived on the scene just as I made it back to the bench, double escort in tow.

Naveen had been flipped onto his back by someone trying to administer CPR. The paramedics moved the Good Samaritan out of the way as other Smithsonian Security personnel worked the inquisitive crowd backward. I scanned their faces, searching for the white-blond man. But the gawkers, shifting as they watched, were just an average mix of curious tourists and nosy locals. I recognized some from my ride on the carousel.

I steeled myself to look down.

There was no doubt. Naveen was dead.

I bit my lips tight. He'd wanted to talk with me. He'd poked me in the back not ten minutes earlier. He'd claimed to have important information.

Most of all, however, he'd been alive.

Half his face was covered with dirt from where he'd fallen after the blond man's visit. Whoever had turned him, I'm sure, had been surprised by the body armor. Hard to do CPR on someone wearing Kevlar, I imagined. But even I could tell from here that Naveen hadn't had a chance. The blond man's bullet had done terrible damage. I couldn't believe the volume of blood. It mixed with the dirt to create an enormous black puddle under his body that the paramedics couldn't help but track through.

The sight of sticky footprints as Naveen's lifeblood seeped into the ground made me want to look away. But I couldn't turn my head.

The guys holding me hadn't let go the whole time it took to walk over here. They weren't letting go now, either. They hadn't handcuffed me, but I found myself the object of scrutiny as people around started to take notice.

The old lady in the red shorts pointed from across the circle of onlookers surrounding Naveen's prone form. "I saw that girl running." She turned to her husband. "We saw her running, didn't we, Egbert?" The man didn't have time to respond before the woman pointed again, and with old-lady vehemence called out. "You killed him!"

159

The black guy who'd first grabbed me tugged my arm, "Let's go," he said.

The elderly woman called after us, "Was he a terrorist?"

When I finally sat, it was in a hard plastic chair in what was undoubtedly an interrogation room. My face ached from the hit I'd taken with the camera. At my request, which had come out in little more than a bleat, someone had placed a paper cup of water on the table in front of me. I drank fast, my greedy throat parched from so much screaming.

My two guards had been replaced by two Metropolitan Police officers. One white, one black. Both standing, they looked at me with identical scorn. I'd shown them my White House ID, hoping that would buy me a little consideration.

I drained the paper cup. I guess that had been all the kindness I was going to get.

We'd gone over the events of the afternoon several times, and I'd begged to call the White House to let Henry know what was going on, but they hadn't let me near a phone, yet.

And just when I thought it couldn't get worse, a knock at the door admitted three Secret Service agents. Craig Sanderson, a woman I didn't know, and Tom, whose demeanor was just as professional as ever, but whose eyes bore into mine with an anger that sent white-hot fear racing across my chest.

"Thank you, gentlemen," Craig drawled to the two police officers. "We will take it from here."

They left, but I had no doubt the officers were simply shifting position to the other side of the room's one-way mirror.

"Ms. Paras," Craig said, taking a seat the moment the door closed. "I have a copy of your statement in front of me, but I have to ask: What were you doing on the Mall this afternoon?"

I tried hard not to look at Tom. I wanted, more than anything, for him to know that I hadn't broken my promise.

"Naveen," I began, focusing on Craig as I spoke, "called me." Now I did look at Tom, repeating. *"He* called *me."*

Unruffled, Craig said, "But that does not explain why you were out there with a dead man, a former operative, and why the witnesses believe you killed him."

"I didn't kill him. You've got to know that, don't you? It was a guy. A really blond guy."

Craig sat up. "You mean to tell me that you saw the killer?"

"Yes," I answered, surprised. "Didn't they tell you?" I'd gone over my statement with the Smithsonian Security guys and the Metropolitan Police at least five times. I'd made that point very clear. What now became clear to me was that the security staff and the police hadn't shared information with the Secret Service.

"Ms. Paras," the woman spoke up. She, too, had a drawl. Where on Craig it came across frighteningly passive, on her it sounded demure and inquisitive. "Why don't you tell us exactly what transpired here this afternoon?"

"Can I call Henry first?" I asked. "He's got to be worried. I should've been back hours ago."

Tom hadn't sat down. Now he pushed an unoccupied chair out of his way, making an angry scrape against the tile floor. "I'll call Henry," he said, without looking at me. Two heartbeats later, he was gone.

I felt my whole body react. He was furious. Once I explained, he'd understand. He had to.

My eyes stayed on the closed door for a long moment.

"Ms. Paras?" the woman prompted.

By the time I got back to the kitchen it was

after seven. With the president and First Lady out at a charity event at the Kennedy Center, it was very quiet. My shoes made soft noises as I made my way to the kitchen. Other than those standing guard at their posts, I didn't want to run into anyone else tonight. I wanted to gather my things and make my way home, hoping for a chance to connect with Tom along the way. I needed to explain myself.

Henry sat at the computer screen. He twisted his bulk around as the sound of my tiptoeing. "Ollie," he said, standing, "what happened?" He moved toward me. I let myself be enveloped by those big arms, and even though it hurt to press my bruised forehead against his chest, it felt so good to be held. "I was so worried."

"What did they tell you?" I asked into his chest.

I felt his grumble of relief. "Not much. Agent MacKenzie called here. At first I thought you'd been injured, but he said you were all right."

I broke away from him. "How did he sound?"

"How did he — ? Ah . . . yes, I understand. Tom. He was . . . professional. Terse and to the point. Nothing more, nothing less. He told me that you would be late returning."

Henry glanced up at the clock. "I didn't re-alize he meant this late. What on earth hap-pened? We heard about the shooting at the Smithsonian. Did you see it? Are you a wit-ness?"

I wanted to tell Henry everything. He had such a positive outlook on life and he seemed to see everything so clearly. I could've used a dash of his insight. "I'm not supposed to talk about it."

He nodded. "I understand." But his slight frown said just the opposite.

As he returned to his computer musings, I gathered a few things, added a couple of notes to my plans for tomorrow, and started to head out. "Henry," I said, suddenly remembering, "I didn't pick up your book."

He didn't turn. "It's okay."

His words were quiet, resigned. "It's okay." That bothered me more than if he'd made a joke or teased me about forgetting.

"See you tomorrow," I said, hoping for something more.

Henry nodded, but didn't say another word.

My shoes made their quiet squeaks across the floor, taking me through the dim hall toward the East entrance. I passed the wall of windows to my right, wondering who was out there in the night, and what they were planning. The sooner I got out of here and was able to call Tom, the happier I'd be.

"Ollie?"

I spun, gasping. I sucked saliva down into my lungs, which threw me into a coughing spasm. "My God," I spluttered. I hadn't heard Paul come up behind me. Bent in half, and supremely embarrassed, I held a hand up to cover my mouth.

He looked ready to slap my back. "I'm sorry, are you okay?"

I was already recovering, so I stepped just out of his reach. "Yeah, I just got scared is all."

"After this afternoon's excitement, I'm not surprised."

"What . . ." I coughed again. "What do you know?"

He looked off into the shadowed recesses of the long hallway as though considering what to say next. "You've had a tough day."

I thought of Naveen. I thought of how close I'd come to sharing his fate. "It could've been worse."

Paul nodded. "Which is why I waited for you tonight."

My stomach clenched — as though someone had reached in and squeezed. "You did?"

"About the executive chef position . . ."

165

he began.

Here it comes. I'm out. My actions today killed my chances. I knew it.

When it took forever for Paul to finish his thought, I prompted him, holding my breath even as I said, "Yes?"

"The First Lady believes . . ."

The fist around my stomach tightened.

". . . it's imperative that you *are* present when Laurel Anne has her audition."

I let my breath out. All I could think of was that I wasn't being fired. As disappointed as I knew I should be by Paul's pronouncement, I was elated that they hadn't decided to toss me out on my butt. Yet. And, I seemed to still be in the running for the promotion. After all that had transpired today, I took this as a positive sign. "All right," I said. "That's good news, right?"

Paul gave me a pointed look. A "don't get your hopes up" look. "Mrs. Campbell said, and I quote: 'If I decide that Laurel Anne's talents are the right choice for the White House kitchen, Ollie will be reporting to her.' " He shrugged with the resignation of someone imparting bad news. "She thinks it's a good test to see if you work well together."

"Sure," I said in a small voice. "Of

course."

"See you tomorrow, Ollie."

"Yeah."

The walk to the McPherson Square station gave me the opportunity to try Tom. I called him three times. It rang before it went to voice mail. That meant he had his phone turned on, but wasn't taking my calls. The first time that I got his voice mail, words failed me and I hung up. The second time, I started to explain, but was cut off by a disembodied voice letting me know my recording time was up. The last time I just apologized.

As I took the escalator down toward the rushing trains, I gripped my cell phone tight. "Please call," I whispered. The little display registered NO SERVICE and I got on the first train to Crystal City, with the firm belief that there would be a message from Tom waiting for me by the time the train emerged into the night at Arlington.

I walked from the Metro to my apartment holding the cell phone in my right hand in case it rang. Just to be certain that I hadn't missed Tom's call, I checked the display every so often as I slowly closed the short distance from the station to the apartment complex. Too slowly. I weighed a thousand pounds.

But the night was clear. Despite the plethora of lights from the surrounding buildings and those from the nearby airport, I could make out stars. Hundreds. One of them, bright and winking, made me stop to make a wish.

I held my breath and waited.

But the phone still didn't ring.

Maybe it wasn't a star, I reasoned. Maybe that one had been Jupiter.

A quick cold breeze shot past as I trudged up the walkway. Chilly night. Matched the state of my mood right now.

I worked up a smile and said hello to James at the front desk. While my building wasn't posh enough to have a real doorman, James tried hard to fit the bill. He took his job seriously, manning the front desk and walking the corridors each evening in a sort of pseudosecurity endeavor. He and two other fellows traded hours, and for their trouble they got a hefty reduction in their rent. James's white hair caught glints from the recessed lighting above, and he nodded a greeting.

"Who were those two fellas who came to visit yesterday morning?" he asked.

That was just yesterday? It seemed like months ago. "Friends of mine," I said.

"We talking about the same two fellas?" James asked. He was ready for conversation, but all I wanted was to grab an elevator and get to my apartment. "They didn't want me to buzz you. They showed me Secret Service ID, so I let them by. They looked pretty upset. Is anything wrong?"

I punched the "up" button, and was rewarded with an immediate "ding." At this time of night, there wasn't a lot of activity up and down the shafts. "Everything's fine," I said and sighed with relief when the elevator doors closed, cutting off further commentary. I punched the button for thirteen. I didn't put much stock in superstition, but other people did. Which is why I'd chosen the floor. Rent was cheaper.

Mrs. Wentworth must have been waiting for me, because she popped out of her door the moment I stepped off at our floor. "Olivia," she called, waving a sheet of paper at me with her free hand — the one not gripping her cane. "Come here."

Rather than taking the right to my apartment, I veered left to hers. "I have to —" I began, but she cut me off.

"Is this you?" She thrust a computer-printed page at me and pointed an arthritic finger at its color picture. "I found this on

169

the Internet. Did you really kill a terrorist today?"

I grabbed the sheet. "Does it say that?" I asked, scanning the article, looking for my name and hoping desperately not to find it.

"No, of course not," she said. "They don't say who killed the terrorist. But I figured it must be you. You had those two Secret Service men come visit you last night, and then you were there when this terrorist got shot."

I should have known Mrs. Wentworth would have found out that Craig and Tom were Secret Service — probably from James. Fatigue loosened my lips and I blurted, "He wasn't a terrorist."

"A-ha. Then this is you."

"Where?" I asked. "I don't see anyone in this picture that looks like me."

"Right there." She pointed to Naveen's prone form, dead center of the crowd. Her finger moved to the picture's very edge, where the side of a nose and a slice of cheek had made it into the shot. Barely. "That's you, isn't it?"

"No," I said. I looked closely. It could've been me. "I wasn't there," I lied.

Her pale eyes sparkled and a grin played at her pursed lips. "If you weren't there, honey, then that's the first thing you would've said."

Wily old lady. I should've been more careful, but my weariness was taking its toll.

"I should go."

"So, did you kill him?"

My stomach wrenched. In a way, I guess I had.

"I'm really not sure what happened there." That, at least, was the truth. "Good night, Mrs. Wentworth."

Her skeptical eyes watched till I shut the door. Leaning against it, I realized I still had the cell phone clamped in my hand. My knuckles ached.

A swift glance at my hall clock — Tom should've called by now. It had been a helluva day. "Come on," I pleaded with the little phone. "Give me a chance to explain."

It took all my effort to push myself off the door and get ready for bed. There were no messages on my home answering machine, not that I expected any. If Tom called, he would use my cell. I pulled on a pair of cotton pants and a T-shirt, brushed my teeth, and stared solemnly at my reflection in the mirror. I was different tonight, in a way I couldn't explain. But my eyes told the story.

Suddenly not tired at all, I grabbed my butterfly afghan — my nana had made it for me — and pulled it tight around my shoulders as I made my way out onto my balcony. No chairs, so I sat on the hard concrete. There wasn't much of a view down below, but high above was a wide swath of sky.

My cell phone sat next to me, silent as ever.

The breeze was cold. The night, very quiet.

I gazed up at the stars and thought about Naveen.

CHAPTER 14

Bucky was kneading dough when I walked into the kitchen the next day.

"Good morning, Ollie," he said.

Bucky's uncharacteristic good cheer, coupled with the bleak looks I got from of the rest of my colleagues, stopped me in my tracks.

Cyan met my eyes. "What are the bruises from?" she asked, pointing to her own forehead as she stared at mine.

"Altercation with a camera," I said. "Long story. What's going on?"

She then glanced over to Henry, who turned away. Marcel appeared to be muttering to himself as he worked at a floral sculpture made entirely of sugar. Bucky whistled. It was the happiest I'd ever seen him.

"What happened?" I asked.

Cyan broke the news. "Laurel Anne's coming tomorrow."

173

"What? She can't."

Bucky stopped whistling. "Oh, yes she can."

"But . . ." I protested. I'd been here late last night when Paul told me I was required to be present for her audition. He hadn't said anything about moving up her audition day. "But we have a state dinner next week."

"Yes," Henry said. "Due to unexpected circumstances, however" — he gave me a look that told me my actions yesterday had had more repercussions than I'd anticipated — "Peter Everett Sargeant III believes it is in the White House's best interest to get Laurel Anne in here as soon as possible." He turned away again.

Bucky added, "Sargeant says that her audition is merely a formality now."

I'd done it, all right. By agreeing to meet Naveen, I'd seen a man get murdered, nearly gotten killed myself, jeopardized my career, endured interrogation by the police, and alienated Tom. I swallowed hard. And I still didn't have the commemorative pan returned to me for Henry's retirement party.

Looking at my mentor's back right now, I realized that was the least of my worries. Henry was angry. He had chosen me to be named executive chef. And I'd blown my chances. I'd blown them spectacularly.

"Well then," I said with forced energy, "it looks like we'll have to work twice as hard today to get the state dinner arranged, doesn't it?"

Cyan and Marcel looked at me as if I'd gone stark-raving nuts. Bucky went back to his dough. But Henry's big head came up, and he turned. I thought I detected a glimmer of pride in his eyes. At least I hoped it was.

"Yes," he said, "that's exactly what it means."

By six o'clock, we'd come up with three preliminary menus, all variations on a theme involving American cuisine with the two countries' unique flavors as accents. Bucky and Marcel had gone home an hour ago, Cyan was just finishing her preps for the next day, and Henry and I were hashing out the remaining state dinner details, including filling out orders from our vendors and contacting the sommelier to have him begin choosing suitable wines. Aware of the added complication of having to pass Sargeant's taste test, we'd decided to develop these three menus, with interchangeable courses. Sort of a mix-and-match plan.

We had a hunch that, if he remained true to form, Sargeant would toss aside at least one of our offerings. Probably more.

The intensity of our planning had taken my mind off my troubles with Tom, but now, as Cyan called good night, I thought about her going home to her boyfriend, and I pulled my cell phone from my pocket. I hardly ever kept my cell phone with me at work. But today I had.

No messages. Still.

The disappointment made my heart hurt.

"Ollie," Henry said, pulling me out of my reverie.

I tucked the phone away again. "Yes?"

He tapped at the computer screen. "Why did you remove the pine nut appetizer from our submission list?"

Work was the best panacea for a broken spirit. "The prince's wife," I said, reaching past Henry to dig through my notes. "We have a reminder here that she's allergic to nuts. The pine nut appetizer was the only item that might've caused an issue."

He stopped and looked at me. "You ready for tomorrow?"

Tomorrow.

The kitchen grew suddenly quiet, as though the entire White House was holding its breath, waiting for me to say her name out loud.

"Laurel Anne's big day," I acknowledged.

I focused on a small spot near the ceiling so I wouldn't have to see the lie in Henry's eyes when I asked him, "This audition really is just a formality, isn't it? She's got the position wrapped up already, doesn't she?"

Henry didn't answer.

Eventually, I lowered my eyes to meet his.

"Ollie," he said in the paternal tone I'd come to know so well, "if that's what you believe, then that's exactly what will happen. If you give up, then she wins. With no effort." His mouth curled down on one side and he shook his head. "Seems to me an executive chef ought to earn her position, not have it handed to her on a silver platter."

Paul Vasquez knocked on the wall as he entered the kitchen. "I don't mean to interrupt, but Ollie has a visitor."

Could it be Tom?

"The Metropolitan Police need you to look at some mug shots," Paul said, dashing my hopes, "to see if you can identify the man from . . . from yesterday. They wanted you to come down to the station, but I convinced them you were needed here. I know how busy you are with everything you've got going this week."

I guess my face must have communicated my disappointment, because Paul was quick to jump in and ask if this was a bad time.

"No, it's fine," I said, just as Henry agreed and told me he'd wait for my return.

Before heading off with Paul, I gripped a handful of Henry's tunic and leaned close to his ear. "I am not giving up."

Unable to recognize anyone in the police photos, I made my way back to the kitchen about a half hour later. Along the way, I passed our social secretary coaching her team through this foreshortened lead time. "Nothing's impossible with the right attitude," I heard Marguerite say.

The team had set up a large felt board where they tacked, removed, and retacked names to devise the dinner's seating arrangements. This was a tough one. I wasn't even sure all the invites had gone out yet. I couldn't imagine the logistical nightmare the social office faced for this event.

When I got back to the kitchen, I found Henry just outside the door, in conversation with Peter Everett Sargeant and a man I'd never met before.

Henry called me over. The new man, wearing a smartly cut suit, full beard, and blue patterned turban, turned slowly at my approach. His hooded eyes were expressionless, yet I was aware of his immediate and thorough inspection of me. I ran the dossier information I'd studied through my head and deduced he must be a representative of Prince Sameer.

"Ambassador Labeeb bin-Saleh, allow me to introduce my first assistant, Olivia Paras," Henry began.

Sargeant interrupted. "We're finished here." He started to guide the ambassador away.

Henry continued as though Sargeant hadn't spoken. "Olivia, you and I will be working closely with Ambassador bin-Saleh and his assistant, Kasim."

I smiled at bin-Saleh. I knew better than to shake hands. He bent forward, slightly, in acknowledgment.

Bin-Saleh's words were melodious as they rolled out of his mouth. "The prince and his wife very much anticipate sampling your talent for food making."

"And we are honored by your presence," I said. "I look forward to working with you and your assistant."

"Kasim," he said, "has not been well on our journey, and he has retired to his room at the house of Bah-lare for the evening."

I knew he meant to say Blair House, the expansive residence across the street where visiting dignitaries were usually accommodated.

"I'm sorry to hear that he's ill," Henry said. "I hope he recovers soon."

The ambassador bent forward again. "I will intend to convey your pleasant wishes."

"Yes, well," Sargeant interrupted as he insinuated himself between Henry and bin-Saleh in an effort to guide the man away. "The ambassador has had a long trip, and I'm certain he would prefer to retire for the evening." To us he added, "We will continue this tomorrow afternoon at two o'clock."

I blurted. "Tomorrow afternoon?"

Sargeant fixed me with a cool stare. "Yes, Ms. Paras," he said. "Two. That will give me time to prescreen the menu items you're proposing for the state dinner."

Did he mean that we were supposed to create our menus for him by tomorrow morning?

As he and bin-Saleh turned away, I called after them. "Wait."

Sargeant's eyes glittered. Ooh. He was not happy.

Bin-Saleh simply blinked, his expression mild.

We needed clarification — tonight — and I knew this was my best shot. I didn't like to air grievances before guests, so I tried to keep my voice neutral. "You do remember that Laurel Anne is coming tomorrow, right?" I asked. Then, with the hope that wishing made it so, I added, "Or has she been rescheduled?"

"Of course I remember that Ms. Braun is due here tomorrow. And thank goodness for that." Sargeant looked to bin-Saleh as though sharing a joke, but the ambassador said nothing. He blinked again, still without expression.

Henry's hand grazed my shoulder blade. I didn't know whether he was encouraging me to continue or warning me to stop. But I pushed. "She's taking over the kitchen for the day. The whole day."

Sargeant rolled his eyes. "Yes. That's why Mrs. Campbell and I are planning to conduct the taste test tomorrow morning — eight thirty sharp. With Laurel Anne here, the First Lady and I will have much to look forward to. Now," he added, "we have other staff members to meet. Good night."

Bin-Saleh bowed our direction. Henry nudged me. I was so flustered by Sargeant's pronouncement I almost forgot to respond.

"What are we going to do?" I asked, the moment they were out of earshot.

Back in the kitchen, Henry scowled. He was silent for a very long time. "How early can you get here tomorrow?" he asked.

"I can stay all night."

"No." He shook his head. "Go home. Sleep fast. You'll need every bit of energy and strength tomorrow. I'll call the others. We'll meet here at four and get as much done as we can before the 'star' arrives." He smiled down at me. "It's just been one thing after another lately, hasn't it?"

I pointed out the doorway, in Sargeant's direction. "And I can tell you exactly when it all started."

I took Henry's advice to get home quickly. My cell phone was out of power — not that it mattered. As I rode the Metro to my stop, I realized that Tom wasn't going to call. Not now. Not until the whole Naveen situation was settled. Or maybe, I thought — with a sudden lurch to my gut — he might never call again.

Last night I'd felt the weight of the world pressing me down. Now, as I walked to my apartment building, I realized I'd never felt so low.

Tonight was much worse. I couldn't even summon enough hope to wish on a star.

The last twenty steps to the building's bright front doors were up a gentle incline, but it took all my energy to climb it. As I reached out to grasp the front door handle,

I heard footsteps behind me.

"Ollie."

I turned.

Tom crossed the driveway, closing the distance between us in ten steps. His face was set, his expression unreadable. "You got a few minutes?"

CHAPTER 15

We passed the front desk without James saying a word beyond, "Good evening." He raised his eyebrows and gave me a look that asked a thousand questions. All of which I chose to ignore.

Tom and I started into the elevator, but a woman who lived several floors above me called out for us to hold it. The twentysomething blond shot in as though finishing a run and stood in the small area's center, effectively keeping us silent for the entire ride up to my place. Tom looked good. So good. I was sure the blond had to notice him — who wouldn't? — even as she studied the rising floor numbers. Tom was strong and trim and the sight of him, so near — with the way the ends of his hair twisted this damp evening — took my breath away.

He wore a pair of pressed khakis and a dark polo shirt open at the collar. I caught a whiff of aftershave. That was a good sign.

At least I hoped it was. He never wore any scent at work — only when we went out. He claimed he only ever wore it to impress me because I liked the smell so much.

Then again, he might have come to break up, officially, with a plan to spend the rest of the evening looking spiffy and gorgeous, and smelling great for some other woman. But he wasn't eyeing the blond's obvious attributes. He was staring at the numbers, too.

The elevator's climb to the thirteenth floor was agonizing.

"Excuse me," we said in tandem, when we finally arrived. Tom followed me down the carpeted hall, his soft footfalls reassuring and terrifying at the same time. I begged the fates not to let Mrs. Wentworth waylay us tonight as I fumbled to let us in. I couldn't get my hand to work right — couldn't get the key into the lock.

Tom said nothing.

I let him step past me when I finally got the door open. As I shut it behind us, I remembered Henry's admonishment to "sleep fast." Glanced at the hall clock. Almost nine. I had to be up again by two. But Tom's face made me realize some things were more important than sleep.

"We need to talk," he said.

185

We were both still standing in the tiny hallway. "Are you hungry?" I brushed past him and caught wind of the soft spicy aftershave again. My heart beat faster and I swore I could hear it banging inside my breastbone. I cleared my throat. "Want something to drink?"

I ducked into the kitchen, partly to open the fridge and pull out a beer for Tom, and partly because I couldn't look at him right now. I needed to compose myself before I spoke one word of apology. I'd had all day to think about what I'd say to him, but right now my head was in knots, not to mention my tongue. I wanted to tell him how sorry I was that I'd tried to meet Naveen, but the truth was, given the circumstances, I didn't see how I could have handled it differently.

I'd been frightened yesterday. More than ever before in my life. I'd seen death and I knew what he looked like. He was short and white-haired, with pale blue eyes. And his hands had been on me.

I stared at the bright inside of the refrigerator, not seeing anything. When I blew out a breath, it trembled through my chest. I don't know how long I stood there, cool air rushing at me, but Tom reached around and pushed the door shut.

"Ollie."

I finally looked up at him.

"You lied to me."

"I didn't."

He flexed his jaw. "You told me that you were not going to try to contact Naveen again."

"He called *me."* I splayed my fingers across my chest, my voice betraying my anxiety. "I told you that. I must have said that a hundred times already. I didn't try to contact him."

"Oh, come on." Tom's expression hardened. "Give me just a little credit. The only way he could have called you is if you called him first."

"But I didn't . . ."

"You told us. You told us right here," he said, jamming his finger toward the floor, "that you weren't going to pursue this. How long did you wait till Craig and I left before you tried calling Naveen again?"

"I didn't call him." Shaking my head, I tried to continue, my voice rising in frustration. "After you left, I stopped. I swear I did. Remember, we talked about it the next day?"

"Uh-huh." He was biting the insides of his cheeks. He only did that when he was really angry. "One problem with your story, Ollie. If you never called him, then how did

187

he get your number?"

I shook my head again. "I don't know. I can't figure it out. I was going to ask him, but . . ."

Tom's gaze shifted to the room's near corner. "It doesn't add up."

"But . . . you and Craig found my number — because I called the D.C. Jail," I said, trying to make sense of it all. "Maybe he did the same thing."

He fired me a look of disdain. "Unlikely. And even if he did. Even if I give you that. Even if I believe you — and God, Ollie, I want to — why didn't you tell me you were going to meet him?"

"He asked me not to."

Tom stared.

My words sounded small, lame. "He said there was a leak. High up. That he couldn't trust anyone."

"And you believed that? You trusted him more than you trust me?"

"No, of course not."

He asked me again, his words coming out measured and crisp. "Then why didn't you tell me you were meeting him?"

I had no answer. Everything seemed so clear all of a sudden. He was right, I should have told him. My voice was low as I tried to explain. "I couldn't tell you. I promised you . . . and if I would've said anything, you wouldn't have let me go."

"Damn right I wouldn't have let you go," he shouted. "You could've been killed out there!"

"Shhh."

"I will not be quiet. Damn it, do you have any idea the danger you're in?"

With a suddenness that took my breath away, I understood. Tom was worried for me. "But I'm okay now," I said. "I didn't get hurt."

The look in his eyes told me I didn't comprehend.

"Not yet," he said, turning away.

"What do you mean?"

He blew out a breath and faced me. "Ollie, you are the only person we know who's still alive who can identify the Chameleon."

My knees went weak. "That's who killed Naveen?"

"Yeah." He nodded. "You came face to face with the world-class assassin. And he came face to face with you. We've done our best to keep your description and name out of the news media. Just like we did with Naveen." He closed his eyes. "For all the good that did him."

"Oh." I sat hard on one of my kitchen chairs, trying to process it all. Finally, I

189

asked, "But . . . where were the guys?"

"What guys?"

"Secret Service. I thought you told me that you had him under surveillance."

"Yeah." Tom paced the small area. "Naveen lost them. He must have known he was being watched. He shook the tail."

"I was so afraid of any agents recognizing me that I was hoping he would lose them," I said. "Now I wish they'd have been there. They might've saved his life. Tom," I began, to stave off the storm brewing in his expression. "Listen —"

"No, you listen. For once, okay? Just once, you listen to me."

I tightened my lips.

"Yes, there's more, and you'll be hearing more about precautions we're taking. Yes, Little Miss Nosybody, Naveen gave us information. Good information. But he was supposed to get us more. He didn't. Because he was killed trying to meet you."

I opened my mouth to ask a question, but thought better of it.

"Could this new information be what Naveen wanted to tell you?" Tom asked rhetorically. "I don't know."

Of course it was, I thought. But Tom paced again, talking more to himself than

190

he was to me. He rubbed his face with both hands.

"Is there anything I can do?" I asked.

"We know the Chameleon is planning something big. We don't know what it is."

I nodded.

"At this point, all we can do is be alert. Keep watch for anyone who fits his description." Tom heaved a deep sigh. "We'd like you to talk to a sketch artist."

"Sure," I said. "Of course."

"Good. I'll arrange for you to meet with him tomorrow. Right now you're our key witness. We need that sketch as soon as possible."

My heart sank again. Was that the only reason he came here tonight? To smooth things between us enough so that I'd cooperate?

"As soon as possible — just in case he gets me, huh?"

Tom flashed a look of such anger, I leaned back. "Do not ever say anything like that again, Ollie. Do you understand?"

"Yes," I answered. There wasn't anything else I could say.

"What's your day look like tomorrow?"

I gave him a quick rundown about the taste-testing and Laurel Anne's audition. He rubbed his face again. I began to realize just how much frustration I had caused.

"What time are you going in?"

"Three thirty."

Tom looked stricken — then glanced at his watch as he moved toward my front door. "Damn it, Ollie," he said. "You're not going to get any sleep tonight."

I gave a helpless shrug.

"Didn't I just tell you we all have to be alert?"

He moved for the door.

I stood up. "But —" I couldn't help myself. "What about us?"

I wished his expression would soften. I wished he would take me in his arms and tell me everything was going to be okay. Instead he shook his head. "I can't do this, Ollie."

"Can't do . . . what?" I asked in a small voice.

He took a long breath and flexed his jaw. "I think we should take a step back."

His words hit me like a gut-punch. I wanted to say something — anything — to make him change his mind, but no words came.

"I'm sorry," he said. "Maybe this was a bad idea."

"No," I said. "It's a good idea. *We're* a good idea. I blew it. It's my fault. I'm sorry."

A trace of affection flitted through his eyes. He tried to smile. "Maybe, when all this is over," he said, "we'll talk."

CHAPTER 16

There was no good reason to whisper, but Henry and I kept our voices low just the same. It was almost as though we had a tacit agreement to tiptoe around the kitchen, lest we disturb the fates and bring Peter Sargeant charging down upon us, to tell us what we were doing wrong.

Cyan and Marcel showed up shortly after we did. Bucky followed and didn't grouse, not even a bit, about the early start. We'd all been through enough state dinners before to know the drill. Having to produce an amazing and flawless dinner for over a hundred people, including two heads of state in addition to our own president, took enormous effort. The fact that we had to create this event in less than a week demanded nothing short of a miracle.

But then again, we worked miracles in this kitchen every day.

"As soon as we receive approval from all

parties and a guest count," Henry said, "Cyan, you organize the stock we'll need — get in touch with some of the vendors today to put them on alert. Does that work for you?"

Without waiting for Cyan's nod, he turned to Marcel. "I'll need samplings of your desserts — taste is paramount today, designs later — by eight. Is that enough time?" We all knew Henry's questions were simple courtesy. Eight was the deadline. No negotiation there. "Once your creations are approved, be sure to coordinate with Cyan for whatever you need to order."

While Henry continued his orchestrations — with Bucky and with additional directives for Cyan — I watched him. He had a safe, straightforward manner that inspired confidence even while he encouraged us to perform Herculinary tasks. I wanted to cultivate that talent in myself, whether I took over as executive chef or not.

Bucky would contact our temporary help — state dinners required that we bring on additional staff — and we had a queue of folks who waited for "the call." This time the call would go out to several of our Muslim chefs as well. In order to keep *halaal,* butchered meats must be prepared and transported according to rigid standards.

We were prepared for this, and we had many reputable chefs willing to work at the White House on a moment's notice.

Depending on availability, most would be professionals we worked with before — others would be delighted to get their first shot at working in the White House. All of them had undergone rigorous background and health checks, coming to our attention via trusted sources. Temporary pay was nothing special, but working for the White House held great prestige. Every temp hoped that his or her performance would lead to a permanent job offer next time the White House kitchen had an opening.

I made a face. After all that had happened recently, it could be my job they'd be vying for.

"Ollie," Henry said, winding up, "you're with me. We've got less than three hours before Laurel Anne is due to arrive."

Bucky huffed. "It's ridiculous, having her audition today," he said. "She deserves her own day, when everyone's attention isn't pulled elsewhere."

I opened my mouth to argue that she'd had two prior opportunities for her "own day," and that she'd been the one to cancel those. But Tom's visit last night had knocked me for a loop. I didn't feel like arguing.

We made a good team, the five of us. Although Marcel, as the pastry chef, tended to work independently, we all worked to pull together everything we needed for the taste-test offerings later this morning. We would still need to cook many of the items on the spot because we wanted to serve them to the First Lady while they were fresh.

Laurel Anne had sent along her ideas for the day's meals, both for the First Family and for official events. She'd created two menus, and had originally wanted to bring her own ingredients, but we shot that idea down in a hurry. We used only approved vendors, and incoming meats, produce, and other fresh items were checked for palatability as well as for safety. In today's world, you never knew.

With that in mind, we'd set aside several locations for Laurel Anne. She had one shelf in both the walk-in refrigerator and the freezer for her requested items. She also had one station in the kitchen itself that we tried not to encroach on, even before her arrival.

"Knock, knock," came a voice from the hallway.

We turned to see Peter Everett Sargeant enter the kitchen, two men close behind. Sargeant looked like he just rolled out of bed. Although dressed impeccably, as always, his face still had a long sleep-crease down one side and his eyes were tiny. The men behind him, by contrast, appeared wide awake. The first one I recognized as the ambassador Henry and I had met last night, Labeeb bin-Saleh. He was again dressed in a dark suit and again wearing the bright turban. The other man, taller than bin-Saleh by a good four inches, wore flowing robes and walked with a slight limp. He too, had a full beard, but wore his differently than his boss did. Bin-Saleh was natty in an exotic sort of way; this new fellow — who I assumed was the formerly ill assistant — was swarthy. He looked unhappy to be here.

He murmured something to bin-Saleh, who then murmured to Sargeant.

Before beginning introductions, Sargeant excused himself and escorted the assistant down the hallway. We could guess where they were going even before bin-Saleh apologized for the interruption. "My assistant, Kasim, is still recovering from our long journey."

"Welcome, again, to our kitchen," Henry said. I could tell he was thrown by this early morning visit. It wasn't yet five thirty. And we had a whole lot to do before Laurel Anne arrived. Still, he made introductions all around.

"I requested of Mr. Sargeant to allow us visiting you early," bin-Saleh explained. "We are remained on a different time and we find it most difficult to maintain to sleep at unwelcome hour."

"Of course," Henry said.

Sargeant and Kasim returned shortly, the taller man looking somewhat more relieved. Again, Henry made introductions and before Sargeant could correct him, he informed bin-Saleh and Kasim that I would be their primary contact with regard to dietary requirements.

The room went quiet. "I've studied the dossiers," I began. I smiled and enunciated clearly. I knew I had a tendency to talk too fast and I didn't want to confuse them if their command of English was limited. "It is my understanding that the princess is allergic to nuts, is that correct?"

I expected them both to nod. Instead, bin-Saleh turned to Kasim for explanation. Kasim translated — I supposed *allergic* and *nuts* weren't in bin-Saleh's English vocabulary yet. Kasim spoke at length, then turned to us, vehemently shaking his head. "Where did you get that erroneous information?" he asked in accented English. He wasn't angry.

He seemed confused. "The requirements we sent ahead of time were quite clear. Our prince and his wife have preferences, and there are several dishes we prefer you avoid, but what you have suggested is incorrect."

I knew what I'd read in the dossier. There had to be some mistake. I opened my mouth to ask for clarification, but Sargeant's glare kept me silent, even as my face reddened. The three men continued to discuss the upcoming event and I followed along, still stung.

Kasim's syntax was perfect. For the first time I felt a shred of relief. Working with him would be a lot easier than working with Sargeant, or even with the ultrapolite though laconic bin-Saleh.

Henry and I exchanged a glance. It looked like the pine nut appetizer was back on the menu, but it bothered me that I'd gotten bad information. I'd have to look into that.

"We will provide you with menus for approval later today," I said to Kasim. "In the meantime, is there anything we can prepare for you now?"

He closed his eyes briefly and I realized that offering food to a man who was unwell was probably not the smartest thing I'd done today.

Bin-Saleh chimed. "We have taken much

time of you here. Now we must return to the house of Blair. Thank you. We will return this afternoon to discuss the menus." He bent forward again and turned away.

They were only out the door for a half a minute when Sargeant returned, glaring at me. "What were you talking about?" he asked.

I had no idea what he meant.

"The prince's wife allergic to nuts? Where did you get that?"

"It was in the dossier," I said.

"You aren't in the habit of confirming information?"

I was. I always confirmed everything. In fact, I wanted to say, my bringing it up in conversation could be considered a confirmation of sorts. An attempt at confirmation, at least. "Yes, I am."

"Then think before you open your mouth in front of dignitaries again," he said. A little bubble of spit formed in the corner of his mouth. "Did you ever stop to consider that the prince might have more than one wife?"

I swallowed a retort. I hadn't considered that.

"I didn't think you had," he said.

My cheeks pulsed hot with racing blood. But Sargeant was gone and I was glad he couldn't see me.

The kitchen phone rang moments later. I picked it up. Just as Paul Vasquez informed me that the Secret Service was escorting Laurel Anne to the kitchen — more than an hour ahead of schedule, I heard her bright voice call out, "We're here!"

CHAPTER 17

Laurel Anne made a beeline for Bucky. "I hope you don't mind our coming early," she said, flashing her camera-ready smile. "But I wanted to be sure we had plenty of time to set up." She spun to face a technician who tramped in behind her, carrying equipment. "Carmen," she ordered, pointing, "that's where I want to work from." Great. *My* favorite work station. I wanted to protest, but I didn't know how. "I told you it was tight in here," she went on. "I wasn't exaggerating, was I?"

The dark fellow shook his head and claimed a spot, where he began to set up. "Got it." Three other assistants followed him into the kitchen, all bearing clunky machinery. Carmen ordered them into position with quick, terse commands. In the space of two seconds, the place went from tight to claustrophobic. And it smelled of sweaty men.

Laurel Anne spun again. "How are you, Bucky? I miss working with you."

Bucky looked like a fourteen-year-old waiting to be kissed by a supermodel. He opened his mouth to speak, but no words came out.

I wished I could say the same for Laurel Anne, but she whirled, yet again, and raked her nails down Henry's sleeve. How the heck she could maintain such nice nails in this business was beyond me. They weren't overly long, but they were shaped and even. I guessed that things were just different for people on camera every day.

"It's so nice to be back here, Henry. How have you been? I bet you can't wait for retirement, can you? This is such a demanding job."

Henry shrugged. "I find it exhilarating."

"Well, of course you do," she said, in the kind of voice I used when I cooed at puppies, "and that's why it's time to make room for the younger generation." She scrunched up her face in what was supposed to be a smile as she tapped the left side of his chest. "We don't want to get too exhilarated these days, do we?"

Henry's face blushed bright red, but it wasn't from embarrassment. Anger sparkled brightly from his eyes, but he kept his mouth shut. Henry never took guff from anyone, and I didn't understand why he was doing so now, until I spied Carmen behind me, filming it all. His trio of assistants spilled around us, setting up a spotlight with white umbrella reflector, positioning a boom microphone, running extension cords, and setting up a second, stationary camera.

"Get in closer," Carmen said in a quiet voice.

Laurel Anne pulled Henry's arm around her, and she bussed his cheek with a quick kiss.

"Say your line again, sweetheart," Carmen urged.

"It's been too long, Henry." She directed her attention to the camera. "I'm so glad to be back here. It's just like coming home."

Carmen lowered himself to a crouch, filming from the low angle. He mouthed the words along with Laurel Anne as she spoke. I stepped out of the camera's view and watched his lips work and his brow furrow.

A half-beat later, Laurel Anne sighed dramatically for the camera. She tilted her head, and delivered the remainder of her introduction. "Henry, you taught me all I know about *Cooking for the Best*. How perfect it is that I'm back here today, at the White House, where it all began." She turned and kissed Henry's cheek again, then blinked four or five times. I swore it was to conjure up wet eyes for the film. "You will be missed."

"Hey," I said, striding into the scene. "He's not going anywhere yet."

"Cut." Carmen glowered at me, stood up. "Who are you?"

I ignored him and addressed Laurel Anne instead. "It's nice to see you again," I lied.

"Olivia." With the camera turned off, the smile turned off, too. "What are you doing here?" She glared at Carmen, who came to stand next to her. "I thought we agreed that she wasn't to be here today."

Carmen took me in with new eyes. Down to my shoes, up again to my face. Then he turned to Laurel Anne. "This is your competition?"

Okay, so I was at least six inches shorter than Laurel Anne and I didn't usually wear makeup to work — there were far too many times I needed to brush flour off my face — and my fingers were those of a worker, not of a television star. I'm sure I didn't look like much to Carmen, here.

"Olivia Paras," I said, grabbing Carmen's hand and shaking it. "Pleased to meet you."

I must have taken him by surprise — to be honest, I was taking myself by surprise with my forwardness — because Carmen was suddenly struck silent.

He finally turned to Laurel Anne. "It was my understanding —"

"Good morning," Paul Vasquez said, as he entered the kitchen. The smile in his words died almost immediately when he found himself navigating around the equipment to join our little tête-à-tête. "What's all this?"

Laurel Anne's beaming smile flicked back to its "on" position. "Paul will sort all this out," she said to Carmen, then twisted back. "Won't you, Paul?"

He shook his head. If I were to characterize his expression, I'd have to say he was befuddled. And Paul Vasquez was rarely befuddled. "When we agreed to your filming here today, we also agreed that you were only to bring one cameraman."

Carmen said, "Well . . . yeah," stringing the word out. A fireplug of a guy, he placed his hands at his hips and addressed Paul. "One cameraman," he said indicating a tall fellow leaning on the counter near the door. "Jake."

"Then the rest of you need to get out of here. I'll arrange for an escort."

Thank God. There wasn't a day that went by that I wasn't delighted to have Paul as our chief usher.

"Uh-uh." Carmen punctuated his response with a shake of his head.

"Excuse me?" Paul said.

"You specified one cameraman. We agreed. One cameraman needs one sound man" — he pointed to a young guy near the boom — "Sid. One tech." He pointed to the last of the three. "Armand. And one director." His fingers splayed across his chest. "Me."

Paul's lips tightened and he rubbed his eyebrows with the fingers of his left hand. "You've got two cameras."

Carmen acknowledged his observation with a nod. "As director, it is my prerogative to capture my own view. I need the freedom a handheld camera provides. Your cramped conditions here," he gazed around the small area, grimacing, "require that we keep our main camera stationary. That's hardly conducive to creativity."

"Boss?" Jake the cameraman said. "Should I be filming this?"

"Yes, yes," Carmen said, throwing his arms out flamboyantly. "It's all flavor, and flavor is what we are all about, aren't we, Laurel Anne?"

If it were possible, she beamed even brighter.

Of course she did. The camera was back on.

Paul cocked an eyebrow and took a long look around the room.

I couldn't read him, but I could tell he was taking the whole enchilada into consideration. He always did.

"Three things," he said, finally, "and there will be no argument." He ticked off his fingers as he spoke. "One — Henry and Ollie's first priority today is to the First Lady's taste-testing for the upcoming state dinner. Cyan and Bucky can assist Laurel Anne. Ollie will join them once the taste-testing is complete."

Laurel Anne's pretty face fell. She shot me one of the nastiest looks I've ever received, her vehemence taking me aback. I felt myself blanch. Great, I thought. Jake over there caught my shocked expression on tape.

"Two — I will allow this . . . this . . ." Paul looked as flustered as I'd ever seen him, "intrusion," he said with emphasis, "only if the White House is provided a complete and uncut tape of the day's activities."

"No problem, man," Carmen said.

"Lastly — I get final say on what, if anything, from today's activities — is used for broadcast."

"No can do." Carmen shook his head. "As director, I get final say on what stays and what's cut. We worked all this out with Peter Sargeant already."

"Peter Sargeant does not have the authority to grant such requests," Paul said, his teeth tight.

Carmen raised a big hand over his head, as though to dispel further argument. "This is a creative endeavor. We let 'the man' in on our decisions and we lose the beauty. The flavor. It's all about the flavor."

Paul nodded, pensive. I held my breath.

"Laurel Anne," he said, "welcome back. Today the kitchen is yours." To Carmen, he said, "I will personally escort you — and your associates — out."

"But," Laurel Anne sputtered, "we have to film this." She shot frantic glances to Carmen, whose large eyes had gone wide. "We're going to broadcast this as my final episode of *Cooking for the Best* when I get the executive chef position here."

Henry cleared his throat. "*If* you get the position here."

At that, Laurel Anne almost lost it right in front of all of us. I held my breath as she worked her face back into a careful smile and rolled her eyes. "Of course. That's what

I meant. *If* I get the position." With a quick tilt to her head, she faced me. "I'm up against a truly worthy opponent."

I bit my lip, hard, and forced a smile of my own. I wanted to retort, but no matter how I worded it, it could come out badly.

"Can't we please keep filming?" she asked Paul. "Carmen, I know Paul understands how important the creative process is. I'm sure he's just concerned about security. We can compromise on this one, can't we?"

Faced with his pleading starlet and an impending toss out the door, Carmen relented. "Sure, sure. You're the boss, man," he said, clapping Paul on the back.

Ooh. Huge breach of protocol.

Paul was, above all, a diplomat. "Well then," he said, clapping his hands together, "we're agreed." He gave the room another long look, and something behind his eyes made me sad. He didn't like this setup any more than I did, and yet his hands were virtually tied. I knew that he had to juggle Peter Sargeant's newness on the job, while keeping in mind that Laurel Anne and the First Lady shared the bond of having the same home state. He couldn't afford to offend any one of these people, and I knew he wouldn't. The sadness, I believed, was directed toward me and to Henry. He knew that if there was any fallout, Henry and I would be catching the brunt of it.

"One more thing," he said. "I need Ollie."

Carmen raised a dark eyebrow.

"Now?" I asked.

Paul nodded, turned, and strode out the door. I followed.

CHAPTER 18

"Don't be alarmed," Paul said as we made our way to his office. "We just don't want to get into specifics in front of visitors."

I walked double-time to keep up with him, but I couldn't figure out how not to be alarmed. I'd been in way over my head these past several days. I'd been called in, talked to, scolded, reminded of being scolded, terrified, and virtually shut out by my boyfriend.

"Is it about the taste-testing?" I asked. I knew my tone was hopeful, but I couldn't help it. "Do we really need to clear menus through Peter Sargeant first?"

He hesitated. "It's not that the First Lady needs an additional taste-tester," he began. "As we all know, Mrs. Campbell has strong opinions on the subject of meal planning."

That was an understatement. Mrs. Campbell had trained in culinary school herself — the same school where Laurel Anne had apprenticed, of course — and the First Lady often suggested changes. To be honest, some of them were very good ideas. And the ones that were not, she was gracious enough not to argue. Mrs. Campbell, while strong-minded, was not difficult to work with.

I waited for him to continue.

"Sargeant was brought on board to keep a close eye on the White House where matters of political correctness are concerned." As we walked, Paul made a sort of so-so motion with his head. "The president's platform of unity means that he wants us to be attuned to the needs of everyone, regardless of race, creed, gender, sexual orientation, etcetera. Peter Sargeant's job is a lot less structured than most around here. He's to ingratiate himself into all White House areas to be our last line of defense. So that no one makes a mistake that costs us dearly in the press."

I nodded.

Paul turned apologetic. "He's keeping an eye on the menus to determine if anything being served could somehow offend a guest. Or put a guest off in some way. If a country has an embargo against a product from another country, we surely don't want to serve it at an official dinner, do we?"

I shook my head.

We turned the corner. "So, no," he said, finally answering my original question, "this isn't about the taste-testing."

I was about to ask what it was about, when I noticed a lanky young man in Paul's office. He stood.

"Olivia Paras," Paul said, "this is Darren Sorrell. He's a police sketch artist here to help put together a picture of the man you . . . saw . . . the other day."

The man I saw the other day. Of course I knew who he meant. I wondered if the vague wording was for Darren's benefit, or for that of the other folks in the office area who might not yet have heard about the skirmish at the merry-go-round. Though how anyone didn't know by now was beyond me.

"Sure," I said. I didn't know how much good this would do, and I worried about Henry getting things ready for Sargeant by himself. Without thinking, I glanced at my watch.

"This shouldn't take too long," Darren said. And then to Paul, "Is there someplace we can go where it's quiet?"

Twenty minutes later, the amazingly speedy Darren had produced, on his laptop, a likeness of the murderous blond man that matched my recollection. As he'd zipped

215

me through choices of eyes, noses, and face shapes, I doubted my accuracy. Did I really remember, or did I think I remembered? "See him in your mind, Ollie," he coached. "Now tell me: Were his ears more like this," click-click, "or like these?"

Even now, barely two days since the altercation, I couldn't swear that this was what the man truly looked like. Darren printed out a copy of the finished product. I stared at it. It looked like the man I remembered, but had I remembered correctly? In all the excitement, had I really noticed all these details, or was my imagination filling in what I couldn't recall?

"You can keep that one."

I shot Darren a look. Why would I want it?

As if he'd read my mind, he continued. "Copies will be distributed to everyone on staff. The Secret Service and the Metropolitan Police are working together to keep this man from breaching security."

I studied the bland features. Even though the pale eyes that stared back at me were rendered in black and white, I could see their color in my mind's eye. That was probably the only feature I'd been confident about. I understood how this assassin could make himself invisible. He blended. He had no distinguishing facial characteristics. Aside from the fact that he was short in stature, he was blah. A combination of shapeless and personalityless features.

I sighed. "I don't know what good this will do."

Darren packed up his laptop. "Sometimes all we can do is our best, and we have to hope that's good enough."

I folded the portrait in quarters, tucked it into the pocket of my apron and headed back to the kitchen where Carmen was doing *his* best to soothe Laurel Anne's obvious distress. He stepped in front of her, begging her to be reasonable.

"I will not settle down. Not when my reputation is on the line." With her fists jammed into her pale pink apron, she glowered at Cyan. "You call yourself a chef and you don't know the difference between fresh and frozen?"

"Of course I do," Cyan answered, with an insolent lift to her chin. "I ordered fresh asparagus for today's delivery." She held the printout of Laurel Anne's e-mail request in her hand. Now, she pointed. "Right here. Asparagus. Five pounds."

Laurel Anne whipped the page out of Cyan's hand. "I wanted frozen."

"Frozen?"

I don't know who said it. Maybe we all did. Frozen? We rarely used frozen produce, and the word stopped us all in our tracks.

"Yes, frozen. I find it much easier to work with for this particular dish."

Cyan aghast, caught sight of me in the doorway, and shrugged.

"Where's Henry?" I asked.

Carmen shook his big head. "You're supposed to join him in the lower kitchen. Bucky is down there, now. Go on, we're handling this."

I ignored him. "Let me see the list."

Laurel Anne didn't want to relinquish the note, but as I stood there, hand extended, waiting, her good manners apparently won out.

Before Cyan had ordered anything, she and I had gone over the list together. If she'd ordered incorrectly, it was as much my fault as it was hers. "This does not specify frozen asparagus," I began.

"Well, it should have." Laurel Anne's face took on a look so heated it could have defrosted the asparagus, had the frozen stuff been here. She whisked the sheet out of my hand and stormed away, studying it. "Let's see what other screwups I have to deal with today."

Carmen trotted after her. "Sweetheart, I'll send Armand out for frozen. We got ya covered, baby. Don't sweat the small stuff."

"It's not that easy," I said.

He spun. Glared at me.

"We have certain vendors we work with," I explained. "We have specific protocols we have to follow. There is no compromise on that. Laurel Anne knows it."

Laurel Anne had taken a position ten steps away, perching her butt against the counter as she studied her list. Carmen kept his back to her and his voice low. "I'm not about to tell her she can't get her frozen asparagus," he said, holding both hands up.

I sighed again, worried that Henry needed me. I knew I should leave Laurel Anne to deal with this situation herself, but I couldn't allow the kitchen to continue in crisis. "Let me see what we can do, okay?"

Carmen gave an abbreviated nod and went to powwow with his team members, who were still exactly where they'd been when I left.

"Listen, Laurel Anne," I said, "I've got some pull with the vendors. Let me know what else you need and I'll see that it gets here fast. Okay?"

"Puh-lease," she said, dragging her eyes from the list. "Like *you're* going to help *me*."

219

She laughed, but it came out more like a bark than an expression of amusement. "I'd rather use the damn fresh asparagus than have you in charge of getting me what I need. That'd give you the opportunity you need to sabotage my chances. You'd like that, wouldn't you?"

"No," I said, although right now I couldn't imagine anyone less deserving to take control of the White House kitchen than Laurel Anne. But sabotage? "No," I said again. "I would never do anything to hurt your chances."

She rolled her eyes, snapped her fingers at Cyan. "You," she said, pointing. "I'm sure you have just as much pull with the vendors as" — a venomous glance at me — "she does. Get on the phone and get the asparagus here by nine thirty."

Cyan looked to me for guidance, but Laurel Anne wasn't done. She turned to me. "You're supposed to be downstairs with Henry, aren't you? Send Bucky up when you get there."

I went.

Down in the lower kitchen, Bucky and Henry were putting the finishing touches on a sample I didn't recognize.

"What is it?" I asked, leaning closer to

take a whiff. It smelled wonderful — warm and garlicky.

Bucky grinned. "My latest creation. Brussels sprouts stuffed with goat cheese, dill, walnuts, and garlic."

He offered me a sample, which I took, tasted, and pronounced fabulous.

"It is, isn't it?" he said, with contagious confidence.

Henry joined in the admiration. I reminded Bucky about Laurel Anne's audition upstairs. "I hate to see you stop while you and Henry are really cookin' here, but . . ."

Bucky, still reveling in his success, gave us both a wry smile as he took his leave. "You'll include me when you present this to the First Lady?"

"Of course," Henry boomed. "You've contributed a new taste sensation. You're in this now as much as we are."

The small room practically glowed with our combined good cheer.

Finally. Something had gone well.

When Bucky left, Henry asked me how things were going in the main kitchen.

I told him.

His sigh spoke volumes. Rather than dwell on the negative, however, Henry stole a look at the clock before reminding me: "Time's precious. Especially today. Ollie, our First Lady awaits. Let us not disappoint her."

We got to work.

At eight twenty, we were ready. There were two side dishes in the oven just about ready to be pulled out — one of them was Bucky's Brussels Sprouts Extravaganza. Several ingredients for other dishes warmed on the stove, others cooled in the refrigerator. We would put them together to create appetizers, entrées, sides, and garnishes when the First Lady was ready to start tasting. Three of our butlers stood nearby, prepared to serve the food once it was plated.

Marcel e-mailed from upstairs to let us know that he, too, was prepared with three sample desserts for Mrs. Campbell's assessment. We waited for Sargeant's call, eager to get started.

He showed up at the lower kitchen's door at eight thirty on the nose. "Are we ready?" he asked.

"Absolutely," I said. I headed to the refrigerator for the salads.

Sargeant addressed the maître d', a handsome man named Jamal Walker. "You will serve in the library today."

What?

"The library?" Henry asked. "But the

222

First Lady usually takes her taste tests —"

Sargeant silenced him with a glare. "Mrs. Campbell prefers the library today." His nose twisted as though it was unpleasant to have to explain. "We will conduct all taste tests there."

Jamal turned to Henry, who shrugged. "So be it," Henry said. "I've always liked the library."

"You do remember that you'll be preparing two portions of each course?" Sargeant asked. "I'm sampling, as well."

I forced a pleasant expression. "How could we forget?"

Within minutes, Henry and I had plated and garnished seven appetizers, two salads, and three soups. Of necessity, the portions were small, but the preparation still took time. We planned to return to the kitchen for the entrée courses when the first round of testing was nearly complete.

As we started out the lower kitchen's door, Sargeant stopped us, with an "Ah-ah-ah." Apparently his favorite refrain.

Henry and I waited for explanation.

"You are not to accompany me."

"What?" we said in unison.

We were *always* present at taste-testings. It was how we gauged the First Lady's opinion, how we knew what worked and to what extent it succeeded. Or failed. Getting Mrs. Campbell's opinion firsthand was invaluable in preparing future menus.

"Another change," Sargeant said with a prim shake of his head. "There is no need to clutter up the library with two chefs and three butlers."

I started to protest. Little did Sargeant know that Bucky planned to join us, which made three chefs. Even so, the butlers would be in and out, serving, not participating in the discussion. The sizable library would hardly be considered crowded.

Henry had finally hit his breaking point. "Is this your decision, or the First Lady's?"

"I don't see how that makes any —"

"Whose decision?"

Sargeant straightened. "My decision, and I stand by it."

Henry folded his arms. "No. I refuse."

Sargeant looked at him with something akin to shock. "But," he said, clearly thrown, "with the tables I've had set up in there . . . there just isn't enough room . . . Perhaps, I suppose, there would be enough room for you, Henry, but two are too many."

"Fine," Henry said, "a compromise then." He turned to me. "Ollie, will you conduct the taste-testing with the First Lady, please? I will remain here and prepare the entrées and sides." To Sargeant, he raised eyebrows and added, "Bucky will join Ollie for a portion of the taste-testing as well. Will that arrangement be suitable?"

He didn't wait for Sargeant's answer.

"Get going," Henry said to me.

I caught the sparkle in his eyes, even as fast panic rushed up my chest. I'd never conducted a taste test on my own. I'd done it plenty of times with Henry, but never had I sat in the position of executive chef for this important duty. I knew I could do it, and do it well, but high stakes — not to mention marinated steaks — were on the line.

I was thrilled.

I wished I could call Tom.

Mrs. Campbell stood when we walked into the room, welcoming our little entourage. I almost felt like Laurel Anne but with butlers instead of cameramen to assist me. The thought made me grin. Mrs. Campbell caught my expression and smiled back.

"Let me begin by apologizing for the minimal forewarning you were given on this state dinner," she said. Her crisp apricot skirt-suit and pale print scarf at the neck complemented her trim frame. Gently coiffed dark hair. With hands clasped in

225

front of her, and deep smile lines at her eyes and mouth, she looked more like a kindly librarian than the First Lady of the United States of America.

Sargeant made an exaggerated show of directing the waitstaff, even though we'd all been through this procedure before and he hadn't. "No apology necessary," he said. He would have continued talking, but Mrs. Campbell interrupted.

"No," she said softly. "I am apologizing." She had one of those voices that made people lean in to hear. Though born and bred in Idaho, her accent made it clear that she'd spent many years in the Deep South of her husband's home. Turning to me, she continued. "You and Henry have worked miracles in the past. I know how much effort is required to come up with a creative menu. For you to do it on such short notice is remarkable. I thank you for your patience and your considerable effort."

"My pleasure." I was just a little bit flustered by her speech, but she wasn't finished.

"My husband has a unique opportunity to bring two opposing nations to the same table. It is up to us." She glanced about the room. "It is up to each and every one of us to give this initiative the very best chance of

226

success."

With that, she reclaimed her seat.

Showtime.

"I will be conducting today's taste test," I began, gesturing the first butler forward. Mrs. Campbell seemed unsurprised by Henry's absence. "We've prepared two portions of each item."

Now she looked perplexed. "Two?"

Sargeant took a chair next to her. "I'm sampling as well."

She glanced at me. I kept my expression neutral. This was not the time nor the place to air dirty laundry. Her face tightened, almost imperceptibly. A beat later, she smiled. "Well, then, Mr. Sargeant, you and I are the lucky ones, aren't we?"

He sniffed, looking over the first item the butler placed before them. "Yes," he said slowly. His expression said, "That remains to be seen."

I took a seat nearby, pulled out my notebook and pen and paid attention.

Four samples later, Mrs. Campbell had pronounced all but one extraordinary. Sargeant had eliminated two, grudgingly complimented the others. He claimed the first to be too bland, the third to have too strong of a garlic flavor.

I nodded for Jamal's first butler to serve

number five. This next one was an appetizer that included chocolate liquor as an ingredient. I expected commentary as soon as the First Lady and Sargeant read the ingredients list and I was not disappointed.

"Can't serve this," Sargeant said, pushing the plate aside.

I knew what was coming.

Mrs. Campbell had already raised a forkful to her mouth and seemed to be enjoying the appetizer. "This is wonderful, Ollie." To Sargeant, she said, "You haven't even tried it."

He snapped a finger at the provided list. "Chocolate liquor." He shook his head, staring at me. "You should have done your homework. Muslims are not allowed any liquor of any kind."

"I did do my homework," I said quietly. Maybe if I spoke like Mrs. Campbell did, people would lean forward to hear me, too. "Chocolate liquor has no alcohol. It is considered *halaal* by Muslims — which means that it's approved for consumption."

"I know what *halaal* means," he said.

"You may be thinking of chocolate liqueur." I spelled the two words for him, emphasizing the difference. Mrs. Campbell was paying close attention to our interchange so I made sure to keep my voice upbeat — helpful. "That would be considered *haram*. And not allowed."

"I still think —"

The First Lady interrupted in her understated way. "Ollie, you are quite certain that all the ingredients in this appetizer are suitable for our guests?"

"I'm certain that all the ingredients in *all* our selections are suitable."

She graced me with a smile. "Well then, Mr. Sargeant. I would hate to pass up serving this delightful dish over a simple misunderstanding. Ms. Paras has made it clear that we will be quite safe serving this. Additionally, our guests' chefs will go over our choices and note any inadequacies based on their requirements. Now, why don't you take a taste and rate it on your sheet before we move forward? I'm sure you'll adore it as much as I do."

Sargeant looked ready to spit a mouthful of appetizer at my head. "You've kept detailed instructions on how to prepare each of these items on file, have you not?"

I nodded. "Yes."

"They've been added to the recipe system? All of them?"

"Yes. We've made that our standard procedure."

"Good." He took a moment to scribble a

229

note on his taste-testing evaluation sheet. "I'm concerned. If Laurel Anne Braun takes over the kitchen sooner than expected, she'll need to access these files. I don't want any mishaps."

The First Lady's brow furrowed. "Mr. Sargeant, I have not yet made my decision regarding the appointment of the executive chef."

"Yes, of course," he said. "My mistake."

Bucky accompanied the waitstaff as they wheeled in the cart laden with our entrées and side selections. Sargeant's mouth tightened when Bucky sidled next to me. The moment the butlers stepped back, I stood up and began.

"The first accompaniment we have for you today is an invention from our assistant chef, Buckminster Reed."

The First Lady glanced over at Bucky, who beamed.

I took my seat.

As Mrs. Campbell and Sargeant started in on the first main course and the Brussels Sprouts Extravaganza, Bucky's foot shook with the rhythm of nervousness. We had a cloth-covered table before us; no one could see the furious movement except for me.

I watched the First Lady's reaction. I

watched Sargeant's. Bucky bit his lip.

Mrs. Campbell seemed about to speak, when Sargeant interrupted. "The flavor is . . . good," he began. "But why on earth did you choose Brussels sprouts? Now that I'm overseeing the kitchen staff I've taken it upon myself to do some research on food, and Brussels sprouts are one of the most hated vegetables. In fact, I believe it's the number-one most hated vegetable in the nation — of all time." He gave a tiny head shake, his mouth pursed. "Yes, I do believe that's a fact."

Bucky's mouth gaped. He looked to me.

I might not like my colleague overmuch, but if I were ever to take the position of executive chef, I'd have to learn to stand up for my people.

I stood. "Mr. Sargeant, if you and Mrs. Campbell don't like the taste, the appearance, or the presentation of that particular dish, we have several other choices for you to sample."

Sargeant scratched his pen across his notepad, not looking up. "Good."

I wasn't done. "But, I suggest not dismissing this item just because of Brussels sprouts' reputation. As you tasted yourself, this is an excellent side dish. We would never serve anything we believe our guests would

231

hate." I worked a smile, glanced over at the First Lady, whose expression was unreadable. "What do you think?" I asked.

She put down her fork. "I think the combination of dill and walnut with the goat cheese is unusual and quite wonderful. I would be proud to serve this to my guests."

I could almost hear Bucky's exhalation of relief.

"But," she continued, "I have not done the research that Mr. Sargeant apparently has taken upon himself to do. This upcoming state dinner is, perhaps, the most important one my husband will ever host. I'm afraid that, for this event at least, I must rely on Mr. Sargeant's expertise."

Expertise? The man had no expertise. He was a protocol guru and knew nothing about food preparation. He probably went online to look up the top-ten most-hated vegetables and used the tidbit he found there to position himself as an authority. I'd read the Brussels sprout report myself, when it came out. In my humble opinion, Sargeant was skewing the results. Something had to be the "most-hated" — that's what happens whenever there's a poll. But just because folks were judging based on the boiled, bitter, tight-packaged greens their mothers served them as kids, didn't mean that these tender, garlicky offerings from Bucky should be dismissed out of hand.

My mind raced. I didn't know how to react without my words being seen as a confrontation to the First Lady's decision — one with which I most heartily disagreed. A quick glance at Bucky confirmed he was deflated, angry, embarrassed.

What would Henry do?

I said, "The official dinner scheduled for August has a cauliflower side dish on the menu. Would you consider allowing us to replace it with Bucky's Brussels sprouts creation?"

Sargeant began to shake his head, but this time Mrs. Campbell interrupted.

"What a clever suggestion, Olivia. Yes, I believe that would be an excellent change. Thank you."

CHAPTER 19

Back in the kitchen, Cyan's hand slipped. A cabinet door slammed shut with a bang.

"Cut!" Carmen yelled, and lowered his camera.

The crew relaxed.

Laurel Anne's million-dollar smile dropped like rotten tomatoes on hot cement.

Jamming his free fist against his hipbone, Carmen advanced on Cyan. "What the hell is wrong with you? I told you all — no unexpected noises." He turned to face the rest of us. "Control, people. We gotta maintain control." He wagged his wide head, the mop of black draping over the front of his face when he finished shaking. "I need a goddamn cigarette," he said, and stormed out the kitchen doorway.

I hoped he knew there was limited smoking on the White House grounds. And that he'd have to be escorted to the designated smoking area and escorted back. Each administration set its own policy regarding tobacco. President Campbell occasionally perched an unlit cigar in his mouth, but I'd never seen him smoke one here, or anywhere. Why the news media folks cared one way or another was beyond me. But these days, every tiny tidbit of a politician's life was fodder for commentary.

Carmen's departure notwithstanding, Jake continued to film.

Laurel Anne paced the small kitchen. Fury emanated from her like heat from a banana flambé. "I can't believe I'm doing this," she said. Grease splatters covered her pink apron. It was her third one, at least — she might've changed aprons again while I'd been out of the room. "They wouldn't let me bring in a wardrobe or makeup person, can you believe it?" she asked rhetorically.

I returned my attention to the computer to finish recording the results of our taste-testing. Henry stood over my shoulder as I noted which items had been approved, which rejected, and why. We had a comprehensive list of possibilities out there. Some we'd try again someday, others we knew better. But we kept them on file, just the same, for reference. No such thing as too much information where individuals' tastes were concerned.

Despite Sargeant's dark cloud of input, and Bucky's disappointment, I considered the taste test a success. We had the equivalent of three complete menus to submit to our guests' dietary consultants for final approval.

I typed while eavesdropping on Bucky's conversation with Henry. Poor Bucky. He chopped artichoke hearts even as he dissed Peter Sargeant. "Good thing I'm not an alcoholic," he said in a low voice. "I'd be tempted to break into the cooking sherry today."

"Will you be done soon?" Laurel Anne asked.

She repeated herself twice before I realized she was talking to me.

"I'm finished right . . ." I hit "Save" and "Exit" as I spoke. ". . . now."

"It's about time. Not only do I have to work with half a staff," she flung an arm toward the other end of the kitchen, "but I'm stuck trying to impress the First Family on a day when the president's wife is probably stuffed from your taste-testing."

She had a point. A good one. I'd questioned Sargeant's wisdom on the timing of this audition, but he'd made it clear that I just couldn't see "the big picture."

236

And as much as I didn't care for Laurel Anne personally, I could empathize with her plight. I wouldn't want to be auditioning today either. At this point, however, there wasn't much to be done. I attempted to soft-pedal. "Mrs. Campbell didn't eat much," I said. "I'm sure the little bit she sampled this morning —"

Laurel Anne plunked her hands on the countertop and spoke through her teeth. "Listen, I don't need you to tell me what to do. What I need are bodies. I've been short-handed since early morning. I'll never make the lunch and dinner deadlines unless you get off that damn computer and start helping get things done."

I bit the insides of my cheeks to keep from lashing back. Next to me, Henry made an unintelligible noise, then brought his lips close to the back of my head. "It's her kitchen today, Ollie."

A reminder to go with the flow, which I knew all too well — even if Henry hadn't prompted me. Difficult as it was to take with a smile, I wasn't about to complain. But taking the high road didn't make Laurel Anne any easier to deal with.

She wiggled her fingers and turned. I followed.

As far as I could tell, Laurel Anne had

done nothing in the past hour. Nothing of substance, in fact, since she'd arrived.

I stole a glance at Marcel. His head tilted, his aristocratic nose wrinkled, he studied a set of directions Laurel Anne had provided him. When left to his own devices, he was brilliant — unstoppable. I knew Marcel well enough to recognize that his expression, his stance, and his pursed lips were precursors to a major eruption.

Cyan chopped lettuce. Bucky still had a pile of artichokes to work through. Henry was stuck boning fish, the worst job of all.

Or so I thought, until Laurel Anne gave me my assignment. She stopped at the wide, piled-high-with-detritus sink, pivoted, and smiled. "Here's your station."

"Clean up?" I said, "But . . ."

She silenced me with a look, then leaned close so only I could hear.

"I'm not stupid," she said in a minty-breath hiss. "I'm not letting you *anywhere* near the food." Righting herself, she spoke louder then, so that everyone understood. "If we keep one person dedicated to sink duty, we'll be that much more efficient."

No one grumbled, but I caught pity in my colleagues' eyes. I knew why. This wasn't just scut work: This was Laurel Anne sending me a clear message.

Carmen returned, looking no more relaxed from his cigarette break than he had before he left. Laurel Anne scurried over to talk with him.

I stared at the sink. Long-dissipated suds gave way to floaters — pieces of lettuce, onion, chicken, fish, grease. I plunged my hands into the tepid brew and fought the heaviness in my heart as I faced reality. Cooking for the White House had been my dream. A dream I'd achieved through hard work and determination. I loved it here. But Laurel Anne's shrill directives sounded my wake-up alarm. This dream was about to end.

I pulled the drain open, sighed, and took a moment to stare over my shoulder, watching Laurel Anne direct Carmen, who then directed everyone else. If this was how she behaved when the camera was running, I shuddered to think what this kitchen would be like when she thought no one was watching.

Water swirled around my submerged hands — a descending vortex of spinning waste — and I thought about my ultimate goal to become the executive chef at the White House. My chances of achieving the position were about the same as any of these churning foodstuffs showing up on the president's plate tonight. Worse, when Laurel Anne got the nod — and we all knew she would — I'd have to find a new home.

"Sorry," Cyan whispered, dropping off her cutting board and knife sink-side. "She wouldn't let us keep the mess under control. Said to leave it. I didn't know she meant it for you to clean up."

"No problem."

Cyan gave me a wry smile and started on her next task.

The five of us had always maintained a clean-up-as-you-go mentality. We handled our messes individually. There were wait-staff folks we could press into service when necessary, but we kept their participation to a minimum because of space issues. We just didn't have the room for extra people in this kitchen, so we made do ourselves as much as possible.

I pulled bowls, utensils, and hollowware from the drained basin, metal scraping against sink's stainless steel sides, clattering when a fork took a nose-dive from my fingers.

"Keep it down," Carmen shouted.

I twisted long enough to meet his glare. He must have read the expression on my face because his hands came up in a placating gesture. "I know I haven't called 'Action' yet, but quiet is a good habit to cultivate." The corners of his mouth curled up grotesquely. I guess it was supposed to be a smile.

I turned my back on him, rearranging the crusted baking pans as silently as I could, filling them with hot sudsy water and letting them soak while I attacked the remaining stack of dirties. Before I could wash, however, I needed to remove all the floppy, wet food lumped at the bottom drain.

Just as I plopped stringy chicken fat into my left palm and reached for a fish part with my right, Cyan was back.

"Ollie," she said, but this time her whisper held a note of urgency, "what does she mean by 'sauté over quince'?" She twisted around to ensure that Laurel Anne wasn't watching, as she pointed to the back side of a pale pink, plastic-encased index card.

I read the loopy script twice — why Laurel Anne handwrote her directions rather than printing them out was anyone's guess — but I still couldn't decide what was meant by sautéing over quince. "What are you making?" I asked, just as quietly.

Cyan flipped the card and I scanned the recipe.

"People!"

Carmen clapped for our attention.

We turned. I gave Cyan a little shove, propelling her toward her station with the hushed reassurance that I'd figure things out. Her grateful smile worried me. I had no idea what Laurel Anne wanted with the butter, onion, egg, artichoke, grape, and quince concoction she'd assigned to Cyan.

The area was small, but Carmen raised his voice anyway. We all stopped moving. "Everyone has a job, yes?"

We nodded.

"Wonderful," he said. He stroked Laurel Anne's left arm like one would a very tall dog. "You all keep doing your . . . thing, whatever it is. As we film, our star here will walk among you. What I want you each to do is to greet her with a smile, *but don't stop what you're doing.* She'll reach in, make some adjustment, and then you smile at her again, say 'Thank you,' and you're done. Got it?"

Marcel stepped forward, wagging an index finger. "No, no, no." In his other hand, he carried a pink note card. He slapped it onto the countertop next to Carmen. "I 'ave been very agreeable to your demands zis morning. But I do not allow the executive chef to dictate my methods." He cast a pointed glance at Laurel Anne. "And neither will I allow *her* to tell me how to prepare my

242

masterpiece. I can not — how you say — compromise my integrity by preparing this . . . this . . . *ordures.*"

Carmen turned to Laurel Anne, who shrugged. The rest of us waited, wide-eyed. So Marcel wasn't the only one who considered today's menu garbage. I just hadn't realized how worked up he'd become.

Carmen tried to placate our pastry chef. "Let's take a look at what Laurel Anne assigned to you," he said. "I'm sure we can work things out."

"No!" Marcel said, thrusting his shoulders back. He jammed a finger against the small pink note. "Do you see what she has given me for direction? *Sacre bleu!* I will not accept assignment from one so clearly untrained."

"Untrained?" Laurel Anne asked, giving an angry wiggle. "Before I went to Media Chefs International I attended the prestigious California Culinary Academy, where I worked my butt off."

With a comedian's perfect timing, Marcel twisted his head, made a show of inspecting Laurel Anne's backside, and said, very clearly, "I think not."

She stamped her foot. Literally. "How dare you!"

Cyan giggled. My hand flew to my mouth.

I knew I shouldn't laugh, and I was about to suggest we all take a moment to settle down when Henry pushed his way into the little group, forcing all parties to take a step back. "Marcel is correct," he began. "I do not control his portion of the meal. We do, however, *confer.*"

I knew Henry well enough to understand that his emphasis on the word *confer* was meant to impress upon Laurel Anne the importance of teamwork.

The subtlety was lost on her. Lost on Carmen, too. The two began arguing that the success of the final broadcast of *Cooking for the Best* required they take a little liberty with procedure.

As Henry strove for compromise and Marcel strove for calm, it became clear to me that Laurel Anne and Carmen were unwilling to budge on anything.

Bucky joined their little group but didn't say a word. I got the impression he wasn't quite sure whose side to take this time.

While they "conferred," I dried my hands and studied the recipe Cyan had given me. She tiptoed over. "I can't make sense of that," she said, with a cautious glance at the growing mêlée.

Laurel Anne was one of those people who didn't list ingredients first. She included

244

each individual item and its quantity as it was utilized. Side one of the card gave directions for the eggs, butter, artichokes, and onion. It ended with "sauté over." Side two began with "quince" and continued with the tossing of grapes and the additions of sugar and heavy cream. "What's it supposed to be?"

"A quiche."

I wrinkled my nose. "Didn't she do her homework?" I asked. "We sent all sorts of information about the Campbells' likes and dislikes. President Campbell hates quiche."

We kept our backs to the agitated crowd of chefs and camera crew, but stole occasional glances to check on their progress. Things were growing more heated by the moment. Even Henry, who almost never got riled, was speaking more slowly than normal, his face red with the exertion of keeping his temper in check. As though by tacit agreement, the combatants all kept their voices low, out of respect for the White House protocols, I hoped, and not because Laurel Anne didn't care for noise.

"You know what I think?" I asked Cyan.

"What?"

Turning the card over, then back, then over again, I gave her the only explanation that made sense. "She's got two recipes here. She must have started one on the front, and finished the second one on the back. Quiche. Quince. Makes sense. It's alphabetical."

Cyan turned the card over a few more times. "Duh," she said. "You're right. But now what do I do?"

"Is this for lunch?"

"Yeah."

I thought about it. "Don't make the quiche. It's just a bad idea." I tilted my head toward the computer. "She probably meant to assign you the fruit recipe anyway. Check our database of recipes. See what you can come up with using the ingredients on the back. Make that. As long as it's a success, she'll never know you substituted."

"Thanks. You're a doll."

"Yeah, well," I said, "in about two seconds, you're going to be the only person in this kitchen who thinks so."

With that, I turned and strode toward the furious group, calling out for them to stop. This was getting ridiculous. We were in the White House kitchen, for crying out loud. And I refused to let it be treated this way. "Marcel," I called. He ignored me.

I tried again. "Henry!"

I couldn't believe this was happening in our kitchen. Conflagrations of this sort

246

would not, and should not be tolerated in the home of the president of the United States. The only reason nearby Secret Service hadn't intervened, I knew, was because we had our doors closed, and the cleaning staff was running the floor buffers in the hallway, masking the rapidly escalating argument.

That was it. I clapped my hands together loudly, just like Carmen had done earlier. "People!" I shouted.

They stopped and stared.

I held up my left wrist. "It's almost noon. Back to work."

CHAPTER 20

"And so ends another exciting day in the White House kitchen."

My colleagues didn't react much to my pronouncement, other than to shoot me derisive stares. Henry, perched on the computer stool, rested his florid face in deep hands. "Thank God that's over." He raised his eyes to meet mine, and then scanned the room. "But . . ." I could hear his bright-side-tone returning, "I'm sure that if Laurel Anne is chosen to replace me, things will go much smoother than they did today." One shoulder lifted. "At least she won't have a camera crew following her every move."

Cyan leaned against the countertop, her arms folded, head down. She lifted it to say, "You wound up being the lucky one, Ollie."

"How so?"

"She shrieked at me," Cyan said, squinting for emphasis. "Shrieked. I thought the quince thing was supposed to be served in a compote glass. But noooo . . ." She strung the word out. "Laurel Anne wanted it served like a parfait instead." She returned to staring at the floor. "She could have just asked nicely. At least you weren't working with food today. That kept you safe from her attacks."

I sneaked a glance at Bucky, expecting him to rise to Laurel Anne's defense. He didn't. Just like the rest of us, he'd found a comfortable spot — leaning in the doorway — and stared at nothing. Even prim and proper Marcel reclined, sort of. He sat on a step stool, elbows on knees.

"Oh," he said, leaping to his feet. "I have forgotten."

Henry raised weary eyes. "What?"

Marcel checked his watch, then the wall clock, then his watch again — all in the space of two seconds. His eyes popped as he spoke. "The ambassador — oh, his name escapes — the Muslim ambassador — he is due here in fifteen minutes to discuss menu changes."

No one moved.

"Marcel?" I said quietly, "are you sure?" I knew it had been a trying day for all of us, Marcel in particular, but we always got more notice than this.

He collapsed back onto the step stool.

249

"Oh, it is my fault. My grievous fault. It was I who answered the telephone during the . . . the . . ."

Bucky supplied: "The meltdown?"

Henry snorted a laugh. Elbows on the countertop, he covered his face with his hands as his shoulders shook.

Cyan started to laugh. I did, too. Even Bucky turned away, his grin belying his normally taciturn expression. Marcel looked confused but cheered by the room's sudden lightheartedness.

I tried to hold back, but bubbles of laughter accompanied my words. "We need to get ready for the ambassador."

Henry planted both feet on the floor. His face, red with mirth, was a welcome change from being red with fury as it had been earlier in the day. "And so we shall. Troops," he said, as we quieted, "we have yet another battle to face. If they are sending their ambassador here to discuss the menu selections, then we must rise to the challenge — fatigued though we are from Laurel Anne's incursion." He wiggled bushy eyebrows, narrowing his eyes as though preparing for attack. "Where are the ingredients we used for the taste test this morning?"

"I have them set aside," I told him.

"Good. We must be prepared in the event

Ambassador bin-Saleh requests his own tasting."

Cyan groaned — stopped when she caught Henry's frown — and worked up a smile. "I'm rarin' to go," she said.

I spoke up. "I'll print up working copies of the menu items so we can take notes."

Marcel apologized again.

"Don't worry about it," I said, "we all had a lot on our minds this evening. I'm glad you remembered before they showed —"

My words died as Peter Everett Sargeant barged into the kitchen with Labeeb bin-Saleh and Kasim Gaffari close behind. "You will want to speak with our executive chef and executive pastry chef," Sargeant was saying over his shoulder. "They're both here tonight."

He carried a sheaf of papers, and despite the late hour, looked crisp and clean as though it were the start of a new day. He stopped the little parade short, just inside the door.

"Is *everyone* still here tonight?" he asked.

No longer lounging against countertops or doorjambs, we stood in a rough semicircle. I said, "Today was Laurel Anne's audition. It took a while."

Sargeant's face went through a two-second contortion. "So I heard." Sargeant

251

turned his full attention to Henry and gestured Marcel forward. "Ambassador bin-Saleh and his assistant Kasim have just a few questions regarding the items you plan to serve at the state dinner." He stepped back like a well-trained emcee, passing the spotlight on to the next performer.

"It will be our pleasure to answer all your questions," Henry said, bringing me into the group. He called Marcel over, too. "What are your concerns?"

As it turned out, we were able to preserve all our first choices for the meal. Once the ambassador was assured that we knew how to keep *halaal,* his worries were put to rest. He told us, through Kasim's translation, that he'd been worried that our kitchen would equate kosher with *halaal,* when in fact the two were not identical. We knew that, and further assuaged his concern.

Kasim asked if we would be holding similar discussions with the prime minister and his entourage.

"Yes," Henry told him. "We will ensure that all parties agree."

"You will not adjust the menu beyond these parameters without consulting us?" Kasim asked.

Henry started to explain our procedures, when Sargeant piped in, "Certainly not."

Kasim bent toward us. "Then I am satisfied with the arrangements." He turned to
Labeeb, spoke in their native tongue, then
asked in English, "Ambassador, are you
ready to return to our quarters?"

It had been a long day, and even Henry's
jovial face showed strain. I could detect a
bright glimmer of hope that Labeeb would
depart with Kasim, allowing the rest of us
to go home for the night. I held my breath.

"No," Labeeb said. "I am yet unready. I
am . . . intrigued with the usage purpose of
herewith item." He picked up a garlic press
and turned the handles into an upside-down
V while the press-part of the device dangled.
"What is the need of such item?"

Always the perfect host, Henry demon-
strated. He even allowed Labeeb to press
several cloves of garlic till the ambassador
had gotten the hang of it. The room was
cramped, getting warm, and I inched away
for breathing space.

Thoroughly enraptured by our gadgetry,
Labeeb asked to see how another small item
worked. He grinned, white teeth dazzling
against his dark skin. "Very highly techni-
cal," he said. "For perhaps James Bond to
cook, no?"

We laughed. It was funny.

Cyan, Bucky, and I exchanged glances as

253

we huddled near the door. So near, yet so far. It would be the height of impropriety to leave at this point, but my feet ached and I wanted to be home.

I thought about Tom.

As Henry and Marcel regaled Labeeb with more gadget magic, Sargeant made his way to our little group. I already knew what was on his mind. "So," he began, addressing me, "how many assistant chefs does it take to destroy a competitor's chances?"

"We did nothing to Laurel Anne," I said. "She brought it on herself."

Cyan agreed. Bucky said nothing, but he didn't defend Laurel Anne either. I took that as a good sign.

"You're very fortunate," Sargeant said, "that her food presentations to the president and Mrs. Campbell went as well as they did. I know that they were impressed with Ms. Braun's variety. The trout was superb, the side dishes imaginative. Mrs. Campbell particularly enjoyed the Asparagus Hollandaise."

I winced. Hardly what I'd call imaginative. The items she'd prepared were basics I'd mastered early in my career. And the fact that she'd used frozen vegetables for her White House audition was mind-boggling.

Sargeant, still extolling Laurel Anne's virtues, continued. "Oh, and the quince parfait . . ." He pressed his fingers to his lips and kissed them into the air. "Magnificent."

Cyan chimed in. "That's only because Ollie covered Laurel Anne's —"

"Ah-ah-ah," Sargeant said, stopping her midsentence. "The only reason everything worked is because Ms. Braun was able to pull it off. Despite your attempts to make her look foolish."

I opened my mouth to argue, but he cut me off. "She told me everything."

"I'll bet she did."

He fixed me with a stare. "She has no reason to lie. She knows she's as good as in."

My heart dropped. I looked away. Clenching my teeth to keep from an improper outburst, I avoided eye contact with Cyan. Seeing her sympathetic face would have put me over the edge. "Believe what you want," I said. "Are we excused?"

Sargeant rolled his eyes and turned to see Kasim headed our way. "Yes," he said. "Henry and Marcel seem to have matters in hand. You may go."

Kasim and Sargeant began a quiet discussion next to us, while I pulled on my coat and made small talk with Cyan and Bucky. "What do you have planned for tomorrow?" Cyan asked. "You're off, right?"

"Henry gave us both tomorrow off?" Bucky asked. "What, is he nuts?"

"No," I said. "You and I are off tomorrow. Henry and Cyan are off the following day. Marcel — I have no idea. Henry said since we're all prepared, all put together, it should be fine. You both know that it's the last-minute work that's a killer. He wants us all to be rested and refreshed before we tackle those eighteen-hour shifts."

Cyan nodded. Bucky shrugged.

"So, any big plans?" Cyan asked again.

Still in discussion with Kasim, Sargeant edged closer to our position. I started to move past them. "I might go to the gun range," I said. "I can use the practice."

"The one out in Frederick?" Bucky asked. While Tom had been eager to teach me the rudiments of shooting, Bucky was a firearms aficionado. The mere mention of a range outing was enough to make him salivate. I'd forgotten that.

"One and the same," I said. "I've been out there a couple of times."

"You like shooting?"

I did. "It's fun."

"What time you going to be there?"

I shrugged. Tom usually went in the afternoon. "Two, maybe."

"Well, hey, maybe I'll see you there."

Just what I needed. More Bucky on my day off. But then again, I reasoned that if by some wild coincidence Bucky and Tom and I all showed up at the same time, it would look a whole lot less suspicious than if I were there by myself. I could claim serendipity. And then it wouldn't be the least bit odd to invite Tom out for coffee afterward.

CHAPTER 21

Arlington National Cemetery's serene beauty spread before me, beckoning. I hadn't been here in a couple of weeks, but even if it had been years, I knew I'd never forget the way. Despite my late hours the past few nights, I hadn't been able to sleep, so I arrived early, getting here when the cemetery opened at eight. With my fingers wrapped around a colorful bunch of blooms — only fresh-cut flowers were allowed on graves here — I made the long trek past acres of white government-issue headstones. So many heroes. So much death.

And yet, it was the sameness of those headstones that provided quiet comfort. As though the souls of all those buried here whispered, "We served together under one flag, now we rest together, united."

Somewhere in the distance, a lawn mower hummed.

My footsteps *shush*ed against wet grass as

the sun worked its way up the sky, burning off the dew and chasing the chill from the air.

Dad had wanted to be buried here. Mom had been aware enough of that to make Dad's final arrangements with a measure of objectivity, despite her crushing grief. I'd been young. Almost too young to remember him. Mom didn't like to talk about how he died. And I often wondered if the reason I chose to live and work in Washington, D.C., was to be close to the memory of the father I never really knew.

I slowed. Came to a stop. Pulled my sweatshirt tighter around me.

Anthony M. Paras. Silver Star.

I stood quietly for a long time.

"Hi, Dad."

With no one around at this early hour I gave in to my desire to talk to him even though I knew he wasn't really here. I knew that whatever lay beneath the soft, wet grass was just a shell of who my dad had been. And yet, my powerful need to connect won out.

"I might . . . I might be leaving the White House."

Half the conversation went on in my brain, as though my father's spirit could hear both my innermost thoughts as well as my spoken words. "I don't want to go, but . . ."

I mulled over everything — my first encounter with Naveen, his death at the merry-go-round, Tom's disappointment in me, Laurel Anne's audition, and my current failure to make any single facet of my life go right.

"What could I have done differently?"

The breeze wrapped the smell of fresh-cut grass and the sound of the lawn mower around me. My hair lifted and I raised my face to the burgeoning sun asking again, rhetorically: "What could I have done differently?"

I didn't have an answer. And despite the calm my visits to Arlington usually brought me, I wouldn't get an answer, either.

I bent to place the flowers on his grave. "Keep an eye on me, Dad."

At the range that afternoon, I realized I'd picked a perfect day to come shooting. The combination indoor/outdoor location was ideal no matter the weather. But today bright sun in clear skies warmed the otherwise cool day and brought out crowds of eager marksmen, everyone cheered to be outside enjoying the beautiful weather.

Tom would want to be here today, too. I

knew it. So that made the day even more perfect for arranging an "accidental" meet.

I got there before one thirty. There was plenty to keep me busy, indoors and out, and I was determined not to give up on catching Tom till they closed the place at five. Of course, once I started target practice, I could keep shooting for hours. And while it was great fun, I never lost sight of safety issues. The range guides kept a close watch on everyone, too. As long as they made sure other patrons took the same care with firearms that I did, I knew I was safe.

The range had storage facilities, so I stopped at the front desk first to pick up my nine-millimeter Beretta and purchase some ammunition. I wore a fanny pack that I'd bought here on an earlier trip. It looked just like an ordinary, albeit large, waist-purse, but a second zippered compartment behind the purse was designed to hold a firearm.

I chose the closest open station, the third of five positions under a cement canopy that shielded us from the sun. I readjusted my ear plugs — snugging them in tighter to protect my hearing. With every spot active, the sound of popping gunfire could be deafening. Literally.

I loaded my magazine, slammed it into place in the Beretta's grip, released the slide, squared my safety goggles tight, and popped my Chicago Bears hat on my head. Ready to go.

My first several shots went wide as shell casings danced out of my gun. My target: a black and white bull's-eye, maybe twenty-four inches wide, fifty feet away. Even though this wasn't considered a difficult shot, I was out of practice. Whenever a bullet hit, it made a fluorescent green hole. No mistaking where my off-center shots went, or even when they missed entirely.

I wanted a bull's-eye.

No, I amended. I wanted them *all* to be bull's-eyes.

Which meant I needed a lot more practice.

As I reloaded, I took the opportunity to check out all the other patrons under the canopy. No Tom. But just about everyone wore round-necked, long-sleeve shirts and jeans, baseball caps, goggles, and ear protection, and it was a little difficult to be sure. The shirt I wore was bright yellow, not just for safety reasons, but because it was a shirt Tom had seen before. Maybe he'd recognize it — and say hello.

There were two other sets of stations on the far side of the main office. I gave myself a thirty-minute time limit at my current spot. After that, I'd take a walk and see what the rest of the range had to offer.

Head up, shoulders back. Arms outstretched, slightly bent. Hands around the grip. My trigger finger rode straight along the firearm's frame, not inside the trigger guard, not yet.

I concentrated. With the gun's sights set on the target's center, I gently eased my trigger finger into position within the guard. I took a long, slow, deep breath, let it out, and squeezed.

Off the mark. Damn. I'd pulled up. Just enough to leave a fluorescent green ding on the edge of the target's outer circle.

A half-hour later, my arms were sore, I smelled like cordite, and there were four people waiting their turn under the canopy. I collected my target via the overhead pulley, packed away my pistol, and headed down to the front office again, where I ducked into the restroom. I washed my hands thoroughly to get the lead off, and removed my goggles and ear plugs.

My face was dirty where the glasses hadn't covered it, and my hair had gone flat. I decided to keep the hat on — it looked better. A quick glance at my watch convinced me it was time to put the plan into action. This was Tom's favorite time of the day to come shooting.

The second set of stations was full, too. I stood well behind the yellow safety line and pretended to watch. My prior visits here convinced me that target shooting was largely a male-dominated sport. Today there were no females up front, and two of the older gents who worked the grounds smiled and waved me over.

They leaned on push brooms as they conversed. Whenever the range was declared "cold," as it was every hour or so, they'd move in, sweep the casings from the concrete floor and dump them into the nearby garbage drums. Bill was taller, Harold shorter, but both wore overalls and skin toughened from years of being outdoors. Bright white skin remained tucked deep inside cheerful wrinkles. "How've you been, honey?" Harold asked.

"Busy," I said, "how about you?"

Bill snorted a laugh. "Tell me about it. You see the crowd over there?" He snapped a thumb over his shoulder. "I'll be chasing brass all afternoon."

"I was over there before it got busy." Casually, so as not to arouse the male protect-our-brother mentality, I asked, "Have you seen Tom MacKenzie here today?"

Harold's eyes narrowed. "The guy who

brought you here the first time? The Secret Service guy?"

I nodded.

Bill asked, "You didn't come together?"

"No."

They exchanged a look. Harold's eyebrows raised, and he thought about it for a couple of seconds. "Yeah, he's here."

Bill pointed to the range's far side. His look said he was reluctant to share the information and all of a sudden I realized why. "Is he with someone?"

The two men leaned back from their brooms, surprised. "No," they said in unison.

"He's practicing pretty hard today," Harold said. "Never seen him so focused." He shrugged and shared another glance with Bill. His eyes twinkled. "Maybe he's taking his frustrations out, or something. You should probably go over there and say hey."

"I think I will," I said.

By the time I reached the farthest set of stations, I'd convinced myself that this was a stupid move. I'd apologized to Tom. I'd been rebuffed. Appearing here now would only make him feel claustrophobic and I risked pushing him further away.

I was about to turn back when I caught

sight of him.

I couldn't help myself. I drew closer, watching him as he nailed that target — *pop — pop — pop — pop — pop — pop.* Bull's-eyes, every one.

He didn't turn. Didn't seem to notice anything or anyone around him, save for the occasional glances side-to-side when shooters in his periphery moved or changed firearms. Harold was right. He was focused.

From my position behind a small shed, I could watch without looking too obvious to passersby, and if Tom should turn, I'd be able to duck behind the shed quickly and avoid any uncomfortable confrontations.

I felt like a high-school girl, gazing adoringly at my crush.

And I felt stupid being here, unwilling and afraid to approach him.

Tom switched the Sig Sauer to his left hand. Firing off-handed, he consistently hit within the second circle of the round target. When he stopped, he shook his head as if disappointed in his performance.

I thought he did great, but I couldn't bring myself to tell him so.

When he changed firearms again, and began practicing with his revolver, I realized he was winding up. He always finished with the Smith & Wesson six-shooter, and even if he had several speed-loaders on hand, he'd be finished soon.

What was I was doing here? This was silly. Again, I felt schoolgirl crush monsters devouring my usually solid self-esteem.

I fingered the brim of my Bears cap — and decided to punt.

Under bright blue canopies strategically placed around the range, the owners had set up vending machines and washroom facilities for the comfort and convenience of their patrons. The nearest oasis was about a hundred yards away. If Tom finished soon, he'd be thirsty, and he'd probably stop here before heading back to his car.

I trotted up to the vending machines, hoping at least one offered ice cold water. My lucky day. I dug two dollars out of the front pouch of my purse. Two bucks for water was highway robbery, but there wasn't much choice.

"You come here often?"

I turned. The man who spoke to me was just an inch or so taller than I was, with dark brown hair and even darker eyes. Tanned, but not leathery, he'd either spent yesterday in a tanning booth or an afternoon being sprayed that color. For being at a shooting range, he was oddly dressed. Short-sleeved gray button-down dress shirt, navy blue Dockers, and polished loafers. He smiled, inched closer. A little too close. I backed up. "Often enough," I said.

"Let me buy you a drink," he said. "What do you want?"

"I've got it." I stepped forward to insert the first of the dollars into the slot, jamming it in fast and following up with the second dollar so my new friend didn't get any ideas to help.

"Oh, is the lady taken?" He smirked and glanced back toward the shed where I'd been watching Tom shoot. Had this guy been watching me?

I hit the machine's wide blue button and heard my relief tumble to the bottom shelf. "She is now," I said.

Letting the cool water trickle down the back of my throat, I strode away. Fifteen steps later, I realized I'd been rude. I thought about the guy behind me — he was just being friendly.

Maybe I'd been too hasty. Not with this guy in particular, but in my attitude. I'd rejected him out of hand because he tried to pick me up. A pessimistic thought caught a beat in the background of my mind. I tried to ignore it, but it played there nonetheless: If Tom and I broke up for good, I'd be encountering these Vending Machine

Romeos and their brethren everywhere. Worse, eventually I'd be seeking them out.

I wasn't interested in Mr. Tan Boy, but I shouldn't have been so discourteous brushing him off.

That little bit of remorse was enough to make me turn.

Romeo was following me.

He smiled. But not the kind of smile you use to pick up a girl.

I picked up the pace.

The shooting station was still about fifty feet away.

Behind me, Romeo's shoes chafed the asphalt. His pace picked up, too.

I had a sudden flashback to the merry-go-round. It couldn't be. Could it?

I turned again.

"Just a minute," he said. "Wait. Please. I have to ask you something."

The "please" almost stopped me. But in a heartbeat I decided I'd rather be rude than take my chances. Something about this man was unpleasantly familiar. "No!" I dropped into a flat-out run. Up ahead I saw Tom packing up, getting ready to leave. "Tom!"

He turned, gave me the oddest look. "Ollie? What are you doing —"

I stumbled as I reached him. Tom grabbed me by my wrists — holding me at arm's length. My brain ticked off that "distancing maneuver" tidbit despite my panic. "That guy," I said, panting, pointing behind me. "He's following me. I think he's —"

"Hold on a minute," he said. "Who?"

And just like at the merry-go-round, he was gone.

"It was the same man," I said. "It was the Chameleon."

We sat in my car, Tom staring at me as if seeing me for the first time.

"How can you be sure?"

From my pocket, I pulled the picture that sketch artist Darren Sorrell printed for me and now I spread it out against my steering wheel. For some reason I carried it everywhere, thinking it might come in handy. Hoping it wouldn't.

But now it did. I shook my head. Could it have been the same guy? There were similarities in height and build, but the coloring was different. And I couldn't be sure about the face.

"Just . . ." I hated it when I faltered over words. "Just . . . I just feel it."

"But you're not sure."

I didn't know what to say, what the right answer was. I couldn't swear it was the same man I'd encountered at the merry-go-round, but it *felt* the same. "His hair was different. And this guy wasn't pale. And his eyes were a different color."

"But you're convinced it was the same man."

Skepticism in Tom's tone. His expression, too. I couldn't blame him, but I knew what I felt. "I am."

"Why did you come to the range today?"

Yikes. Good time for a fib. "I needed the practice."

"And you believe the Chameleon followed you here?" Tom's tone was half-disbelieving, half-coy, as though he saw all this as a manufactured stunt to get back together. I could understand why it looked suspicious. But I couldn't dismiss my very real fear.

"You said yourself I'm the only person who can identify him."

"Okay, calm down," he said. "It might have just been a guy who wanted your number. He just got overeager. Guys do that sometimes."

I usually hate when people tell me to calm down, but I had to face facts. Tom could be right. I could be overreacting. I took a deep breath and gave it one last shot. "Listen, there was something about this guy that felt familiar. Felt wrong. And he followed me. He chased me. And he disappeared into the crowd, just like the other day."

"You get a good look at him?"

"I did."

"Do you think another visit from the sketch artist will do any good?"

"So we can have two versions of the Chameleon floating around?" I gave a laugh I didn't feel. "We already know he blends into the background. What good would it do?" Morosely, I added. "And I have to face it, you're right. I'm not even sure it was the same guy."

"Two minutes ago you swore it had to be."

I dropped my head into my hands. "I'm confused."

A long moment passed, both of us quiet.

Tom broke the silence. "For what it's worth, Ollie, I'm confused, too."

I waited, but he didn't say anything more.

"I guess I should get going," I said.

"Yeah."

I still waited. He finally said, "You going to be okay?"

"Yeah," I lied.

I watched him drive away before I started my car.

Some fun day off.

Chapter 22

For the second time in less than a week, I was awakened by pounding at my door before the sun was up.

"Hang on," I called as I navigated through my dark apartment. What time was it? I squinted at the digital readout on my stove as I scurried past the kitchen. Three in the morning. The door cracked again. Sounded like someone banging against it with a stick.

It had to be Tom. Who else could it be at this hour?

I peered out the peephole.

Mrs. Wentworth had her cane in the air, ready to bring it down against my door again. Before she could, I swung it open.

"Mrs. Wentworth," I said with alarm. "Are you all right?"

"Of course I'm all right. Damn foolish question. Could I be standing here in the middle of the night talking to you if I weren't? Let me in."

When an elderly neighbor lady says "Let me in," you let her in.

I turned on a hallway lamp and ushered her into the living room, thanking heaven that the place was clean. "What's wrong?" I asked.

"Let me sit, first."

"Can I get you something?" I asked, thinking how ludicrous the question felt at three in the morning with both of us wearing nightclothes. But I didn't know what else to say.

Mrs. Wentworth was tiny in a formerly tall sort of way. She stooped as she toddled over to my leather sofa. Giving it a glance of distaste, she changed trajectory and headed into the kitchen. "Hard chairs are easier to get out of. I'll have tea, if you got it. No caffeine."

The bright overhead light gave the kitchen a surreal glow. I filled two mugs with water, placed them in the microwave, and sat. Mrs. Wentworth had hung her cane over the back of her chair and folded her gnarled hands atop the table.

"Don't you use a teapot?" she asked.

I bit my tongue. I normally would use a teapot, but I'd opted for the microwave in the hopes of moving this impromptu visit along a little faster.

"Would you like anything else?" I asked. "Cookies?" What I really wanted to know was why she was here at this crazy hour, but she seemed in no hurry, content to study my kitchen's décor.

"You make the cookies from scratch?"

"Yes."

"I'll have some."

She took one of my Crisp Triple Chocolate Chip cookies but didn't eat it. Instead she finally turned her shrewd stare in my direction. "Don't you want to know what I saw?"

What I wanted was to go back to bed. But I was raised to be polite. And now that I was awake, I sure as hell did want to know what was so important that had her banging on my door in the middle of the night. "What did you see, Mrs. Wentworth?"

She took a mouthful of cookie, and then took her sweet time chewing. "You did a nice job decorating the place. How come you don't have a boyfriend here?"

Taken aback, I stammered. Then lied. "He's working."

She nodded. Finished the cookie.

"I didn't think he was here. That's why I chased the guy away. Knew you didn't have anyone here to protect you except me."

"Chased? What guy?"

She jerked a thumb toward my door. "He

was trying to get in here."

I stood. "Tonight?"

"Just now. I chased him away."

I opened my mouth, but the microwave dinged, cutting off further comment. I used the distraction of steeping tea to gather my thoughts before asking, "Why don't you tell me what happened — from the beginning?"

Mrs. Wentworth's eyes sparkled. She clawed another cookie from the plate. "I heard the stairway door open," she said. "You know nobody here ever uses the stairs."

She waited for me to nod before continuing.

"I happened to be near the door, so I peeked out the peephole."

"You happened to be near the door?" I couldn't keep the skepticism from my voice even as I placed the steaming mug in front of her. "It's three in the morning. Why weren't you in bed?"

She fixed me with that intelligent gaze again. "I'll be sleeping permanently one of these days, you know. I don't plan to waste my time doing it now."

With no idea how to respond to that, I took a sip of too-hot, pale tea.

"And you should be grateful I haven't keeled over yet. The guy I saw creeping around here was up to no good."

"Who was it?"

"How should I know?" she asked with asperity. "He was trying to break into your door, not mine. Maybe it's someone you know."

Suddenly weak at the knees, I sat. After today's encounter at the range, I felt vulnerable. Mrs. Wentworth's pronouncement fed into my newfound paranoia.

Determined to keep a firm grip on logic, I said, "Couldn't it have been James? Or one of the other doormen? Or maybe one of the custodians?"

"Would James be picking your lock?"

I gasped. "You're sure?"

"Honey, I may not be fast on my feet, but there's nothing wrong with my eyes."

I stood. "I'll call nine-one-one."

"Already done."

As if on cue, my buzzer rang, making me jump. "Yes," I said, pressing the intercom.

James tried to sound official, but his voice came through tinny. "Police here for you, Ms. Paras. Is there a problem?"

Mrs. Wentworth eyed me over the top of her tea mug.

"I need to report something, yes," I said. "You can let them come up."

"Should I come up there, too?" James asked.

"You better keep an eye on the door," I said to him. Mrs. Wentworth nodded her agreement. "By the way, James, was there anyone down there looking for me a little while ago?"

"You mean that one Secret Service guy? I haven't seen hide nor hair of him."

"No, someone else. Anyone else."

"No, Ms. Paras. No one's come through the door since before eleven. That's when I locked up. Anybody'd have to ring the doorbell after that."

"Thanks, James."

When the police arrived, Mrs. Wentworth gave them a surprisingly detailed description of the would-be intruder.

"Short," she said. "No taller than five-three, I'd say. He had a clean-shaven head, dark skin."

Two officers stood in my tiny kitchen. One male, one female. Both in their late twenties. Both buff but looking wide at the hips with all the equipment they wore. The female officer, Duffy, sat next to Mrs. Wentworth and took notes. "Black?" she asked.

Mrs. Wentworth shook her head, clearly enjoying the attention. "No, more like tan. Like somebody who lives at the beach."

At my sudden intake of breath, they all turned.

"You recognize this individual?" Rogers, the other officer, asked.

"Yes," I said. "No . . . well . . . maybe."

Twin stares of annoyance from the two cops. I could practically read their minds. They were thinking this was simply a case of boyfriend troubles — that I knew who the intruder was, but was trying to protect him.

Hurrying to dispel that thought, I explained. "Today . . . er, well, I guess I mean yesterday . . . a guy followed me. That's what he looked like. He was tan. Very tan, like he sprayed it on or something. Except the guy at the range had dark hair."

The annoyed looks were replaced by quick concern. "He followed you home?" Duffy asked.

"No." I went on to tell them about my experience at the shooting range.

Rogers asked, "Do you have a gun on the premises?"

"I do. He made me so nervous that I brought it home with me."

"You have a permit?"

"Yes," I said, "of course."

"May I see it?"

"The gun or the permit?"

279

"Both."

I wanted them to jump up and set off to find the guy who'd been at my door — to figure out how he'd gotten up here without James being aware of it — but instead I found myself questioned and my gun examined. They seemed impressed by the fact that I worked at the White House.

"What about the guy?" I asked, as they pronounced everything in order and admonished me to keep practicing.

Duffy said, "We'll talk with the doorman, run prints on your door — don't touch your outer doorknob until we —"

"He was wearing gloves," Mrs. Wentworth said around a mouthful of cookie.

The officers' eyebrows raised as though impressed. Duffy turned to Mrs. Wentworth. "Is there anything else you can think of that could help us identify the guy?"

She thought about it for a long moment, and I could see her replaying the scene at my door in her mind. "Yes," she said slowly, stringing the word out. "When I opened the door and yelled at him, he said something. Shouted it, in fact. Like I scared him."

We all leaned forward.

"I did frighten him, you know. I said that I'd already called nine-one-one."

"What did he say?" Rogers asked.

Mrs. Wentworth shook her head. "It was another language. I couldn't understand the words, but I most certainly understood the meaning. That's when he took off down the stairs."

And downstairs, James hadn't noticed anything amiss. How did the guy get out? How had he gotten in?

My building's lack of a security staff had never bothered me before. Now, goose bumps raced up the back of my neck.

Before they left, the officers inspected my locks and told me they were as good as I could get. Rogers said, "No signs of tampering . . . But if somebody really wants in . . ."

I must have blanched because he quickly added, "If you hear anything suspicious, call nine-one-one."

I thanked them, thanked Mrs. Wentworth.

She grabbed a handful of cookies and tottered back to her apartment, leaving me alone, unable to sleep, knowing that nightmares awaited me whether or not I closed my eyes.

CHAPTER 23

I debated calling Tom. Decided against it.

Our last conversation had left me feeling foolish. As though I'd manufactured the incident at the range as an excuse to see him. He had promised to report my sighting, but I'd gotten the distinct impression that he didn't really believe it was the Chameleon who'd approached me. Now, after last night's unpleasant happening, I wondered if my cover was totally blown. Did the Chameleon know who I was and where I lived?

It scared me. More than I cared to admit.

What would Tom say? Warn me to be more careful? Tell me to sleep with my gun under my pillow?

Would he come racing to my rescue to protect me from the Chameleon?

No.

I slid my Metro pass through the gate's reader on my way out at McPherson Square, shuffling with the crowd toward the exit — keeping alert for anything, anyone — out of place.

I needed to get used to the fact that Tom wasn't there for me anymore.

The thought depressed me. But I couldn't let the weight of disappointment slow me down. Reminding myself that a fast-moving target is a whole lot harder to hit than a static one, I practically shot from the station's maw to the White House's Northeast gate. I should tell someone here about the attempted break-in. But who? Tom told me that my involvement — from the very start when I whacked the pan against Naveen's head — to the incident at the merry-go-round, was considered confidential. I didn't know who, beyond Tom, Craig Sanderson, and unknown higher-ups were in on it.

By the time the White House front lawn came into view, I'd worked up a sweat, and my breaths came fast and shallow as I slid my ID through the card reader.

Freddie wasn't in the booth this morning to answer the shrill beep. "Hi, Gloria," I said as the woman came out of her building to double-check it was me.

"You okay?" she asked.

Now that I was inside the gate, I felt enormously better. With Secret Service at every turn, and snipers atop the roof, I knew I was safe from the Chameleon here, at least.

"I'm fine," I said, as I tucked my pass away and wiped my dotted brow. "Warm today, huh?"

"Supposed to be midseventies this afternoon."

She gave me a funny look as I walked, more sedately now, to the East entrance.

"What are you doing here?" I asked Henry when I got into the kitchen. "You're supposed to be off today."

He turned from his hunched position at the computer. "Change of plan," he said, his face making the transformation from furrowed-brow to bright. "You and I are going on a field trip. I thought about calling you last night, but I knew you'd be in early anyway . . ." He glanced up at the clock, "but this is really early, even for you."

I donned my tunic. "Couldn't sleep."

The kitchen was quiet for a long moment as Henry returned to his document. He hadn't turned on many lights, and I took a deep breath — the scent of disinfectant over the lingering smells of yeast and garlic — and was comforted by the closeness of it all. This was my haven. I could happily live here. I pictured the adjacent storage area, and wondered how easily I could convert it to a sleeping space until I felt safe in my apartment again.

I smiled at the absurdity of the plan. Not a chance I'd escape the Secret Service's notice. For one thing, my pass would alert them that I hadn't left for days. And showering each morning might prove problematic.

Still, a girl could dream.

"What's so funny?" Henry asked.

I wanted to tell him about my early morning visitor, about the range, but I couldn't start down that path without betraying confidential information. Or compromising the plan to keep me safe. Oh, yeah, that plan was working.

"Nothing, really," I said. "What kind of field trip?"

He hoisted himself off the stool, and clapped his hands. "We are going to Camp David."

"Today?"

"Yes, ma'am," he said, brushing past me to pull out his stash of favorite recipes. "On a helicopter."

Henry looked and sounded like a little kid who'd just been promised a pony ride. I couldn't help grinning — his excitement was contagious.

"What time?"

"They'll call for us after nine. We're in charge of dinner there tonight. The Camp David kitchen staff is already preparing some basics, and getting ready for our arrival. But! The president specifically requested our presence." He graced me with a look that said "Impressive, huh?" and then went back to rummaging through his file. "This trade agreement summit must be pretty important to insist that you and I oversee the meals. This time there is a real possibility for cooperation. The president realizes that, and he is doing all he can to make it a reality."

"I'd say. These two countries have been at war with one another for . . ." I blew out a breath. ". . . for as long as I can remember. If President Campbell is able to facilitate a trade agreement, it'll be an important first step toward achieving peace in the Middle East."

"Here." Henry handed me three recipes, having tuned me out in favor of planning meals. "Let's figure out what we need to make these."

We were shepherded to the helicopter just after nine, leaving Marcel in charge of the kitchen during our absence.

The presidential helicopter, *Marine One,* had already shuttled President Campbell and his guests to Camp David. The rest of the delegations attending the summit would arrive either by separate air arrangements or chauffeured motorcade.

The helicopter taking the two of us to Camp David was one of the ordinary, run-of-the mill designs. The Secret Service fellow who led us toward it seemed to view it as no big deal.

I found it incredibly exciting.

An earphone-wearing man in a flight jacket held up a gloved hand, motioning us to wait outside the marked perimeter while the enormous blades whirled overhead, their movement making loud *whup-whup* noises in the otherwise quiet morning. I held my arm up to shield my face from dust zipping into my eyes.

"Henry! Ollie!"

We turned. Craig Sanderson trotted toward us, papers in hand, his short hair flipping up from the copter's air current. "Did we forget something?" I asked Henry, shouting to be heard.

"No. I have everything here." He patted his laptop case.

Craig wasn't out of breath, but he had to raise his voice over the sound of the rotating blades. "This has just been released," he said, handing a flapping paper to Henry, and another to me. The look he gave me was anything but friendly, and as soon as I saw the face on the picture, I knew why.

Henry leaned in, firmly holding the paper by both ends. "Who is this?"

Craig explained that the White House, and indeed all of Washington, D.C., was on high alert for the assassin known as the Chameleon. He pointed to the face I'd described to Darren Sorrell, the face that stared up at us now. "This is the most recent composite we could come up with. We're notifying everyone at Camp David. This guy's slippery, and we want him caught."

"I've heard of this Chameleon," Henry said, nodding. "Someone has actually seen him?"

I felt myself blush.

Craig nodded, without looking at me. "We think so. Just keep a close eye out, all right? We believe he's targeted President Campbell. That's why these trade negotiations were moved. It will be more difficult for the Chameleon to attempt an attack in the new location; Camp David is much less problematic to secure than the White House — but until we tell you otherwise, anyone who looks like this, or who behaves in a suspicious manner, should be reported immediately."

I thought about my decision to not tell Tom about the attempted break-in.

Dumb move. I should've swallowed my pride and called him last night. I opened my mouth to tell Craig, but the pilot shouted for us to board and Craig jogged away.

Next chance I had to talk to either one of them, I decided, I would.

The seventy-mile trip from one landing strip to the next was the most exciting I'd ever experienced. I was part of something big. Henry had been to Camp David before, but this would be my first time. There was a separate cooking staff at the retreat, so we were rarely called in to participate. This business summit could become a turning point in world history, and I was proud and elated to be part of it.

We circled the camp once before landing. The 125-acre retreat in Maryland's Catoctin Mountains was just as breathtaking as Tom had proclaimed. He'd been here before, too, several times, and he couldn't get enough of it. I could see why. Below us, cottages, paths, and gorgeous mature trees covered the top and one side of a small mountain. Lots of rocky terrain. Lots of greenery. I caught sight of a small portion of the security fence, and the agents who guarded it.

I sighed deeply. I'd be safe here.

The place was bustling with arrivals when we set down. We were directed up a path to the camp commander's office. On the way, we watched limousines navigate the roads to the various cabins to drop off riders before setting off again to the staff parking and guest barracks farther north.

Neither Henry nor I would be staying the night, and as we walked the path I regretted that. An idyllic spot, there were tennis courts, a staff pool, and that deep green smell only a forest of cool trees can provide. I breathed in the springy newness. For the first time in days, I felt alive with comfort. I vowed to put aside my worries about Tom, my worries about being a target for the Chameleon, and concentrate on doing the best job I could while soaking up the sense of well-being that pervaded this place.

Henry must have sensed my contentment; he smiled and winked.

I could understand why Franklin Delano Roosevelt had originally named this Shangri-La. It was, indeed, a haven. It had been called Camp David since before I was born, when Dwight Eisenhower renamed the retreat in honor of his grandson.

As I followed Henry and our guide, a kitchen staffer named Rosa Brelczyk, I found myself wishing the original name had endured. Jimmy Carter had chosen well when he staged his peace talks here.

Rosa kept us to the right on the long path. Round and short, she had the smile of a saint, and she maintained gentle chatter, welcoming us as we walked. All the cottages on the premises were named for trees: Chestnut, Hickory, Dogwood.

A limousine cleared the gatehouse and passed us on our left. The car stopped just outside the Birch guesthouse. As we approached I saw Ambassador bin-Saleh and his assistant, Kasim, alight. Accompanying them was a woman, dressed in a full *burqa*, her face and body completely obscured by her flowing blue garment.

Henry whispered. "That's the princess."

"How do you know?"

"Watch," he said.

As though he'd timed his comment, two women emerged from Birch, both also fully covered, but in fabrics far less opulent than the silk of the princess's. They flanked their mistress and all three kept their heads together as they disappeared back into the cabin.

"I see."

"Labeeb told me there were three women in their party: the princess and two hand-maidens."

I raised an eyebrow. "Handmaiden? What is this, the Middle Ages?"

"Labeeb's word." He shrugged. "Seems to fit."

Rosa veered right at a large, beautiful building. "Aspen Lodge," she said brightly.

"We're working in the president's cabin?" I asked.

She nodded, still walking, passing the front entrance. "The north wing houses the kitchen. We've been anticipating your arrival, Henry. Yours, too," she said to me, but I could tell she didn't remember my name. "I hope you're used to working in tight quarters. We have a lot of . . . help . . . here today."

She wasn't kidding.

"There are so many people," I said to Rosa after being introduced to the entire Camp David kitchen staff and a couple of others — chefs from the two visiting digni-taries' countries.

She gave me a rueful smile. "The kitchen isn't the only place that's crowded. Not only do we have the summit leaders here, but each of them brought along several ambassadors, foreign ministers, legal advisors, defense ministers, public relations advisors . . ." She gave an extended sigh. "From what I understand, they've all had to cut back on the size of their entourage. As it is, we're stretching ourselves to make do."

The word *entourage* gave me a little start. It reminded me of Laurel Anne's audition, of the day we'd endured with her in control. If you could call it that. I swallowed hard as I thought about this glorious refuge and all it represented. And the fact that I might never come back.

Bringing myself back to the present, I nodded. "We met only a couple of the ambassadors at the White House when they stopped by for a visit. And I haven't even seen the prime minister yet. Mostly, the guests and their people stay offsite. This," I said, looking around, "is a whole lot more cozy."

She laughed. "That it is. And you'll interact with people you've only seen on TV up till now. Come on, let's get you set up."

Ten minutes later, aproned and toqued, I noticed Henry in deep discussion with the two other chefs. I deduced from their expressions that they weren't comprehending everything Henry was saying.

I edged closer to their huddle, and Henry

waved me in.

"This is Olivia," he said, taking extra care to enunciate his words. "She works with me." He pointed to himself.

He then introduced the two men. The first, Avram, was an older fellow; he had at least five years on Henry. He was tiny, almost effeminate in his bearing, and because he had his toque in his hands instead of on his head, I could see straight over the top of his shiny pate. The second man, Gaspar, was taller than Henry — wider, too. His dark features and loud voice combined to produce an imposing presence.

They'd been arguing, in a Tower of Babel sort of way.

All three men smiled at me, and Henry took the opportunity to tell me that they had met before, several times, at chef summits, held every August, in places all over the world.

Avram and Gaspar had a decent command of the English language, and since I knew a little bit of French — in which they were both fluent — we were able to get by. Whenever stumped, we lapsed into hand motions and food-charades. By the time we'd settled on the upcoming dinner menu, we were proficient at deciphering each others' needs.

Avram held up a finger. He dug into his apron pocket and pulled out a folded paper. It was a copy of the list of foods the First Lady had taste-tested. "Here," he said, pointing to one of the items, "is good, not spiceful?"

I ran my finger down to see where he indicated. While everything we planned to serve at the upcoming state dinner had been approved by both camps and was both kosher and *halaal*, we still understood that our guest chefs might have questions. They didn't disappoint. "Not spicy," I said, fanning my mouth and shaking my head. "No."

His face broke into a wide grin.

A separate section of the kitchen had been set aside for Avram's preparations to allow him to keep kosher. Separate utensils, kept on hand for this express purpose since the Camp David Accords, were pulled out and Avram pronounced the setup satisfactory.

Gaspar grabbed the note from Avram's grasp, lifted it up near his eyes, then pulled reading glasses from his pocket. He grunted twice as he followed the list with a fat finger.

Avram didn't seem to mind — he apparently didn't see Gaspar's snatch as anything but professional interest. In fact, he tilted his face upward to watch the taller man peruse the list and Avram asked a question in a language I didn't understand.

I glanced at Henry, who shrugged.

Gaspar answered Avram, again in a language unfamiliar to me and it surprised me to realize that these two were more alike than I would have expected. I said as much to Henry.

"That's why the chef summit is so special," he said. "There are no politics. We put aside our countries' differences to come together, to learn, to grow. Mostly, to cook. I'm glad you're seeing this Ollie. It's good experience for you before you go to your first summit."

"*If* I go," I corrected him. "I'm pretty sure Laurel Anne has already made her travel arrangements."

He waved a finger at me.

Avram, Gaspar, Henry, and I set to work together, surrounded by a bevy of helpers including our own Camp David staff and one assistant each from the two other countries.

While we worked, we talked. And despite the language difficulties, we got plenty done in a short period of time.

Until the room went suddenly quiet.

I looked up.

At the kitchen's doorway, a Marine, at attention.

A charge of fear ricocheted through our friendly atmosphere.

"What happened?" Henry asked.

The young man in uniform spoke clearly, but quietly. "Dinner plans have changed. President Campbell, Prince Sameer bin Khalifah, and Prime Minister Jaron Jaffe will take their meal in Hickory. They will be joined by . . ."

He rattled off more names of other political bigwigs.

Avram asked why the change. I didn't understand his exact words, but I knew what he meant. The Marine understood, too. "You will be contacted soon with regard to further details. In the meantime, the First Lady and Princess Hessa bint Muaath will take their dinner at Aspen cottage."

He pivoted and left.

The moment he was gone, our group began buzzing. What was that all about?

CHAPTER 24

One of the sous-chefs, Jessica, cut her hand badly enough to warrant medical attention. I volunteered to take her to the dispensary, and together we walked back up the same path Henry and I had taken from the helicopter pad. Jessica and I moved quickly, with me holding her hastily bandaged hand above her heart level to stem the bleeding.

The staff at the dispensary didn't waste time. They went to work on Jessica, throwing thanks to me over their shoulders — an effective dismissal.

As I passed Birch cabin on my return trip, the front door swung open and Kasim emerged. He called to me to wait. Again he wore the traditional full-length robes of his culture. Today they were brown. With a bright red turban atop his head, he towered over me by a foot and a half, at least. Back in D.C., with the temperatures warming up nicely, Kasim must have sweltered. Here, at the higher elevation and beneath the canopy of trees, I'm sure he was much more comfortable. He seemed less tense, although I noticed he moved slower than he had in the past. I asked him how he was feeling.

"I am much improved," he said.

"If I may say so, you look better."

He blinked acknowledgment, and I wondered if I'd breached protocol by commenting on his appearance. Henceforth I promised myself to watch my words.

He changed the subject. "I have several questions with regard to the final dinner and to preparations at this location. Your Mr. Sargeant is not present here?"

"No, he's not." When Rosa had explained how each of the delegates had cut back their staff, she hadn't mentioned Peter Everett Sargeant III. It wasn't until later, after we'd begun dinner preparations, that we found out he hadn't been included on the list of invitees. I was exceptionally happy to realize that when it came down to it, the sensitivity director wasn't as necessary as he thought he was.

"Shall I then speak with you about these matters?"

"Of course you can . . ." I hedged. I didn't want to sound like someone who passed the buck . . . "but Henry is executive chef," I said. "I'll be happy to help you any way I can. I'm on my way back to the kitchen now. Would you care to join me?"

He nodded. "The princess has asked me to see to it that dinner is *halaal.*"

"I can assure you, it is."

A gentle smile. "And I can assure you that my princess will not be content until I have overseen the preparation facility myself."

"I understand."

"Are you staying in that cabin?" He pointed to our right, a smaller structure adjacent to the president's cottage named Witch Hazel.

"Not me." I laughed. "I don't know who's in that one. Maybe one of the Cabinet members."

"I would expect the president's staff to be housed close by. Your accommodations are elsewhere?"

"The staff has its own section." I pointed far north and a little bit west of our position. "There are barracks out that way — I've never seen them, but they're supposed to be nice — and there are even recreational facilities for those off-duty." I sighed. "I wish we *were* staying here tonight."

"You are not?"

I shook my head. "No, Henry and I are heading back after the evening meal."

Emotion flashed in his eyes. Regret? Sympathy? I couldn't tell. "This is a most beautiful setting," he said. "And I am most fortunate to have been chosen for this assignment — I certainly understand your desire to remain here. I find myself very . . . content . . . to spend the next several nights on these premises in anticipation of the successful completion of our trade agreements."

We were silent for several footsteps. A golf cart whirred behind us and we stepped aside. Two Cabinet members sped by. They were both clad in Camp David windbreakers — and were both looking quite pleased. They acknowledged us with twin nods.

"Where is Ambassador bin-Saleh?" I asked, when Kasim and I continued walking.

"He will join the prince in . . ." He paused before pronouncing it. "Hickory . . . for dinner."

"Oh."

"You disagree?"

Embarrassed to come across as disapproving, which my "Oh," probably had, I quickly explained, "When we were in the kitchen earlier, they announced the guests who would be dining in Hickory. I noticed that your name and Ambassador bin-Saleh's were not among them."

"Ah," he said, "I understand your confusion. The ambassador originally was to remain in our cabin" — he pointed behind us toward a small structure near Birch — "with me. But after speaking with the prince, it is agreed that recent events in Europe have demanded the ambassador's presence at the discussion table."

Before I could stop myself, I asked, "We heard something was up, what happened?"

Another golf cart passed us, its riders so intent in their discussion that they didn't acknowledge us. They wore cool Camp David windbreakers, too. I wondered if there was a way to get one of those for myself.

"It is on your network television news, so there is no reason not to share the information with you," he said gravely. "It is a good day for peace. The French have announced the death of a well-known assassin."

"The Chameleon?"

"You know of this assassin?"

"Just a little," I said, suddenly confused. It couldn't be. He'd been after me. Just yesterday. This morning, in fact. Something didn't make sense. "Are you sure?"

"The French authorities, acting on word from an informant, discovered the assassin attempting to detonate a bomb in Paris."

Kasim's mouth set in a grim line. "This was during very busy hours yesterday and could have easily devastated the entire city. The *gendarmes* were able to prevent him from setting off the explosion, but he could not escape this time. He was shot."

I stopped walking. "Wow." At the moment, it was all I could say. If the Chameleon had been killed in Paris yesterday, then it couldn't have been him running after me at the gun range, or trying to break into my apartment.

Instead of a world-class assassin after me, I was being stalked by your run-of-the-mill criminal. Or maybe I wasn't being stalked at all.

"This happened yesterday?" I said. With so much on my mind, I hadn't paid any attention to the news.

"Yes," Kasim said as we walked into the loud, busy, heavenly smelling kitchen. "The French authorities waited until they were certain of the assassin's identity. They made the announcement just hours ago and the wires have picked it up."

"Thanks," I said. "I didn't know."

"There is much to be grateful for in our world tonight."

Waiters hustled the completed meal over to

Hickory, where it would be plated and served to all our delegates and honored guests. We'd originally expected to serve dinner just outside Aspen Lodge, where an enormous table had been set up in view of the putting greens and pool, but plans changed. President Gerald Ford had once entertained an entire delegation outdoors. For myself, I preferred serving and dining indoors. No wind. No gnats.

Henry and I worked next to each other, putting the finishing touches on the meal we would serve to Mrs. Campbell and the princess. Because he didn't have a national representative dining with the women, Gaspar took the opportunity to rest; his assistant retreated to the barracks.

From his corner seat in the kitchen, Gaspar threw out occasional suggestions for arrangement or garnish, all of which Henry and Avram took in stride. I saw it as an opportunity to learn new techniques and was thrilled to be surrounded by three giants in the field.

Which reminded me of something that I didn't understand. When Avram set off to get ingredients out of the refrigerator, I moved closer to Henry.

"Why are we here?" I asked him in a whisper.

He shot me a quizzical glance as he twisted sprigs of parsley. "Because of the importance of these meetings." He pointed to the desserts. "More raspberry on that one."

"What I mean is . . ." I added more raspberry. "Camp David is obviously fully staffed, and the prince and the prime minister have their own chefs . . ."

He waited.

"Why fly us — you and me — out here? I think they could have handled everything perfectly with the staff on hand."

Henry graced me with one of his "here comes a lecture" smiles. "You and I are President Campbell's best. Today is the first day of important negotiations. It sets the right tone for him to bring us here, to show that he understands the magnitude of these talks. We are a symbol of the president doing his utmost, of offering the best he has."

I nodded. I hadn't thought of it that way.

"And when we leave tonight, to return to the vital job of preparing for the state dinner, we will have imposed ourselves on the Camp David staff and on these two visiting chefs. Imposed," he repeated, "in a very good, very powerful way. All remaining meals served during these negotiations will be seen as our progeny."

"That's heavy."

He winked. "Heavy as whipping cream."

In an unusual turn of events, we chefs were called upon to serve courses in the Aspen dining room. Highly uncommon, but then again, the entire atmosphere at Camp David was different. Everyone was more relaxed here. It was as though serenity hung in the fragrant air, just waiting for us to take a deep breath and share it.

I tied on a fresh apron before meeting the First Lady and her guest. It wouldn't do to have raspberry splatters all over my chest as I served the women their first course.

When I voiced my concerns about taking on the added responsibility of actually serving a meal, Henry waved a hand in the air as if to say this would be no trouble at all. I had two assistants: one Camp David regular and one Muslim assistant, both female. That was the primary reason we'd been tagged for service. Our waitstaff tonight was predominantly male, and we'd been given explicit instructions by Kasim to have only females serve the princess.

Fair enough.

Just before we served, the three of us stopped to give the food-laden cart another inspection. We'd begin with soup: a light combination of vegetables, lemon, and coriander, accompanied by an assortment of breads prepared without lard or milk.

I was particularly proud of tonight's entrée, a roasted squab — boned by our Muslim assistant — stuffed with curry-coconut flavor-infused rice. I couldn't wait to see if our menu passed muster with the princess. Still clad in the sky-colored robes, she sat erect, hands in her lap. Behind, the handmaidens sat, dressed in pale beige gowns and scarves that covered only the lower portion of their faces. Across the table from the princess, the First Lady smiled. Dressed more casually, in linen slacks and a plaid gauze shirt, she licked her lips twice before saying, ". . . and walking trails. Do you enjoy walking outdoors?"

One of the handmaidens blinked, tilted her head, then stood to translate in the princess's ear.

The princess faced her handmaiden — or so I assumed, because it was impossible to tell through the fabric precisely which way her attention was turned — and whispered in return. The handmaiden said, "No. The princess does not," before returning to her seat.

Mrs. Campbell's smile didn't fade. I gave her credit. In her position, I'd be wishing for a face-scarf of my own.

I smoothed my apron, gave the cart one more check, then grasped its stainless-steel handles. My assistants fell in behind me.

"Good evening, Olivia," Mrs. Campbell said with obvious relief.

The princess immediately leaned back, then lowered her head.

I made eye contact with the First Lady, then turned to our guest. "Good evening, Mrs. Campbell, Princess Hessa."

She didn't acknowledge me, and I worried that I'd made some gross faux pas by addressing her directly. The First Lady didn't miss a beat. "Thank you for preparing this lovely meal," she said, with a smile powerful enough to banish my princess-addressing doubts, "This soup looks deli—"

Before she could finish her sentence, the princess stood. Her handmaidens rushed to her side. The two girls chattered in high-pitched foreign voices, until the princess quieted them with a raised hand. She gestured, and one of the assistants rushed to the door, summoning Kasim from outside.

He brought his face close enough to hear the handmaiden whisper.

I stood, soup bowl still in hand, unsure of

my next move.

"I am sorry," Kasim said a moment later. "The princess begs your indulgence to be excused."

Mrs. Campbell had already come to her feet. Concern tightened her gentle features. "Of course," she said. "Would the princess prefer to have dinner served in her own quarters?"

Kasim asked the handmaiden in their native tongue. Then he listened. The handmaiden spoke softly; I couldn't hear her.

Facing us once again, Kasim said, "We thank you for you kind hospitality, but the princess is overheated and does not care to eat at the moment."

Mrs. Campbell looked as puzzled as I felt. "I hope she's not ill," she said. "Please let us know if there's anything we can do."

Kasim thanked her. The two women left to escort the princess to her cabin. Kasim watched after them, looking confused. "I shall return to my cabin as well," he said. "Good night."

Mrs. Campbell said, "Good night," to Kasim and then looked at me.

"Did I do something wrong?" I asked as my assistants swept in to clear away the princess's place settings.

"No," the First Lady said, her forehead

wrinkled. "I don't understand what just happened." She sat.

I placed the bowl of soup in front of her.

"Is there anything we can do for you?"

"No," she said again, drawing out the word. "I made certain to familiarize myself with their customs, and yet . . . I couldn't get her to talk with me. At all." Her expression relaxed, turned almost despondent. "I hope I haven't inadvertently done something to impede my husband's efforts."

"I'm sure you haven't," I said.

She smiled up at me with a mixture of gratitude and regret. "Thank you, Ollie." With a glance at her soup, she finished the sentiment she'd begun before the princess's peculiar departure. "This *does* look delicious. Thank you."

When I returned to the kitchen, enough of the waitstaff was back from Hickory, and I was spared further serving duties. I never minded pitching in. No one did. But the scene with the princess unnerved me. I didn't want Mrs. Campbell to associate my presence with such a negative moment. Not when she still had her executive chef decision to make.

We cleaned up as the waitstaff hustled, and before long Henry and I were ready to go. Right on schedule. I smiled. If there was one thing White House and First Family staff members were good at, it was punctuality. Avram and Gaspar were scheduled to remain at Camp David for the duration of the trade talks, a prospect that delighted them both. Henry and I thanked them for all we learned, and we wished them well over the coming days and in the future.

The path back to the helicopter pad was much darker now that dusk had settled. I breathed in the damp greenery, again, and wished I could stay just another day. "It's gorgeous here," I said, throwing my arms out to encompass the expansiveness. "It's so peaceful, so . . . calming. It almost makes me forget . . ."

"Forget what?" Henry asked.

I dropped my hands to my sides, remembering all that had transpired before my trip to this Shangri-la. Although the Chameleon was dead, and my fear of him now gone, I still had the stalking-weirdo issue to deal with. Not to mention my concerns about my future with Tom. If I had a future with Tom. Too much to burden Henry with, so I shot him a rueful smile and said, "Boy troubles."

He laughed.

We were passing Birch, our footsteps making soft shuffling noises, when we heard it.

Strange noises — coughing, crying, and gasped directives in a foreign tongue. The cabin's front door stood open, and one of the handmaidens who had been approaching from the opposite direction rushed in, accompanied by a man I hadn't seen before. The door slammed shut behind them.

We stood in the shadows, watching.

"What do you suppose that's all about?" I whispered to Henry.

His lips drew into a line. "I have no idea."

Back at my apartment that night, I couldn't wait to turn on the news, but I had one very important stop to make first.

Mrs. Wentworth answered almost before I finished knocking.

"There you are," she said. "I've been worried."

"Why, did anything happen while I was gone?"

She shook her snowy head. "Nope. All quiet. But you're late."

"I am," I said. "Busy day. But I wanted to stop by and thank you again for what you did last night. I don't know who the guy was, but I'm glad you were awake. I hate to think what would have happened if you weren't."

She wrinkled her nose and gave a sidewise

glance, snorting. But I could tell she was pleased with herself. "Turns out there's been a rash of break-ins."

"There has? In our building?"

She shook her head. "Not just here. Nearby, too. Three in the complex across the street. All three in one night. Five more about half-mile away. They figure the fella who tried to break in here was expanding his territory." She licked her dry lips. "Police called me today. Wanted me to look at some pictures. But I didn't recognize the guy who was here."

"Wow," I said. I hadn't been specifically targeted after all. Relief washed over me like an unexpected sun shower.

"Your boyfriend coming to stay tonight?"

"No."

Feathery eyebrows tugged upward. "Why not? He should be here. To protect you."

"I'll do okay," I said, then thanked her again and said good night.

"Oh, I get it," she said as I made the short trek to my apartment door.

I turned.

She waved her cane at me. "You two better make up pretty quick. You never know if that creep will try again."

"Good night, Mrs. Wentworth."

■ ■ ■

"Police in Paris tonight confirm that the elusive assassin known as the Chameleon is dead." The handsome anchorman averted his gaze slightly off camera — as though to direct viewers' attention. On cue, the scene shifted and my television screen became the street just outside the Louvre. In the background, over the shoulder of the onsite female reporter, I could make out the familiar, I. M. Pei-designed glass pyramid, which served as the museum's entrance.

My tape was in, my VCR was set on "Record," and I sat forward, watching intently.

The American reporter fought to speak over the rain and winds that buffeted the Parisian avenue. She pushed damp hair off her face, and spoke with somber inflections. "It is here, at the world-famous Louvre, the largest museum in the world, that the Chameleon intended to wreak havoc on not only his target, French President Pierre La Place . . ." — the network cut to a stock photo of the smiling world leader, hand raised in greeting — ". . . but on priceless history, art, and innocent bystanders as well.

"Other than the Chameleon, whose true

314

identity is being withheld until further notice, no one was injured in yesterday's gunfire. Authorities from Interpol are not commenting on how they learned of the Chameleon's plans in time to protect the president, but there is much celebration tonight as a mysterious killer's long reign of terror comes to a bloody, and final, close."

The anchorman provided a few more details about the shooting, and explained why Interpol had delayed announcement of the Chameleon's death. Apparently he'd been such a master of disguise that they hadn't been immediately certain that the man shot at the scene was truly the Chameleon. According to reports, and "respected sources," there was no doubt at all that the French *gendarmes* had rid the world of this terrible assassin, once and for all.

The scene shifted again, and there, big as my twenty-seven-inch screen would allow, was an artist's rendering of the Chameleon's face. Had they drawn this picture after he'd been killed? I didn't know. What I did know was that he didn't look at all like the man I'd seen at the merry-go-round. He was darker skinned, with dark hair and dark eyes. I waited till the segment came to a complete end, before stopping the tape, rewinding, and freezing the man's face to study it.

I pulled out the artist's rendering.

Not the same man. But then again, this was an individual who made his living occupying other identities. The broadcast hadn't said a word about his height or build. From the drawing onscreen, the face was slim enough to be right. The cheeks slightly concave, the shape of the face narrow, though not long.

I stared at the screen, then at the drawing in my hands. Then back at the screen.

Maybe. But it was a stretch.

I already knew that the prospective suitor at the range and the potential intruder at my door couldn't have been the Chameleon. Not possible for the assassin to have been here and in Paris at the same time. But the merry-go-round guy . . . that was another story. That man had *murdered* Naveen. I'd seen it happen — it was a scenario that would play before my eyes again and again for the rest of my life.

Tom and the rest of the Secret Service had assumed the killer was the Chameleon. I'd assumed so, too. Comparing these pictures made me second-guess that assumption.

With a sigh, I folded the paper and put it away again. I didn't know who killed

Naveen. Maybe I never would.

In the White House kitchen all the next day, we were at full staff and would remain so for the duration. Tomorrow a slew of temporary help would descend upon us to prepare for the dinner, just over forty-eight hours away.

The most important consideration in preparing a meal of this magnitude was the preparation. And not just food preparation: The timing of pre-work, the organization of manpower, the boiling point of both water and tempers, all had to be taken into account when preparing for such an event. Which meant that until this dinner was over, I needed to put my personal issues aside. Tom hadn't left any messages. Hadn't stopped by to visit, either.

I'd expected him to call last night, when word of the Chameleon's demise hit the news. But, nothing.

It was time for me to face facts. To put things into perspective. Right now, nothing was more important than our upcoming state dinner and the trade agreements in the Middle East it might represent. This state dinner, perhaps the most important one we would ever experience, was Henry's swan song, his crowning glory — the meal that would be talked about for years after his retirement.

I sighed. This might be my swan song, too. But for a whole different reason.

Jamal, the maître d', would be in charge of Wednesday night's event. He and I stood over the large gray bins that held different varieties of china that the White House possessed. We anticipated a full house, 140 guests, seated at tables of ten in the State Dining Room.

"I suggest the Reagan china and the Wilson china," Jamal said, as he scrutinized his records. The Campbells hadn't yet decided on their own style of dinnerware for their White House legacy and we were often required to combine settings when entertaining a large group of guests. "Both are elegant, yet understated. Or —"

"No, unfortunately," I said, interrupting him. "Both of those," I pointed, "have gold in the design. Since many of our guests are male Muslims, we have to take into account that they are not allowed to consume food served on silver or gold."

Jamal nodded. "Serving trays, too, then?"

"Yep."

We had several options open to us, but I knew we needed to make a decision quickly if we were to move forward. "Surely we aren't the first administration to welcome Muslim guests to our table," I said, "so let's take a look at what serving pieces were used the last time the kitchen faced this situation."

Jamal said he would take care of it, and left.

Peter Sargeant took that moment to drop in. His eyes scanned the whole of the storage area, then focused on the china before me and announced that I needed to be aware of our Muslim guests' requirements before making snap — and uninformed — decisions that could easily ruin the negotiations that President Campbell was so tirelessly working to facilitate. He then began a lecture, attempting to inform me of the Muslim rules.

"We know the protocols," I said crisply. "That's why Jamal and I were here. We've already dismissed these." I pointed to the bins. As I continued, my voice rose. "We were already coming up with alternatives before you arrived."

He blinked, evidently surprised by my "Back off, bucko," attitude. It took mere seconds for him to recover. "You're wasting your time, here," he said. "I've already seen to that."

"You have?" I was curious. "Which china

did you choose?"

"Since when do I answer to you?"

Like I'd been slapped, I froze — speechless. Grasping for composure, I decided to face this bully once and for all. "Mr. Sargeant," I began, "we apparently got off on the wrong foot, somehow." I didn't add that our "wrong foot" was a direct result of him targeting me for harassment. "I'd like to rectify that."

If he'd been taller, he would have looked down his nose at me. "I see no need."

"You see no need?" I repeated his words, disbelievingly. "And why is that?"

"Ms. Paras, you may not want to hear this, but since the truth is always the best approach, I will tell you, for your own good, that I believe your days here are numbered. Specifically, I see your tenure at the White House coming to a close immediately after Laurel Anne is named executive chef. I see no need to cultivate a 'relationship' with you if you won't be here next week."

When he said Laurel Anne's name, he smiled. Like a teenager with a bad crush.

"Well then," I said, fighting the sting of his words. "I will leave you to your china choice." I brushed past him.

"Ah-ah-ah," he said.

I turned.

"I just came from informing Henry. You should know, too. The atmosphere at Camp David did not agree with the princess. She is back at Blair House with her assistants. Her chef remained at Camp David with the prince, so our kitchen may be called upon to assist with meals."

I nodded acknowledgment.

"Kasim will act as liaison between the White House and Blair House."

"He's back here, too?" The poor guy. He'd been so content at Camp David.

"Is there a reason he shouldn't be?"

I was in no mood to argue anymore. I said nothing. As long as I worked in the White House, I intended to maintain dignity in my position. "Thank you for letting me know," I said, and then left the room.

Kasim did, indeed, stop by the kitchen to inquire about obtaining ingredients for Blair House. Peter Sargeant accompanied him. Cyan, Bucky, and I offered to make anything the princess required, but Kasim demurred. "If the items we discussed will please be delivered to Blair House," he said, "the princess's assistants will prepare her meals."

"Is she well?" I asked.

"Thank you for your concern, yes, the princess is much better now that she has returned to the apartments."

"Has the social secretary discussed dinner with you?" I asked. "Has she explained how the courses will be presented?"

Kasim nodded, addressing us all. "I am pleased to say that Ms. Schumacher has been very thorough. The prince and princess, as well as the rest of our delegation are aware of the finger bowls, if that is your concern."

It was. Guests at our official dinners often didn't know what to do when presented with a doily-covered plate, glass bowl of water, fork and spoon. Waiters placed these finger bowls before each guest after the main course. Once a guest was finished availing himself of its cleansing benefits, he was supposed to move the doily and bowl to the side and place the fork to the left and the spoon to the right. This indicated that the guest was ready to be served dessert. I couldn't count the number of times this tradition had resulted in confusion. I was glad Marguerite had taken time to explain the procedure to Kasim.

"Don't you have something to do?" Sargeant asked me.

I bit the insides of my cheeks. Hard. "Yes," I finally said. "I have a great deal to do."

"Then why aren't you doing it?"

I could take a hint.

Kasim held up a hand. "Your indulgence. Please. I have a question."

"Yes?" I said, happy to be doing anything that might irritate Sargeant.

"Are you" — his wide brown eyes made an encompassing gesture about the room — "the entire staff? I cannot see how so few of you will accomplish such a substantial endeavor."

"We have many more chefs arriving tomorrow," I said.

"I have not seen others." His gaze corralled the room again. "I have only seen those who are here, now."

Sargeant started to interrupt. Kasim waved him away, focusing his attention on me.

Pleased to be granted the limelight despite Sargeant's disapproval, I continued. "We have temporary staff members scheduled to arrive tomorrow. They'll be here at eight, and Cyan and Bucky," I gestured, "will take them through what needs to be done. Most of these chefs and assistants have worked with us before. That's nice because they know our procedures." I smiled. "I'll be here by ten or so, and I won't leave until everything is perfect for the next day's dinner."

Sargeant butted in. "You're not coming in

until ten? Why not?"

"That's how we set up the schedule."

"That makes no sense. Come in earlier. This is an important dinner. We can't have the kitchen working at half staff."

Henry joined the conversation from across the room. "Peter, let me assure you. Everything is covered. We are all well aware of the importance of the state dinner and we are equally well-prepared. *I* scheduled Ollie to come in at ten tomorrow. I'm also coming in at ten. We are not needed here any earlier than that."

To me, he said, in a gentler tone, "You mentioned stopping at Arlington tomorrow morning, right?"

I nodded, not giving voice to my answer. I didn't want Sargeant asking why I visited Arlington. Henry knew that before big events I liked to take a few moments there. Even though my dad wasn't a part of my life — not really — he was all the family I had here. Spending a few minutes at his graveside gave me peace.

"Why on earth —" Sargeant began.

As though to protect my private rituals, Henry interrupted. "We will be here very late tomorrow evening. Cyan and Bucky will handle the early shift, Ollie and I will handle the later shift, which is when things have a tendency to go wrong. We will ensure that they don't." Henry glanced over to our pastry chef. "Marcel keeps his own hours as he sees fit."

Mollified, Sargeant stopped arguing.

Kasim thanked us for the insights into the workings of our kitchen.

"Watch it!" Bucky cried.

Sargeant stood to my right, Kasim to my left. As one, we pressed ourselves against the countertop avoiding Bucky's race to the sink, flaming skillet in hand. I felt the waft of heat as he rushed past us. He dropped the pan in the sink, clunking it loudly. Water on the hot surface sizzled and smoke billowed upward.

"Why didn't you use baking soda to put that out?" Henry asked.

Bucky spoke over his shoulder. "It was out of reach, this was faster."

Kasim blinked several times. "The smoke," he said. "It is affecting my contact lenses." He turned away, blinking more rapidly. Cyan, too, seemed to be struggling as the dark cloud spread through the room.

"Should have used a fire extinguisher," Sargeant complained, loud enough for Bucky to hear.

With his back to us, Bucky answered. "And have to fill out a dozen reports in triplicate to explain why it wasn't a breach of security that caused me to use it? No thanks."

"Geez," Sargeant said. "It's bothering my contacts, too." He coughed, blinked several times, and caught a lens in his palm. Keeping his head down, he tore out of the kitchen, anger radiating from him like the heat off Bucky's pan. Kasim followed Sargeant, and Cyan brought up the rear, her eyes streaming from the smoke's irritation.

Marcel, Henry, and I braved the haze, while Bucky — apparently unaffected — washed the burnt skillet. "Can I clear a room or what?" he asked merrily.

We flicked the exhaust fans to high, and soon Cyan returned. "Where's Sargeant?" I asked. "And Kasim?"

She shrugged. "Gone. Kasim said he was heading back to Blair House, and Sargeant said he had plans for tomorrow he needed to solidify today."

"Bucky," I said, slapping him on the shoulder, "how can we ever thank you?"

At nine o'clock the following morning, I got off the Metro at the Arlington Cemetery stop. About twenty people got off at the same time. A family of four with a stroller, some couples, a group of tourists, and a couple of stragglers. We all followed the signs to the Arlington Visitor Center and a few of us branched off from the first-time visitors, clearly knowing where we were going. I was back for a another visit sooner than my usual interval, but with everything that was going on I felt the need.

Another woman and two men headed in the same direction as me. The woman, in her sixties, grasped a bouquet of cut flowers as she headed toward the Tomb of the Unknown Soldier. A man with a briefcase and a rapid pace quickly outdistanced the rest of us. The other man carried a small potted plant. I knew that sort of arrangement wasn't allowed in Arlington. I wondered if I should say something, but I decided it was too late. He'd brought the thing, and if it gave him happiness to leave it there, so be it. The cemetery workers would remove it as soon as they saw it. And this guy would probably be none the wiser.

He walked the same direction I did, though far off to my left, like a wing man. I tried to figure out who he'd be here to visit. A parent? A sibling? I couldn't tell his age. He wore a baseball cap over long, red frizzy hair, a black T-shirt that read LINCOLN CITY, a blue short-sleeve dress shirt open over the T-shirt, and baggy blue jeans. He walked with a loping gait but he was short, so he didn't get far fast.

I was about to give into my helpful-Hannah instincts and mention the restrictions on grave decorations when he veered off far left and disappeared around one of the buildings.

An omen. I wasn't supposed to say anything.

Alone now, I made the quiet trek to my father's grave. Clear skies with a wind so harsh it nearly knocked me sideways, it was cool enough to need my hoodie, warm enough to promise a sparkling day ahead. I would miss most of it, sequestered in the kitchen until every possible last-minute issue had been covered, but I planned to enjoy this peaceful respite while I could.

Somewhere beyond my vision to the far right, a lawn mower did its job, the sound coming in spurts as the wind quieted and rushed up again. With 260 acres to manage here at Arlington, it always seemed a lawn mower, or four, hummed nearby. I crested a rise and noticed that the section next to my dad's was in the process of being mowed. I loved the smell of the fresh-cut grass, and the cool dew damp of the morning. The intermittent roar of the nearby machines didn't bother me. It was nice to have a reminder of life, of continuity, of normalcy as I visited those who'd died for the freedoms I took for granted every day.

My hair lifted, twisting as it escaped my hood. I sighed, enjoying the sensation.

"Hey Dad," I said aloud. Nobody near to hear.

As always, the only answers were the calls of birds, the push-pull *shush*ing of the wind, and the ever present activity in my own mind. I sought to quiet my thoughts, to take in the calm that surrounded me here. To let it take root in me so that the next several days would go as smoothly as I wanted them to.

Whether or not I had a job at the White House when all this was through, I could do no less than my best. Ever.

"You understand that, don't you, Dad?"

The whirr of the nearest lawn mower shifted from active cutting to soft idle. I glanced up. A worker, just beyond a copse of trees, swung out of his grass-cutting seat and waved over another worker in a white pickup truck, towing a wood chipper. The pickup driver stopped, got out, and the two men trotted a couple hundred feet behind the mower and dropped to their hands and knees, searching the ground. I wondered

329

what was lost.

Had the lawn mower not quieted just then, had the wind not taken that moment to still, I might not have heard the out-of-place noise to my left.

I twisted my head to see the red-haired guy in the baseball cap walking toward me. No potted plant in his hands. Evidently he'd found whoever he was looking for. I smiled a hello. This was a big place; he must have gotten lost. I figured he needed directions back to the Metro.

But as I took a step toward him, my skin zinged an early warning. The man's expression wasn't right. His face, getting nearer by the step, was angry, determined . . . and familiar.

CHAPTER 25

Tunnel vision swallowed my awareness. Flash fear held me immobile. A rush like a giant wave crashed in my ears as my terrified brain took forever to delineate options. Torn between running — to where? my mind screamed — and fighting, indecision froze me to the spot.

One second, maybe two.

It felt like hours.

The killer from the merry-go-round reached behind his flapping shirt to his waistband and I spun away, knowing he had a gun and a bullet meant for my brain.

My feet pounded the grass. Silenced by fear, I zigged to my right between headstones, wondering, absurdly, if ducking behind one might render me invisible. I knew I should scream, but irrationally decided it could slow me down.

Stupid, stupid.

I needed cover. I raced for the trees.

My screams finally came as I skip-stepped past more headstones. In perfect alignment, so low to the ground, they offered nothing in terms of cover. I didn't have my own gun with me — of course not — and I didn't know what else to do. I ducked to my left this time, remembering Tom's admonishments about moving targets.

On the wind, I heard a pop, like a cap gun. I didn't turn.

Fifty feet away, a hundred? I couldn't guess — I didn't care — the groundskeeper and pickup driver still knelt on the grass far behind the riding lawn mower, searching the ground. I called to them, but my voice whipped away on the swift wind.

A horrifying thought occurred to me. What if the groundskeepers were in cahoots with the man chasing me? What if I was supposed to run to them, seeking safety, only to find myself trapped?

I shut my mouth, concentrating every muscle on moving forward, racing, running, putting distance between me and the killer.

Life didn't flash before my eyes. Ideas did.

My late-to-the-party brain finally kicked in with a suggestion, and I swerved left then right, then left again.

Another pop.

He was shooting at me.

Dear God, why?

Because I'd seen him at the merry-go-round.

Thirty more steps. Twenty.

I counted as I ran, leaping as my short legs strove for long strides, repeating: Don't fall.

Don't fall.

Don't.

Fall.

Ten more steps.

A noise, a shout.

To my far right, the groundskeeper got to his feet, gesticulating, hollering. Even if these workers weren't in league with the killer behind me, I knew I'd never outdistance the killer behind me in time to reach them. They were too far.

They continued to shout, but I couldn't make out anything over the hum of the motor, now three steps away.

Two.

One.

I bounded into the seat, taking precious seconds to shift the lawn mower into gear and jerk the front wheels far to the left, directly into the runner's path. The mower lurched forward, too slow, too slow. I leaped off the other side. The groundskeeper ran at me from behind. The killer ran at me from my left. The pickup truck driver must have known what I had in mind, because he came at me, too.

Too late. I made it into the white pickup, pulling the door shut out of habit and slamming the vehicle into gear.

I floored it. The equipment bed behind me bounced over the uneven ground and I prayed it wouldn't overturn.

Perspiration beaded down my face, puddling at my collarbone. Desperate sweat caused my shaking hands to slip on the steering wheel. I stole a quick glance in the side view mirror where I saw the two groundskeepers shaking their fists and shouting. I could see their mouths moving, but I couldn't hear a word.

The killer was gone.

Again.

Blowing out breaths, I fought to achieve enough calm to make sense of all this. I needed to drive to the entrance, or one of the maintenance locations. I needed to talk to people I could trust.

I drove the long aisle of grass between white headstones, apologizing to the dead upon whose graves the tires trampled. It felt wrong. Everything felt wrong.

At the first road, I took a left, my mind still not working the way it should. What had happened? If the Chameleon was dead, then who was this?

Only one option made sense. It *hadn't* been the Chameleon who'd killed Naveen. Someone else had killed him. And that someone wanted me out of the picture.

Still shaking, I pulled the truck to the side of the road, and stopped. By now the groundskeepers would have called in the theft of the pickup. I was sure to be arrested soon. I needed to know what I could or couldn't say about Naveen's killer to these local authorities. I needed to think. I needed to call Tom.

I eased off the brake and dug for my cell phone, heart pounding again. But this time for a completely different reason.

I heard sirens in the distance. Coming for me. I knew it and felt a combined sense of relief, fear, and agony knowing whatever happened next would prevent me getting to work on time. Poor Henry.

With resolve, I increased pressure on the gas pedal. The visitor's center was far off, but I knew how to get there. But before I did, Tom had to know. I pulled up my cell phone, ready to dial.

The click to my right should have warned me.

I didn't react in time.

335

The passenger door flew open and the pale-eyed killer pointed his pistol right at my head.

Without thinking, I jerked the wheel to the left and slammed the gas pedal hard as I could, praying I wouldn't flood the thing.

I didn't.

The killer fell away; I heard his grunt as he hit the ground. He got a shot off. It hit the pickup's back window, making me scream, shattering the glass into an instant zillion-piece spiderweb.

Sirens grew louder.

My cell phone remained in my right hand as I gripped the steering wheel and drove for my life. I thought I heard another shot hit the truck, but when I heard it again and again, I realized it was the memory of the hit replaying in my mind.

I watched through my rear- and side-view mirrors, not looking where I was going.

Flashing lights directly ahead.

I hit the brake, held my hands up, shouting, "I'm not armed," as the pickup was swarmed by police.

I'd gotten away.

But for how long?

CHAPTER 26

I was lucky, in more ways than one. Both groundskeepers — the man with the lawn mower and the one with the pickup truck — were bona fide cemetery workers. And both had seen the killer chasing me. Not well enough to offer a description, but well enough to support my claim of hijacking the pickup in order to save my life. The shot that took out the pickup's rear window helped, too.

Once the police officers who surrounded me understood that I wasn't a threat — the cell phone practically had to be pried from my petrified fingers — they were more than willing to allow me to call the White House to let Henry know, again, that I'd be late, although again, I couldn't tell him why.

I was beginning to believe that Laurel Anne might be the best choice for executive chef after all. It seemed that everywhere I turned, I was involved in trouble that prevented me from doing my job.

I sat in a small cemetery office with a paper cup of water in my hand, waiting for my ride. The police had generously offered to escort me back to the White House and I'd accepted. No way was I getting on the Metro again. Not a chance.

My cell phone wasn't receiving service, so I got up and walked the short hallway, until near the windows, I got a signal.

Tom answered on the second ring. "Hey," he said, without his customary joviality, "what's up?"

Words failed me. I opened my mouth, but nothing came out. It was too much. The weight of it all crushed my throat closed.

"Ollie," he said, tersely. "I got a busy day here. Can I call you later?"

Like a geyser, I burst forth all at once. "He tried to kill me. He's here in Arlington. He shot at me. I stole a truck."

"Say that again," he said. "Slow."

"The guy who killed Naveen. He's here."

"How do you know?"

"He tried again, Tom." I hated the desperation in my voice, hated the water shaking in the cup from my unsteady hand, but I couldn't help myself. "He tried to kill me. Today. Here. Just now."

"Where are you?"

338

"Arlington Cemetery." I enunciated carefully. Hadn't I just said that?

"Where?"

I looked around. I had no idea. When they'd bundled me into a car and driven me here, I'd blanked out. "In an office." I looked out the window and realized where I was. "In the administration building."

"I'll be there in fifteen."

"Wait," I said. "I've already given my statement. They're going to drive me back to the White House."

"No," he said, and there was something different in his voice this time. It scared me. "I will come get you. Do not leave there."

"But," I said, glad of his concern, but worried about him now, "you said you have a busy day. They're finding someone to drive me, right now. I'm not hurt."

"Ollie." The frightening tone was back. "Do not go anywhere with anyone. I will come get you now. Do you understand?"

I nodded and realized he couldn't see me. My voice was croaky. "Yeah."

"Promise me."

"I promise."

CHAPTER 27

Tom was silent for the first full minute of our ride to the White House. Like a chastised child I sat near the passenger door staring out the window, unsure of his mood, unsure of mine, and utterly unable to explain what had happened out there by my dad's grave.

"We need to talk," he finally said.

"I need to get back to the kitchen."

"This is more important."

I couldn't believe that anything was more important than working on tomorrow night's state dinner, but I didn't argue.

We whipped past cars, well over the posted speed limit. I thought he'd drop me off at Pennsylvania, but he didn't. He continued to E Street, signaling to the guard who protected the closed avenue. In all, the trip had taken us half the time it should have.

"I never come in this way," I said.

Tom waited till we were within the White

House grounds to stop the car. He pulled to the side and turned to me. "Ollie," he said. "There's been a development."

My stomach made a flip-flop and I knew what he was going to say. "What?" I asked.

"The Chameleon isn't dead."

Now my stomach twisted. "Oh my God."

"Yeah."

We were both silent a long moment.

I fought to keep calm, but my heart raced and I felt suddenly lightheaded. "It was him at Arlington," I said.

"I'm sure it was."

"He got away."

Tom stared at me. "We'll get him Ollie. I promise."

"Why is he after me?" I asked. "I saw him, sure, but I thought he was here for some big assassination plot. Isn't that what Naveen was trying to tell me?" I told Tom about the attempted break-in at my apartment and I reminded him that it was the same night the fellow at the range followed me. I thought they were all related and I said so, even though I didn't think it made any sense at all. "The Chameleon didn't come all this way to target an assistant chef."

Tom shrugged, draped an arm over the steering wheel and stared out at the grounds. "You're a loose end. You're a li-

ability. This guy hasn't had his successes —
if you want to call them that — by leaving
loose ends." He studied his hand. "Don't
leave here tonight without me, okay? I'll
make sure you get home safe."

I started to say, "I'll be fine," but thought
better of it after what had just happened.
"Thanks."

He put the car in gear. "I'll sleep on your
couch."

Henry and I walked five sous-chefs through
their individual responsibilities for tomorrow night's dinner. We'd worked with all of
them — three men, two women — before,
and they understood what we wanted, and
took to their tasks with such confidence, it
allowed Henry and me to take a breather to
visit Marcel's corner of the kitchen.

Before we did, Henry pulled me aside.
Over the sounds of pans clattering on stove
burners, whisks against stainless-steel pans,
and cabinets opening and closing, we didn't
worry about being overheard. "There's
something else going on, isn't there?"

I wanted to say, "Yes, yes!" but instead, I
asked, "Going on with what?"

He pulled a paper from his pocket. "This."

It was the picture of the man who'd killed
Naveen. The picture the sketch artist had

come up with based on my description. When I saw it, I assumed Henry had kept his copy folded in his pocket, just like I kept mine, until he said, "They say this Chameleon is dead, but yet this morning, we were handed these pictures a second time. We were instructed to be watchful. Extra careful with everyone we encounter."

He looked back toward where our sous-chefs were hard at work and where the additional temporary staff members kept busy under Bucky's and Cyan's sharp eyes. "I find myself scrutinizing every one of those young people. And yet, I know most of them. I don't know what is going on here. But I think you do."

I hesitated, but it was enough to let Henry know he'd hit the mark. "I can't talk about it," I began. "But —"

"I understand. Of course I do. But —"

"I'm sure I can tell you this much," I said, touching a corner of the drawing. "This man is very dangerous. Whether or not he's the Chameleon."

"Ollie, I'm afraid for you." Henry seemed suddenly old. "Every time there's been some altercation recently, on the White House lawn, at the National Mall, and even this morning, at Arlington . . ."

"You know about that?"

343

"I know that there was a shooting. Again. And coincidentally — again — you called to tell me you'd be late coming to work."

"I'm sorry."

He held up a hand. "I'm not looking for an apology, nor an explanation. I'm simply . . ." Henry ran his fingers through his sparse hair, closing his eyes for a couple of beats. "I'm simply asking you to be careful. Both for your safety" — he gazed out over the banging, clattering, bustling kitchen — "and for your chances at taking over my job." He stared at me, and it hurt to see the emotion there. "I don't want Laurel Anne to take over my home." He sighed. "Promise me you'll watch your step. In everything."

Just like when Tom had made me promise to call him when I needed to leave, I said, "I promise."

"Come on, then," he said. "We have much yet to do."

Marcel's desserts were always breathtaking in their beauty, but this time the master claimed to have bested himself. He held up his hand as Henry and I drew near. "One moment," he said. Then, to an unseen assistant around the corner, he called, "You are ready?"

A muffled, affirmative reply.

Marcel's bright smile gestured us forward

and we followed him. Just inside the next room, a small table butted up against the countertop. The item in the middle was covered with wide white butcher paper, making it look like a sharply angular ghost. I knew from prior experience that Marcel preferred to keep his creations dust-free this way. Cloth had a tendency to catch on his desserts' delicate edges and break them off.

Now he asked us, "You are ready?"

Henry and I nodded.

Marcel and his assistant lifted the paper.

The beauty caught my breath.

Tomorrow night's dessert centerpiece — about twelve inches high — was, indeed, his most magnificent creation yet. Like a giant flame, three distinct tongues of fire twisted upward around a crystalline sphere.

Henry whistled.

I walked around it. "Sugar?"

"Mais évidemment."

If I hadn't been familiar with Marcel's methods, I would've assumed the center-pieces were created from glass. Each twist, representing the three countries in negotia-tions, was colored with each nation's na-tional hues. I bent close to the American one, amazed at how Marcel had been able to spin sugar to such a vibrant red at the base, only to have the color melt away to white and then finish at the very tip with a curve of blue. The crystalline globe suspended in the center of these three twists was painted — if that was the right description — to represent the world. It was held, protected, embraced, by the three nations' "arms."

"Wow," I said. There was nothing else I could say. "Wow."

"Marcel," Henry said, smiling widely, "I bow to your brilliance."

Marcel nodded acknowledgment, beaming.

The sculpture's base was clear, almost colorless. Etched into it — how he'd accomplished such a feat, I'll never know — was the word *peace* in all three languages. On my best day, my handwriting didn't look this good. It was almost as though he'd taken his creations to an engraver to complete.

The thought — engraver! — made me realize that I still hadn't received Henry's commemorative skillet back from the Secret Service. I needed to do that. Even if it was the last thing I did here, I'd get that gift to Henry. I decided to ask Tom about it tonight when I called him for my escort home. I made a mental note.

With another admiring glance at Marcel's

creation, I asked him, "How many do you have left to make?"

"I have completed all of them, of course."

Of course. Since the day I'd met him, Marcel had been the picture of professionalism — always working ahead. With dinner planned for 140 guests tomorrow night — at ten guests per table — Marcel would have made fourteen of these. He amazed me, constantly raising the bar. His pursuit of perfection encouraged me to push myself to be better, always. "They're wonderful," I said.

"They are, are they not?"

And I loved the way our pastry chef took compliments.

"My only concern," Marcel said, with a mournful expression, "is ensuring that each of these makes it safely to the State Dining Room. We cannot allow any breakage. I trust Miguel here," he nodded to the small man who'd helped him lift the cover, "but I do not know these new assistants well enough to trust them with my work."

We briefly discussed the matter, and then left Marcel to finish whatever he could on the rest of the dessert project — the smaller, individual items that would be placed around each sculpture and served to our guests for consumption. Not that they couldn't consume the globes or flames. But who would want to destroy such beauty?

Peter Everett Sargeant was standing in the center of the kitchen when we returned. "I've been waiting for you two."

He pulled out a list, and began reciting, starting with tasks to be done. He kept going despite Henry's assurances that we'd already accomplished all that, and more. Next, he launched into his version of what we needed to do, beginning tomorrow morning. I wanted to jam a dishrag into his mouth, to put an end to his babble. We'd been through the rigors of state dinners over and over again before he'd ever stepped foot in the White House. We didn't need this intervention.

"Although most of your support personnel have worked in the White House before," he continued, "I do not have all their resumes. I need a copy of each curriculum vitae so that we have that information on hand when we need to fill permanent positions here."

Henry said, "I make the hiring decisions for the kitchen."

Sargeant gave him a funny look. "Ms. Braun has made it clear that when she takes over the kitchen, she will require my assistance in these matters. Assistance I am most happy to provide, might I add."

"Ms. Braun is not the executive chef!" Henry's voice boomed. "And she won't ever be, if I have anything to say about it." Face red, he moved in close to Sargeant, towering over the little guy, pointing his finger. "I will thank you to remember that you are not responsible for making that decision. And, Mr. Sensitivity Director, I will also thank you to remember that Olivia Paras is in contention for the position. Your constant innuendo that Ms. Braun has the position wrapped up — over my trusted and capable assistant — shows a tremendous *lack* of sensitivity."

The room went suddenly silent except for Henry's heavy breathing and the slight backward shuffle of Sargeant's shoes against the floor.

Leaning back now, Henry worked a passive expression onto his face. In a most civilized voice, he asked, "Is there anything else before you leave?"

Sargeant hesitated, then said, "Yes. Yes, there is. Princess Hessa is due here shortly."

"Here?" I said. "Tonight?"

Sargeant said, "Yes, tonight," so matter-of-factly that we might have been discussing a network sitcom schedule. Henry and I exchanged looks.

"Why?" I asked. "It's late. Heads of state never come for visits this late at night. And, even if they did, there'd be ceremony, a big hoopla." Incredulity made my words race. "The president and Mrs. Campbell are still at Camp David until tomorrow afternoon. There's no one here to receive her."

"*I'm* here," he said with a sniff.

"But . . ."

Henry asked, "What's the purpose of the visit?"

"The princess is concerned about meal preparation for her husband. He has very specific likes and dislikes —"

In that instant, plans for the dinner crumbled like falling rocks. I blurted, "Our menus were approved days ago. It's too late to make changes."

Sargeant cast a withering glance at me, then glared at Henry. "This is your choice for successor?"

"Ollie is right," Henry said. "Everything has been approved."

Sargeant shook his head. "I'll be back shortly with Princess Hessa and Kasim, who will translate. I trust you'll have your issues under control by then."

Once he was safely out of earshot, I looked at Henry. "That man infuriates me."

He patted my shoulder and said, "You

deserve the position of executive chef, Ollie." With a sad look, he added, "But if for some reason you aren't appointed," he sighed, "maybe it is for the best."

I braved a smile. "Maybe it is."

"This," Peter Sargeant said as he strode into our work area, nearly bumping into four assistants in the process, "is the main White House kitchen."

As Sargeant waited for Kasim to translate, he stepped to his right. There were white-clad sous-chefs and assistants in every corner of the space, everyone busy. The clatter of pans, the brief barked questions and orders, and the sizzle as vegetables were dropped into searing olive oil made it difficult to hear over the din.

Kasim leaned close to the princess, who tonight wore a beaded orange *burqa*, again in full headdress. I couldn't make out her features beneath the chiffonlike fabric, but every so often the air current would press the material against her face, giving a sense of the shape of her features. Still, not enough for me to determine whether she'd be considered attractive or not. If a groom wasn't allowed to see his prospective wife before the wedding, it could make for an interesting honeymoon.

Kasim towered over the small woman, holding his beard to the side whenever he leaned down to speak to her. I wondered if he did so because his beard wasn't allowed to graze the princess's coverings, even accidentally.

"Good evening," Kasim said to us. "I trust that our visit does not adversely impact your preparations for tomorrow."

"Not at all," I lied.

Henry whispered, "You handle this, I'll keep the troops busy."

Although we'd sent about half the temporary staff home for the night, with strict instructions not to be late tomorrow morning, we still had more people busy in the kitchen than the small area could comfortably handle. The presence of Kasim, the princess, and Sargeant limited our ability to access certain areas.

Kasim held his hands clasped together at his waist. "The princess appreciates you taking the time to show her around and share your plans for tomorrow."

The princess stood in front of Kasim, Sargeant behind. Now, the sensitivity director was poking his head around Kasim's figure, giving me the evil eye.

Like I wouldn't know how to respond without his input. "I'm delighted to do so,"

I said. "What would the princess like to see first?"

Kasim didn't consult her. They must have discussed the matter before they arrived. "Princess Hessa is most pleased with your choices for tomorrow night's dinner. She would be very interested to sample the cucumber appetizer."

Lucky for us, we always made extra of everything. The item she wanted to taste, Cucumber Slices Stuffed with Feta and Pine Nuts, was being worked on by one of our Muslim assistants, so I led her, Kasim, and Sargeant around the busy assistants to where a tray of items was being prepared.

Just as I was about to pull a completed cucumber slice from the tray, xylophone music pierced the air.

"What's that?" I asked.

The princess reached into her *burqa* with her right hand, and pulled out a cell phone. She answered with a murmur, and held her left hand over her ear.

"Perhaps you should escort the princess to the hallway," I whispered to Sargeant.

To my surprise, he took the suggestion.

I turned to Kasim. "I didn't realize the princess carried a cell phone."

If eyebrows could shrug, his did. "Do you not have one?" he asked, as he pulled a cell phone from beneath his flowing robes. "I carry mine always. As a travel facilitator, it is imperative that I am always able to be reached."

"I do have one," I said, flustered. I realized my gaffe. Because Kasim and the princess came from a Middle Eastern country, I'd made the erroneous assumption that their access to technology was far behind ours. The phone Kasim tucked away, and the one the princess had used, both looked to be state-of-the-art. "What I mean to say is that I didn't realize they worked here. That is, mine doesn't work when I leave the country. Are these the same cell phones you use at home?"

"I understand your confusion. As diplomats, we are required to avail ourselves of technology that spans international borders." He lifted one shoulder. "These are special telephones. The princess insisted on acquiring one before we departed. She is concerned about her children's well-being while she is away. This is one of the reasons she did not prefer to stay at Camp David." He gave a regretful smile. "There was no signal there. And she is quite the devoted mother. She is often in contact with her family."

The devoted mother and Sargeant returned just then. Within minutes I'd walked her through the preparation of the filling for the appetizer without her saying a word. I offered her one to sample, but she waved me away, stepping backward as she did so. Her braceleted wrist jangled bright silver and gold.

Realizing that she might be uncomfortable consuming food in our presence, I offered to package up some of the appetizers for her to enjoy back at Blair House. Kasim translated.

She shook her hands at me again.

There was no pleasing this woman. Nor a chance of getting her to speak aloud.

"What time will you be here tomorrow morning?" Sargeant asked me. "Not late again, I hope."

"Henry and I will be here before the sun comes up," I said.

"How long are you staying tonight?"

Henry joined us. "Is there a reason you need to know?"

Good old Henry, rushing to my rescue.

Flustered, Sargeant stammered. "I . . . I'm concerned about leaving temporary help here unsupervised."

Henry's wide face split into a grin. But it wasn't a happy one. "That will never happen."

"You understand," Sargeant said, "what with heightened security . . . we can't afford to take chances."

"As I said, you can put your mind at ease. But Ollie and I don't plan to stay past ten this evening. We don't want to be exhausted for the big event tomorrow."

Kasim interrupted to ask Sargeant a question. I gathered that the princess was ready to return to Blair House. I'd learned my lesson; I didn't offer her any food. As they spoke, Henry edged closer to me. "I'm worried about you getting home tonight. How about I take the Metro with you and make sure you get in safe? I can call a cab from there."

"Henry, my apartment is ridiculously out of your way," I said, "that's not a good idea."

"It's not that bad," he said. "I don't like the idea of you traveling alone at night, any night. With recent events, you shouldn't be left alone at all."

"I'm okay."

"Olivia," he said.

With a sidelong glance to Sargeant, who appeared to be oblivious to our conversation as he chatted with Kasim, I spoke in a low voice. "I've got someone taking me home tonight," I said.

Henry's eyebrows shot upward. "Who?"

I bit my lip, rolled my eyes, then whispered, "One of the . . . guys."

Henry said, "Ahh," and grinned at me. "I understand." He winked. "Your secret is safe with me."

I looked up to see Sargeant, Kasim, and the princess watching us. Oh great. So much for keeping secrets. Thank goodness I hadn't mentioned Tom by name.

Sargeant eyed me with distaste. But I was getting used to it. "The princess will be leaving now," he said. "Kasim and I will accompany her back to Blair House."

"Good night," we said as the trio left.

Kasim nodded. "And to you."

The princess and Sargeant kept walking without a word.

When the last possible task that could be done, was done, and all the temporary help had gone home, I called Tom. Past midnight, our quitting time was far later than Henry had estimated.

The phone rang twice, then went to voice mail. I left Tom a vague message about being ready to leave.

Henry shuffled in from the other room, yawning. He had his jacket on. "Problem?" he asked.

"No, just a delay."

He considered this, then started for the kitchen's stool. "I'll wait with you."

"That's okay," I said. "I'm sure he'll call back any minute now. He made me promise not to go home alone, so don't worry. He'll be here. Just a little bit tardy."

One eye narrowed. "You wouldn't be telling a fib just to let the old man go home early and grab some shut-eye, would you?"

"No," I said, "I swear."

"Okay then." Relief tugged a smile out of him, but weariness pulled harder. He was exhausted and tomorrow promised to be twice as busy as today had been. We both needed to get some sleep, and there was no sense in both of us waiting for me to be picked up. "You're sure?"

I'd been in this situation with Tom a hundred times before. If he was on duty he couldn't always answer his phone. But he remained aware and always called me back at his earliest opportunity. I forced a smile, knowing that it sometimes took him over an hour to get back to me. "I'm sure," I said.

Fifteen minutes after Henry left, I was still sitting in the too-quiet kitchen, waiting. Despite the fact that this place for all intents and purposes was my second home, I shivered. The hum of the refrigeration units, the occasional *whoosh* of machinery nearby, oddball sounds — they were just part of the background during the day. Now each sounded loud as a shout, and every time some device kicked on, or off, I jumped.

I dialed Tom again.

"Ollie," he answered.

"Did you get my message?"

"Just now. I was listening to it when you beeped in."

There was something weird in his voice.

"What's wrong?" I asked.

"I . . ." He swore. "It's a bad time right now."

"Oh," I said not knowing what to do with that information. "Do you want to call me back?"

He swore a second time. I heard a toilet flush.

"You're in the bathroom?" I asked.

"My only chance to check my phone. Listen, Ollie, I . . . I can't get away tonight."

"You can't?" I looked at the clock. Nearly one in the morning. The Metro stopped running at midnight.

"I'm so sorry. Is there anyone else you can call?"

I started to answer, but over the rushing water I heard a male voice call, "Mac-Kenzie, let's go."

"I'll be okay," I said.

359

"Ollie —"

"Go," I said. "It'll be okay."

I hung up feeling lonelier than I ever had before.

Had I known this, I might've taken Henry up on his offer to see me home safely. But, no use crying over spilled sauerkraut. This wasn't the first time I'd worked past Metro hours. I zipped through my cell's phone book until I found the speed dial for the Red Top Cab company and requested a car be sent right away.

The dispatcher told me it would be just a few minutes. I set out for Fifteenth Street to wait.

Before I cleared the gates, I turned back to look at the White House. The heart of the nation, at night.

Beautiful.

And, right now, peaceful.

I thought about the negotiating country's delegates, still at Camp David tonight. Probably asleep right now. Had they reached an accord? Would the state dinner celebrate new trade agreements that could herald the dawn of peace? I stared up at the sky, wishing I could see more of the stars, but still comforted knowing they were there. Despite the fact that I wore soft-soled shoes, my footsteps brushed against the pavement so loudly. They rang out evidence of my passage, and it made me feel vulnerable.

The statue of General William Tecumseh Sherman atop his horse provided a place for me to park myself to wait for the taxi's arrival. All four of the horse's hooves rested on the ground. An urban legend had begun — I didn't know when or where — suggesting that the placement of a horse's hooves on a statue tells how the rider died. All four on the ground indicated that Sherman died a peaceful death, which was true — if dying of pneumonia could be considered peaceful.

Not all statues were "correct" as far as this legend was concerned, but as I sat on the cement steps I was glad of the thought. Concentrating on peace kept me from panicking.

Then I thought about Sherman's "scorched earth" initiatives.

Not so peaceful.

I stood.

A high-pitched squeal to my left made me jump. A homeless man, bearded and shuffling, pulled an overstuffed wheeled cart in his wake.

He didn't approach me and for that I was grateful. With the Chameleon known for his ability to alter his appearance and blend into the background, I might've decked the guy if he asked me for loose change.

Thirty seconds later, the cab pulled up. Right on schedule. I scooted in. The dark-skinned driver nodded when I gave him my address. Before I closed the door, I asked him how late Red Top provided service, even though I already knew they ran twenty-four hours a day.

I just wanted a look at the guy.

When he answered me, I stared, paying no attention to his words, but close attention to his features. Not the guy at the merry-go-round. Not the guy at Arlington. I was being paranoid, but if it kept me safe, so be it. Contented, I realized I'd been gawking when an extended pause and a peculiar expression on the guy's face brought me back to the present. He'd asked a question.

"I'm sorry, what?" I asked.

"Please close the door?" His accent was thick, Middle Eastern. Not the same as Ambassador bin-Saleh's or Kasim's, but I guessed it came from the same region.

"Sure," I said, and pulled it shut.

I sat back and watched out the window as the quiet city flew by and we made our way into Virginia. The chances of the Chameleon suddenly showing up as a taxi driver — *my*

362

taxi driver — were about a zillion to one, but I knew the assassin had it in for me, and I knew he had resources. What had Naveen said? That higher-ups in our system had been compromised? Was that it? Tom hadn't seemed overly troubled by that information, but I was. It explained a lot.

The worst of it was that with Naveen's death, we still were no closer to knowing what the Chameleon had in store. I was pleased to know that, due to the importance of the trade negotiations going on at Camp David, and the upcoming state dinner, the Secret Service had increased security measures not only around the White House, but in the surrounding areas as well. At least the president would be safe.

Now I just had to hope I was.

Again I stared at the cab driver. This guy wasn't the Chameleon. Of that I was certain. But could he be an accomplice?

The driver must have felt the weight of my gaze because his eyes kept flicking to the rearview mirror to stare back at me. I looked away. He looked away. When I checked again he was watching me. And I watched him.

"Something is a problem?"

"No," I said, lying again. I'd been doing a

lot of that recently. "Have you lived here long?"

He shot me a look of utter contempt.

Great. Now I was the suspicious person.

"I have been in this country fifteen years," he said with no small degree of pride. "I have come here legally and I have made the United States of America my home. I passed all the tests," he said. "I am not a terrorist."

Oh, Lord, now I'd done it.

"I didn't think that you —"

"I see your look in your eyes." He pointed at his own eyes in emphasis. "You have suspicion. What, do you think every Muslim man is going to blow you up?" With that he threw his hands off the steering wheel and the car jerked hard to the left, crossing the yellow lines.

I screamed, but fortunately the absence of oncoming traffic prevented our instant death, and he righted the vehicle quickly.

"Sorry," I said.

He gave me a look that said, "You should be."

I wanted to correct him. Tell him that I wasn't feeling bad for partaking in my own brand of profiling, I was just sorry I'd screamed. I *didn't* assume every Muslim man I encountered was ready to blow me up, but I had an assassin after me. An assassin who made his living by committing murder and slinking away, disguised as . . . as anyone.

If I wanted to look at this guy suspiciously, then it was my prerogative to do so.

"Last time I checked, there were no limits on freedom of personal thoughts," I mumbled.

"What?" he asked. "What do you say?"

The moment of tension now past, I realized that if he'd been in cahoots with the Chameleon, I would've been dead ten minutes ago. "Nothing."

After an extended, awkward silence, I gave him a fair but unapologetic tip, slammed the car door, and thanked the stars above that I was finally home.

CHAPTER 28

First thing the next morning, while the sky was still dark, chief usher Paul Vasquez popped into the kitchen. "Henry, Ollie. Follow me."

The corridor was cool and quiet. Dark. In just a few short hours, the very same area would be filled with fervent reporters, eager politicians, and polite dignitaries. All hungry.

Paul held open the door of the China Room. I remembered the last time he'd called me in here, and I watched his face for some indication that I'd inadvertently stepped out of line again. The fact that Henry was with me ruled that out, thank goodness.

"There's been a change," Paul said as he closed the door.

"In the menu?" Henry asked.

"No." He stood close, the three of us making a tight triangle, tighter than would normally be considered comfortable for a casual discussion. His voice dropped and we edged closer still. "The information I'm about to share with you is being released on a strict 'need to know' basis." He looked at me for a long moment, then at Henry.

We both nodded.

"You understand that you are not to share a word of this with anyone, unless you clear it with me first."

We both said, "Yes."

The tension in his face relaxed, just a bit, and he looked about to smile. "I am extraordinarily pleased to report that negotiations at Camp David have resulted, not in a simple trade agreement, but in a peace treaty." Paul's careful expression gave way to a full-blown beam. "President Campbell has been successful in facilitating a peace agreement between the two warring countries. When this treaty is signed, it will be as big, or possibly bigger than the accords between Egypt and Israel."

Henry and I kept our exclamations of cheer in check, so as not to bring a batch of Secret Service agents bursting in on us. "That's wonderful," I said.

Paul looked as pleased as if he'd facilitated the treaty himself. "It is," he said. "And the reason I wanted you both to know ahead of time is because we're changing plans for tonight's dinner."

Uh-oh. Last-minute changes were never a good thing.

I held my breath.

"We're taking the celebration outdoors," he began.

Henry and I cut him off right there, both of us protesting. Henry was louder. "We can't serve the dinner outside," he said, "we've got everything set up for the State Dining Room. The places are set, the room is decorated, and . . . and . . . there are bugs outside." Vehement head shake. "It would be a disaster."

Paul waited for Henry to finish, holding up a placating hand. "Let me explain and perhaps we can find some common ground here. Because of the success of the accords and the ideal weather conditions, President Campbell prefers to make the announcement of the peace treaty outside the South Portico."

I pictured it. The South Lawn offered plenty of room for the dignitaries, their staffs, invited guests, and the press to spread out. The South Portico and the Truman balcony provided a beautiful backdrop for photos that would, no doubt, find a place in history books for all the ages. I waited for the rest of what Paul had to say.

"What we intend to do, is have the welcoming ceremony, introductory speeches, and official reception outdoors as usual. At that point, the honored guests and their entourages will be invited to partake in refreshments."

"Dear God!" Henry said, "We don't have enough food for the entire crowd."

Paul quickly interjected. "I know. We realize the difficulty. And we've come up with what we think is a workable option given the circumstances. We will have the cocktail hour outdoors at four o'clock in the Rose Garden," he held up both index fingers, "which will include appetizers and beverages. You are authorized to order prepared items from our approved contacts to augment the food you've prepared here. Once everyone is satiated, at precisely five o'clock, the president will announce the agreements. More speeches. Tables will have already been set up for the official signing. The signing will take place immediately, in front of the South Portico. More speeches, again. We anticipate a half-hour's worth of questions and photographs. Shortly thereafter, at precisely seven, dinner will be served in the State Dining Room."

Henry covered his eyes with his hands.

This was no expression of frustration, I knew, nor of surrender. He was thinking, planning, figuring ways to make this work.

He dropped his hands. "Okay."

Paul, who expected nothing less, said, "Good. Let me know if there's anything you need."

I walked to the Rose Garden to see for myself that everything was in place the way Henry and I expected it to be. While I walked, I checked my cell phone. Tom had called and left me a message. I listened.

"Thanks for texting me that you got home safe. I was worried about you. I have to run — there's a lot going on. Call me when you get in. And, don't head home by yourself tonight. Give me a call when you guys are cleaning up. Talk to you later."

I berated myself for not checking messages sooner, but when I dialed his cell, it went immediately to voice mail. I told him I'd made it to the White House safely and I agreed to call him later. I purposely didn't add that I'd taken the Metro this morning. He would not have been amused. As I shut my phone I realized that this crisscross communication, while far from romantic, was promising. He was worried about me.

And I was worried for him. I knew that

today's ceremonies and dinner — even if an agreement hadn't materialized — made for a tempting target. The Chameleon would be wise to stay away today, though. Despite the fact that all the guards knew me and I knew them, this morning I'd been subjected to the most thorough search I'd ever encountered. Freddie and Gloria were both on duty, and Gloria had patted me down. When I'd asked why the extra precaution, Freddie had mentioned Chameleon concerns.

Outside the front gates, in Lafayette Park, demonstrators from the prince's country chanted. Bearded men shouted. All wore traditional turbans and long flowing robes as they gesticulated and yelled. Their vituperative verbal assaults, some in English, others in what I assumed was their native tongue, made it clear that not everyone supported the newly crowned prince.

I turned to Gloria. "I thought camping out overnight in Lafayette Park was prohibited."

She stared through the gates at the angry crowd. "They didn't camp. They started arriving just a little while ago. Heard this is just the first wave, and we've got lots more coming our way. They're protesting in shifts, I guess."

The men screamed, occasionally in unison. Those without upraised fists carried signs. Hand-lettered, they were written in a language I couldn't read. They could have crossed the lines of vulgarity for all I knew. I watched the sweating, angry men and realized that they probably had.

I'd headed quickly to the entrance. Could the Chameleon be in that crowd? I doubted it. From everything I'd learned about the assassin, he had no political ties. No policy he supported. He was a mercenary who went in, got the job done, and raced out again without leaving a trace.

With security heightened to greater tension than I'd ever seen before, the assassin would have a tough time getting close enough to President Campbell today. That, however, didn't mean that Tom was safe.

Now at the Rose Garden, I blew out a breath as I inspected the tables. A centerpiece of yellow and white blooms on each of the seven tables stood taller than the four complementary arrangements accompanying it. Although the smaller bouquets were by no means tiny, they were dwarfed by the taller arrangements. The White House floral designer, Kendra, had pulled the original designs from their places in the State Dining Room and created these centerpieces last minute. Even now, I knew she was hard at work making replacements for the smaller items. Their exposure to the outdoors could make the blooms droop. Like the rest of us at the White House, she strove for perfection.

From across the expanse of the South Lawn I heard the Marine Band practicing. Everyone practiced until there was no chance of error. Even the aides who were assigned to move dignitaries to their proper positions practiced. I heard someone ask, "We've got Princess Hessa standing next to Mrs. Campbell at this point. Is that right?" and someone else answer in the affirmative.

Camera technicians and other media folk had gotten here early and were already setting up. Outside the South Portico, on the North Lawn, and in other strategic spots, high-beam lamps on tall black poles, augmented by light-reflecting umbrellas, waited for important people to arrive.

Two cameramen ran extension cords to their equipment. I wandered nearer to them on the pretext of examining another table. One was short, with a vague resemblance to Laurel Anne's buddy Carmen, and the other one lanky and blond. They ignored me, but I sidled closer, checking them out. Could I recognize the Chameleon if I saw him again? If he were disguised? I had my doubts, but I planned to study every single new face today. If my life was in jeopardy because I could recognize the guy, then I might as well do my best to use that information to pick him out.

"Could you believe security today?" the blond guy said.

Carmen's lookalike shook his head. "It's always bad, but geez. Did they make you take your camera apart, too?"

"Hell, yeah. I tried to tell them that this equipment is sensitive, but it was either take the thing apart in front of them or —"

"— you don't get in," the dark guy finished.

"What the hell do they think I could have in here anyway?" The blond guy held up his press pass, dangling from a lanyard around his neck. "And who the hell would try to look like me, anyway? The uniforms here know me. I've been doing this for months."

They muttered back and forth as I started past them. Nope, I decided. Neither one looked like the face burned into my memory from the merry-go-round. Or from the range. Or from Arlington.

Their talk of tight security made me glad. Maybe we'd be safe today after all.

■ ■ ■ ■

"Over here, over here," Cyan called to one of the temps. "Yeah, that's it," she said as the girl brought the tray of appetizers to the kitchen's far side, narrowly avoiding collision with two other tray-bearing assistants. "Yikes," Cyan exclaimed at the near-miss. Then, waving her hand at the girl who'd deposited the food before her, she added, "Not you. It's just —"

The girl waited.

"Never mind. Thanks," Cyan said, "I think Bucky needs help over there."

"Stressed out yet?" I asked as I worked.

"Most of these kids have been trained in bigger facilities," she said. "They don't get the fact that we have to think about our activity. They can't just jump up and do something. They need to think first. Otherwise . . . disaster."

I smiled at her use of the word *kids*. Cyan was the youngest member of our team and more than half of the chefs she'd hired had mastered technique while Cyan was still learning the difference between a teaspoon and a tablespoon. The fact that she was a White House sous-chef at her tender age was testament to her talent. But we still

375

needed to work on her ability to remain calm during tense situations.

"What color are the eyes today?" I asked, to change the subject.

She leaned toward me and blinked.

"Brown? I don't think I've ever seen you in that color."

"They're new," she said, smiling. "With all the brown-eyed folks traipsing through here these past few days, I thought I'd join the party."

I gave her a quizzical look. "You mean like Laurel Anne?" I asked, "Or Ambassador bin-Saleh? Or Kasim?" As I ran through the names of the brown-eyed people we'd encountered recently, I realized how many there were. "Or . . . Peter Everett Sargeant III?"

She stuck out her tongue. "No thanks."

"I bet the princess has brown eyes, too," I said. "Of course, we'll never see them."

"How is she supposed to eat in front of all the guests if she can't remove her veil?"

I shook my head. "No idea. Maybe I'll ask Kasim."

Just as she giggled, Henry returned from his inspection of the serving tables outside. "Troops," he said, his voice booming loud enough for everyone to hear. The kitchen silenced immediately. "I need my team to follow me," he said.

Cyan gave out some last-minute instructions to those nearby, and I handed cinnamon and powdered sugar to another assistant to mix. We made our way through the obstacle course of temporary help and headed for the door.

"This way," Henry said. Marcel and Bucky got there just as we did, and the five of us tramped to the nearest storage room, where it was blessedly quiet.

"As you know, since plans have been changed, we will be running tonight's dinner by the seats of our pants."

Okay, that was an exaggeration. We had everything planned — micromanaged to the very minute — and even though the outdoor cocktail reception threw our best-laid plans into chaos, we were managing the chaos. Pretty well, too.

Henry read from his list. "Cyan, you will coordinate the staff to ensure the hors d'oeuvres are placed outside at the proper time. The head waiter is assigning a team to you, and we will have less than ten minutes from the close of the welcoming ceremonies until the food needs to be out there. We have to stay on top of this."

She nodded.

"Bucky, you're in charge of dinner's first

two courses."

His head snapped back like Henry had punched him. "Me?"

"Yes." Henry pointed. "I need you to oversee the final preparations just before the food is plated. I've prepared a list of those who will assist you, and you will work together with the indoor waitstaff to ensure the proper plating and prompt delivery of the first courses to the dining room." Rolling wide eyes, Henry continued, "Dennis, our sommelier, is beside himself. He'd planned vintages to complement tonight's menu — he had not arranged for a full assortment of aperitifs. But," he added with a rueful smile, "that's not currently our concern. He will be marvelous; he always is."

"What am I doing?" I asked.

"Before the first guest arrives, we are all gathering our troops to make as many more appetizers as we possibly can in the allotted time. All of us. While Cyan and Bucky direct their people, you and I, Ollie, with the help of some assistants, will be making more appetizers. Thank goodness we made as much as we did, and thank goodness you ordered those extra supplies, Cyan."

She blushed at the compliment.

"Once we have the situation under control

— and I expect to arrive at that state shortly — Ollie and I will take charge of overseeing operations. This event tonight will require *orchestration.* We will probably all step out of our comfort zones." He took a moment to make eye contact with each of us. "And assist where we're needed, whether it's our job or not."

Henry was preaching to the choir. Not one of us approached our positions as a prima donna would — my mind lurched as I pictured Laurel Anne faced with this state of affairs — but Henry's coaching gave me reassurance. He huddled our team before every big event. This was standard. This was reassuring. Suddenly these last-minute changes didn't seem all that insurmountable.

If I ever ran my own kitchen, I'd do it exactly the same way.

At three thirty, with Henry's blessing, I snuck outside to watch the ceremonies, keeping close to the South Portico doors. The prime minister and the prince and princess had arrived in limousines earlier and had been welcomed at the south doors and into the oval-shaped Diplomatic Reception Room with a flurry of pomp and circumstance. After that "official reception," the president and Mrs. Campbell, with the assistance of the well-practiced aides, guided the dignitaries outdoors, amid snapping camera shutters and microphones thrust forward from behind velvet ropes.

Each of the dignitaries found his or her place on a line of artificial green turf that had been rolled out several hundred yards south, where official ceremonies were usually held. Each dignitary's name was marked on the ground with white tape. Every movement of this entire day had been scrupulously choreographed; such preparations were necessary so that an event of this magnitude ran smoothly.

I winced at the loud pops of the twenty-one gun salute and watched as the cameras moved in to capture the president's official inspection of the troops.

The Marine Band, also known as "The President's Own," played several national favorites including "Yankee Doodle Dandy," and two songs I didn't recognize, but I knew must be the national songs of the prime minister's and prince's respective countries.

For a breathless instant, the music stilled.

And then, the Marine Band began the "Star Spangled Banner." When the familiar opening notes of our national anthem sounded, so clear and strong on this exceptional spring afternoon, shivers ran up my back. I blinked once . . . twice, and then again.

As I stood there watching, I marveled. The photographers stilled their cameras, the reporters lowered their microphones. We all stood at attention to salute the most beautiful flag, the most powerful symbol of freedom on Earth. Next to me, the waiters halted their work to place hands over hearts. Several mouthed the words to the song so many of us learned in grammar school.

As always happened, when the lyrics came to ". . . gave proof through the night, that our flag was still there . . ." goose bumps raced across my arms and chest, down my back. I took in a deep breath and thanked heaven that I'd been born here, that my parents' grandparents had come to this country for a new life so many years before. I had much to be thankful for.

I whispered along with the final line, ". . . and the home of the brave."

How true.

I knew I should hustle toward the West Wing, where the appetizers, beverages, and incidentals were being set up for the cocktail reception just moments away.

But I couldn't resist taking a quick moment to sidle near the dais that had been erected just outside the south doors. Atop a carpet of bright red, three tables were being set up, and I knew that the reason they were there — for a three-way discussion for the cameras on the nature of the Camp David trade agreement — was pretext. These were the tables where the president, prime minister, and prince would sit to sign the peace treaty that would change the fabric of life in this world forever. And our president had facilitated this.

Had the day been overcast and rainy, I would have felt just as ebullient. I was part of this moment. I was part of history. As workers placed chairs, tablecloths, and flags in place on and around the dais, I ran my finger along the edge of the signing table. A lineup of miniature flags, representing a myriad of countries, topped the tables with a festive, though profound touch.

Out of the corner of my eye, I thought I saw Tom near the West Wing. Even though I'd been on my way back to the kitchen, I couldn't resist delaying long enough to see him and say hello.

My short legs could only take short strides, and I certainly didn't want to call attention to myself by running, so I walked purposefully toward the West Wing and was disappointed to see Tom catch up with

Craig and disappear inside before I had a chance to talk with him. At least I knew he was here. And that made me feel better. Within the White House gates, I felt so much safer than I did in the rest of the city. I glanced up at the black-clad snipers on the building's roof, pacing with their rifles, keeping a close eye on all of us below.

While at the Rose Garden, where chafing dishes had just been set up, I corralled Jamal. "As a last-minute addition, we've prepared extra fruit trays," I said, pointing to spots on the tables between the silver servingware, "which I think should go here, here, and," I stretched out both arms, "there."

Jamal nodded, asked a couple of questions about timing, and headed back in via the West Wing entrance.

I caught sight of Kasim working his way toward the food tables, dodging workers who carried chairs, tables, and other accoutrements. Kasim was in a robe of navy blue with a brown turban. Poor guy. Today was warming up and even in my white tunic and toque, I was hot. I could only imagine how he felt. He spent his entire life wearing dark clothing in a hot climate. How uncomfortable And he'd been ill recently, too.

I also wondered how he felt, being left out

of the ceremony taking place on the South Lawn. As one of the underlings, Kasim wasn't privy to the big events. Like Henry and I, he was there to make himself available, to facilitate and to assist. When it came to the formal procedures, he was left in the background to make sure things went smoothly for his people.

I was about to ask him if he needed assistance when I noticed Peter Everett Sargeant. He called out to Kasim, who turned. I ducked out of sight, then inched closer to hear.

"This came for you moments ago," Sargeant said, handing Kasim a large diplomatic pouch.

Kasim nodded his thanks. "I am most grateful. The princess was quite distressed to have left these things behind this morning. I will see to it that she receives this promptly." He turned his back to Sargeant, but the shorter man trailed behind the foreign assistant, talking animatedly. He, too, was relegated to the background to assure smooth transitions. The problem was that Sargeant didn't like to be left out.

The last thing I needed was another run-in with Sargeant. I stepped out of their line of vision, behind one of the colonnade's white pillars, and started to make my way back to the kitchen.

"If she prefers me to hold onto anything of hers, I can make a page available to assist."

"Thank you," Kasim said, "the princess will be most appreciative of your offer. But I believe one of her female assistants will be present later."

The words were polite but strained, and Kasim's long-legged, limping strides punctuated his obvious desire to distance himself from Sargeant.

I could relate.

Sargeant scurried double-time to catch up. Decked out in another smartly cut pinstripe suit, this one the same shade of navy blue as Kasim's robes, the two looked like a multicultural Mutt and Jeff. "I'm sorry you missed the opening ceremonies."

"It is my duty to serve my prince and his wife at their pleasure. If I am required here, then this is where I remain." Kasim spoke as he walked. I ducked deeper behind the pillar and hoped to get past them both without being seen. "Just as I am certain that you are more needed here to facilitate than you are out there." He gestured toward the crowd.

"I wanted to take special care of your delivery," he said with a degree of annoyance. "I will join the celebration as soon as I am certain that you and your colleagues are well taken care of."

Kasim wiped his brow and coughed. He stopped, turned, and looked down at our eager sensitivity director. "What I am in need of at the moment, my dear sir, are your lavatory facilities. I am feeling unwell."

"Of course," Sargeant said. "Let me show you the way. I'll take my leave then, and see you at the reception."

"Thank you," Kasim said. He wiped his face again and made a noise that underscored his discomfort. "I may be required to return to Blair House if I continue to feel this unwell."

"Is there anything I can do?" Sargeant said again. Now he started to look as though he'd like to get away from the other man.

"The lavatory."

"Yes, yes, of course."

Just then Sargeant spied me. "What are you doing out here?" he asked.

Kasim lurched toward the doors leading into the West Wing. Sargeant called a Secret Service agent over and asked him to escort Kasim to the washroom that I knew was just outside the Oval Office. The foreign diplomat nodded to me, briefly, looking relieved to be able to get indoors out of the heat.

I nodded back, then turned to Sargeant. "I'm here to make sure things are set up properly."

"And why wouldn't they be?"

I bit my tongue. Literally. Then said. "In the White House kitchen we leave nothing to chance."

"You will not be out here when the guests are."

"I don't intend to be."

He tugged at his suit jacket. "That's all," he said, dismissing me. "Do not let me see anyone from the kitchen out here again. You especially. Are we understood?"

"Yes, sir."

If he was taken aback by my crisp retort, I didn't know it. I executed a quick turn and had my back to him before he could respond. At this point I had nothing to lose. All I wanted right now was to make tonight's event a success — an amazing success — for Henry's sake. This would be our final hurrah together. Whether I stayed at the White House or not, I was determined that Henry would go out with a bang.

As luck would have it, however, I found myself outdoors again, just as President Campbell finished his welcoming speech. I glanced at my watch. Right on time. Paul Vasquez stood near the presidential contingent, and I knew he kept a precise eye on every movement, maintaining an exact schedule.

When President Campbell closed, the crowd burst into eager applause. As it died down, White House personnel moved in to ensure the crowd followed the plan. The Marine Band began playing low background music, which they would maintain until it came time for more speeches.

Leading the way to the Rose Garden, President Campbell walked between the prince and prime minister. Behind them followed the First Lady and Princess Hessa. Although the prime minister was married, he'd come alone to the United States. This was the first I'd seen of him. While the prince and princess were settled at Blair House, the prime minister had been accommodated at a nearby hotel, the best Washington, D.C., had to offer. Despite Blair House's size and accommodations, it was not acceptable to house two delegates in the same abode at the same time. Since the prime minister and his group was smaller, and did not require the same level of privacy that the prince did, he'd agreed to the hotel.

From all accounts everyone was happy,

although it seemed that everyone would have preferred to remain at Camp David.

All but the princess, that is.

I caught sight of Kasim as I made my way to the tables to give everything a last look and to ensure that the food we'd prepared was being displayed properly. Kasim pushed at his headdress, as he made his way back toward the West Wing. He looked sweaty and uncomfortable, eager to avoid the crowd, and I guessed he was again heading to the washroom.

"Were you able to get the diplomatic pouch to the princess?" I asked. He wasn't carrying it, but neither was the princess. If it was something she needed, I worried that Kasim's apparent illness would have a ripple effect on the rest of the day.

I must have startled him because he shot me a strange look, his brown eyes squinting even as he shook his head. "No," he said, "that is, yes. She has what she needs. Her assistant is taking charge."

Within minutes the crowd made its way to the appetizer tables. The important and the beautiful: senators, ambassadors, celebrities, media giants, and star-gazing assistants milled around the grassy area, all smiling. The crowd would thin down considerably before dinner began.

I knew I should head in, but then I saw Tom. He stood, looking smart and strong and brave, wearing a gray blazer, navy slacks, and sunglasses. A curly clear cord wound from his earpiece to inside his jacket. "Hey," I said as I passed.

"Hey, yourself," he whispered, eyes forward. His expression was all business. "You see anybody who looks familiar?"

"Nobody. I think you guys scared him off."

"Don't count on it," he said, never breaking his attention from the hundreds of people in the garden. "Keep your eyes open."

I started back inside, then stopped. "Say, Tom, do dignitaries go through security?"

His face twitched. Enough to know that I was taking too much of his attention.

"Sorry. Stupid question. Never mind," I said. I thought I knew the answer to that anyway. I mean, when the queen of England comes to visit, they don't ask her to put her tiara in a bin and step through a magnetometer. Dignitaries and heads of state were always who they said they were, and security was gently applied. "You going to be here all day?"

He gave an almost imperceptible shake of his head. "I'll be inside."

"It's cooler inside," I said.

He grimaced.

I took another look at the princess, who again, was keeping to herself. One of the two handmaidens stayed close — I assumed to translate. But every time anyone came near the princess to talk, or with a microphone, she turned her veiled head away.

I made my way around the business end of the food, and I noticed that one of the fruit trays was nearly empty. Already. The food was moving faster than we expected and I looked around for Jamal. He was nowhere to be found, so I took the tray and lifted it onto my shoulder, hoping to avoid running into Sargeant. He'd have something disparaging to say about me if he caught me doing the waitstaff's work. But that's how we did things at the White House. We didn't spend time worrying if picking up a scrap of paper or moving a table was someone else's job. If it needed to be done and one of us was there, we did it.

I carried the picked-over tray, making my way to the family dining room on the first floor. We used that room as a staging area for big dinners, and even though it was a considerable walk from the Rose Garden outside, it was still the best place to keep everything we planned to serve.

Henry was on his way out when we crossed paths. "How is it out there? Do we need another tray of fruit?"

"We do," I said. "I figured I'd bring this one in and —"

One of the waiters lifted the tray from my hands and started for the kitchen downstairs. "I'll grab a new one," I said.

Another waiter turned the corner. "Let Brandon do it," Henry said, calling him over.

Brandon looked apologetic. "I'll be back as soon as I can. Mr. Sargeant sent me on an errand," he said. "The princess has requested a female serve her, so he sent me to get Tanya or Bethany."

"I'll do it then," I said. "We can't let the table sit empty for this long."

"Go," Henry said.

I went.

But first: "Let me take this off," I said removing my toque. If Sargeant saw that tall white chef's hat amid the bustling waitstaff, I'd hear it for sure. Without it, no one would pay me any attention.

Henry winked. "Good idea."

Timing-wise, we had only about another five minutes before the announcement. I wanted to be out there, have the tray in place, and make myself unobtrusive before

President Campbell let the guests know the real reason for today's gathering.

Cyan was in the family dining room, orchestrating staff. It would be another two hours before dinner was served, but this was the bewitching time, the time when everything had to be handled exactly right or our careful plans would fall apart. Henry had insisted that, once the food was completely prepared, I stay out of the kitchen. He knew me well enough to know that I'd be in there, doing all the last-minute jobs myself instead of delegating them. He used to say that when I took over as executive chef I'd need to learn the skill set that allowed me to let go, but today he said it differently, "When you're running your own kitchen . . ."

That hurt. He hadn't meant it to, but we both needed to face facts. This was it. By the time Henry retired next week, we were both pretty sure I'd be looking for a new position.

I worked hard to take on more of a management role. Of course, sometimes that meant grabbing a tray of fruit.

The round, crystal tray was piled high with strawberries, kiwi, cantaloupe, grapes, and some of the more unusual choices, such as starfruit. Our temporary staff had spent hours making each piece perfect, and the tray was arranged as though ready for a *Bon Appétit* photo shoot.

I lifted the heavy platter and made my way outside, enjoying the cool air-conditioning as long as I could.

The best way to avoid the hordes of people gathered outdoors was to take the corridor that led through the West Wing before I went outside.

As I passed several of the Secret Service agents along the corridor, I looked for Tom. Not there. I narrowly avoided bumping into a man coming out of the washroom outside the Oval Office. Since he and I were about the same height, I couldn't see his face over the tray, but I could see his slacks. Uh-oh. Sargeant's blue pinstripes. He went east, I went west, and I breathed a sigh of relief when he didn't take me to task about being out among the populace again.

As I traversed the corridor, I watched the activity outside. The White House chief of staff was at the microphone under the lights the two techs had set up earlier. He called for everyone's attention and, for about the fourth time this afternoon, introduced the president of the United States, Harrison R. Campbell.

The Marine Band began "Hail to the Chief," and President Campbell smilingly stepped up onto the raised platform to take the microphone.

The heat rolled over me when the page opened the door. I made my way to the table with the open spot and laid the tray down, making sure to uncover it. A waiter nearby took the cover from me and asked if there was anything he could do.

There wasn't, so I quickly rearranged the table to accommodate the new tray.

The princess, who I thought should have been up near the prince, made her way toward the table farthest from the dais. I didn't want to turn and give her my full attention — somehow I sensed that would make her recoil — but I noticed her slip her hand out and pull a slice of kiwi under her veil.

So the princess does eat after all, I thought.

She took another piece of fruit and then another. With everyone's attention on the president, no one paid her the slightest heed. From the quickness of her movements I had to figure the poor woman was starving. She picked at each of the hors d'oeuvres trays, devouring the small tidbits as quickly as she could get them under her veil. When her hand reached again, she picked up two pieces of Baklava Stuffed with Almonds,

Pecans, and Pine Nuts.

Good thing she didn't have that nut allergy after all.

I smiled, and worked at cleaning up the garnishes that had fallen off trays and stained the pristine tablecloths. From the tiny sounds to my left, I knew she was busy eating, though I detected her inching farther away.

Just then, a young man in navy blue, pinstriped slacks stepped backward out of the crowd. The tables were set up in roughly a U shape and he was at the very end of the U's top, which put him directly to the left of the speakers at the dais. The prince and prime minister had joined President Campbell at his invitation, and the three of them stood together, looking chummy — freezing their movements and smiles for pictures.

With his back to the table the young man didn't seem to know I was there. He wore a white, long-sleeve shirt that looked crisp, but enormous sweat stains created dark moon shapes under his arms. It was hot, but not that hot.

I fussed with the table, making everything look good, and I gave the guy another glance. The side of his face, the shape of his head.

I jerked at the charge of familiarity.

No, I told myself. This guy was not the same guy from the merry-go-round. Not the guy from the range.

Was he?

Pale, yes, but this guy had brown hair.

He was the right height.

I scanned the area, looking for Tom.

Not there.

I froze, my hand poised over the fruit tray. What should I do? I couldn't say for sure that this man was the Chameleon. I couldn't see his face. Not yet.

What could I do?

What was he going to do?

The nearest Secret Service agent was thirty yards to my left. If I called out, I'd alert this guy, cause a disturbance, and he'd get away. He was inching forward, closer to the action. If I ran over to the agent, I could lose sight of him.

And I wasn't even sure this was the Chameleon. He could be a reporter. A cameraman on break. He wore a press ID on a lanyard around his neck and he shifted his weight, his back now completely toward me.

All I knew was that standing here frozen was not the way to go.

Freezing nearly got me killed at Arlington.

I had to move.

I grabbed the next tray of fruit. Almost empty.

Wanting to get a better look at him, I started to ask the guy if he wanted any fruit — when he jammed his right hand into his pocket and pulled out . . .

A cell phone.

Panic, then relief. I nearly laughed in spite of myself.

I looked at him again.

Inched closer.

He pulled another item out, this from his left pocket. It looked like an antenna. A sizeable one. Without dragging his gaze from the speeches in front of us, he connected the antenna to the top of the cell phone and twisted it into place. That was odd. Usually antennae stayed attached to phones. And then I remember Kasim telling me about the specialized models he was required to carry. This one looked a lot like the one he'd shown me that day. Maybe international phones had unique construction.

"Today," President Campbell said, beaming as cameras flashed and shutters snapped, "we are changing the face of the world as we know it. For we are not here today just to celebrate a trade agreement." He paused, waiting for the silence to ripple through the crowd. It didn't take long. "We are here today to celebrate peace. A true peace in the Middle East. Today we sign a treaty ending war between two great countries in that region."

A roar of applause. The president kept a hand on the shoulder of the prime minister to his right and the prince to his left. "Today's treaty promises our children a safer world."

More applause.

The crowd, breathless, waited for the president's next words.

And that's when she screamed.

The princess fell to the ground, gasping for air. Her veil fell askew and I saw a portion of her face for the first time. Her mouth hung open and she made noises humans don't usually make. I knew we needed Kasim, or one of the woman's handmaidens. Or even Peter Sargeant. Where were they? I was about to rush to her side when one of her handmaidens appeared at her side.

"She's having an allergic reaction!" someone yelled. I wasn't sure who.

The crowd rushed to the princess's side. Everyone in the immediate area reacted. Everyone, but the young man in the blue pinstripe pants. He didn't turn.

He didn't turn?

He pointed the elongated antenna of his cell phone at the prime minister.

My mind skip-stepped. He's going to make a call now? From that position?

And then I understood.

"Gun!" I screamed just as his finger grazed the dial buttons.

I threw the plate of food at his head, while rushing at him, prepared to tackle. The plate of food knocked him sideways, throwing off his aim.

Still I was too late.

I heard a *pop*. And another.

The prince jerked back, fell to the ground. The side of his head flowered red.

The young man in the navy slacks turned.

Pale blue eyes met mine.

In that instant, I knew.

The Chameleon.

His gaze flickered. I sensed a split-second of indecision. Kill me first? Or run?

Agents covered the president, the prime minister, the prince. The man with the cell phone gun shoved me to the ground and took off, running not away from the White House grounds, but into the building itself. In the mêlée that erupted, no one saw him go.

No one but me.

I scrambled to my feet and ran after him.

"The Chameleon," I shouted. No one heard. It was chaos outside. But now the Chameleon and I were inside. "Tom!" I called.

The corridors were empty. All the Secret Service agents had rushed out to protect the president.

I stood outside the Oval Office. I had no idea where the man went or what I could do.

"Tom," I called again.

I headed through the corridor to the east end where I knew a guard would be stationed. A guard who would not have moved from his post. But he wasn't there.

I heard a noise behind me.

The bathroom door opened and Kasim lunged out, grasping the walls as he tried to walk.

"Kasim," I said, rushing to his side.

He tried to wave me off, but he didn't look well. His turban was askew again and he headed for the doors.

"Wait," I said.

"Something has happened," he said, "I must be with the prince."

"No, don't go out there. A man —"

The words died on my lips as Kasim stumbled. He caught himself before he fell, but he made his mistake when he turned.

One eye was brown — the other blue. A pale blue.

The Chameleon's eyes.

I kicked at his shin and knocked him completely to the ground. On his feet were strange platform-like shoes, which gave him at least ten inches of height. No wonder the man always walked with an odd gait. And I thought he'd been sick. He'd played us all the whole time.

With surprising agility he threw off the shoes, got up, and came at me.

I ran.

But this time I didn't have a head start.

Kasim, or whoever he was, grabbed me. He smashed his left hand tight over my mouth and nose, cutting off my air. "Your lucky day, Ollie. I'm not going to kill you till I'm safely out of here. You be a good little chef and I'll consider doing it quickly." His voice was low and devoid of Kasim's usual crisp enunciations.

Running, he dragged me backward with him, but I didn't cooperate, making his passage difficult. I knew he needed to get me out of the corridor now. The place would be crawling with agents in about fifteen seconds.

I pulled my lips back, fighting the painful pressure of his hand till I could bare my teeth. I bit him, hard as I could. He bellowed, and I screamed for help again, raising my hands over my head to rake across his face. He shouted expletives at me.

I tore at his beard, my fingers digging into the matted mess, the gum-like adhesive stretching as the artificial hair came off in one clump.

"Freeze!"

I wriggled around. Tom stood at the far end of the corridor, his gun aimed at us.

"Let her go," he shouted.

Kasim pointed the barrel end of the cell phone to my head, his finger close to the number seven. Lucky number.

For someone else, maybe.

"Drop the weapon or she's dead," Kasim shouted back at Tom. He dodged behind me, keeping my head in front of his. It was an impossible shot. Even for Tom.

I didn't think. I reacted. Time to make my own luck. I jammed the heel of my shoe hard against Kasim's instep, scraping downward, using all my weight. It wasn't a lot, but it was enough to make him flinch. He winced and stepped to his right as I tried to break from his hold.

He grabbed me by the hair, yanking me backward, pointing the cell phone pistol at Tom. I heard that popping sound again, just like at Arlington, only much louder in these close quarters. As Kasim fired I fell backward, trying to knock the gun from his hands.

He held onto the gun, but not for long.

Tom had gotten him center mass and again in his forehead. Kasim slumped to the ground, pulling me with him. I yanked my hair free from his grip, my eyes tearing from the tender pain. The cell phone slipped from his fingers, clattering to the floor as his body seized up, trembled, then relaxed.

Blood poured over the back of my neck.

But it wasn't my blood.

The pale blue eye and the brown one were both fixed in a glassy death stare. Kasim, the Chameleon, had finally been killed. I knew it even without checking for a pulse.

For a very long moment, all I was aware of was my rapid breathing and the sound of my heartbeat in my ears. What a wonderful thing to hear.

Then — where did all the people come from? The room was suddenly filled. Secret Service agents, reporters, White House staff. How long had they been here? Had they seen what happened? I couldn't say.

Little by little, noises, sights, smells came back to me.

A tall agent I didn't know checked the

fallen Kasim. Craig Sanderson was there, too. More agents. The tall agent picked up the cell phone pistol. He gave a low whistle and hefted the phone in his hastily gloved hand. "Look at this," he said to Craig. "I heard about these things coming out of Europe. Never seen one before."

Craig snapped at him. "Apparently neither did our security team. We will look into this."

My knees buckled and I sat.

Tom pulled me to my feet, wrapping me in a hug. "Oh, God," he whispered into my hair, "I thought I'd lost you. I thought I'd shot you myself."

I knew I should be worried about what the other agents were thinking, but I was just too shaken to do anything more than hold Tom tight. "I never doubted you for a second."

He murmured something I didn't catch.

Panic made me chatter. I couldn't stop talking. If I did, I thought I might collapse. "How did you know? Where did you come from? Did you see him outside? How's the princess? Was she in on it?"

Tom just shook his head. "All in good time."

I remembered to breathe, and someone shoved a glass of water into my hands. I think I thanked them, but I wasn't sure. All I could see right now was Tom. He'd been there when I needed him most. "You know what they say about saving a person's life, don't you?"

His grin was infectious. "No, I don't. Why don't you tell me?"

"You're responsible for them forever. You saved me. Now you're stuck with me," I said, giddy with relief. "You couldn't get rid of me even if you wore a Teflon suit."

"Ollie, I would never want to."

Now that, I heard.

CHAPTER 29

The rest of the day was chaos. White House-brand chaos. In any other public venue, the afternoon's pandemonium might have continued with hundreds of people running around, screaming. Here, chaos meant ordered disarray. The Secret Service took charge with swift efficiency. They put us under immediate lockdown. Invited guests were placed in the State Dining Room. Reporters, camera people, technicians, and their staff were sent to the East Room.

We all waited, enduring the systematic scrutiny of every person present, and we knew it would be hours — if we were lucky, only hours — before life returned to normal.

Good thing we had lots of food.

The president and First Lady had been whisked to safety. Prince Sameer and Princess Hessa were airlifted to hospitals; she recovering from her allergic reaction, he in surgery after being shot in the head. Prime

Minister Jaffe had been hit, too. A bullet had grazed his shoulder, causing only a minor flesh wound, but he was being kept under medical observation as well. I'd gotten this information from the Secret Service detail that was currently guarding me. Basic information, but enough to keep me satisfied. For now.

I'd been sequestered right away. They told me it was for my protection, but I knew better. They wanted me for questioning, and they needed to ensure that no one talked to me before I spoke with them.

Kasim was dead, and for the first time since I'd smacked Naveen with the pan, I knew I was truly safe from the Chameleon. The four agents assigned to me, three men and one woman, kept me company in the China Room. Of all the places to be holed up. This is where it all began, just about ten days ago. This time, however, I faced the door. I wanted to see what I was in for when it came.

Five other chairs had been placed in the room, along with several coatracks — the China Room often doubled as a coat-check during state dinners. Thinking about our comprehensive pre-dinner preparation made me feel sad. Tonight should have been a sparkling celebration. Henry's last official hurrah. Mine, too. Instead, I sat in this room of empty chairs and lonely coatracks, trying to calm myself.

All the agents remained standing, their faces impassive, their hands clasped in front of them. Outside the room I could hear muted crowd sounds: conversation, movement, the opening and closing of doors.

Eddie, the one closest to me, asked, "Do you need anything?"

"No," I said, "thanks." My voice quivered.

I wanted to see Tom, but I knew he'd be the last person I'd be allowed talk with right now. It was imperative that our statements be taken separately, without any chance of one person's impressions contaminating the other's. I knew this.

And so I waited.

The White House filled to capacity — and then some, a reporter's dream. Five times in the space of ten minutes, eager journalists tried to sneak to the China Room and tried to talk their way into getting an exclusive interview with me. They were pointedly refused. I'd never felt so well-protected in my life. Seconds after terse orders were murmured into microphones, instant backup arrived to escort these wayward guests back to the East Room.

Eventually, three men in suits came in.

No knock, they just barged in — the suddenly open door allowing a three-second blare of corridor noise. I didn't know these men, nor did I know precisely which branch of the government they worked for. Eddie encouraged me to be as thorough and as forthcoming as possible. They took turns. They asked me about the incident, which I answered as fully as I could. Their excruciating politeness made me more uncomfortable than anything else. I was too scared to quip. I licked constantly dry lips, and spoke into a handheld digital recorder that saved every trembling answer I gave, punctuated with many nervous "ums," and "uhs." One of the three took my picture — without forewarning — but what was I going to do if they told me it was coming? Smile for the camera?

Finally finished, they thanked me and left.

"Can I go now?"

"Not yet," Eddie said.

After about a half hour the door opened again. The two agents there stepped aside. Not knowing what to expect, I stood.

Special Agent in Charge Craig Sanderson came in with Paul Vasquez right behind him. Again I felt that flood of familiarity. Last time here, I'd been chastised. What now? Termination?

I swallowed, hard.

Our honored guest, Prince Sameer of Alkumstan, had been shot in the head. I'd knocked the Chameleon's aim off from his target, the prime minister, and the resulting shot might've cost the prince his life. If he died, would I be held responsible? Had I inadvertently saved one man only to cause the death of another? The countries in question had been warring for decades. These were nations with suspicious tendencies, short tempers, and long memories. Termination of employment might be the least of my worries right now.

"Sit," Craig said to me. He gestured for Paul to take the wing chair opposite mine and he pulled up a seat for himself.

I sat.

Paul spoke first. "You're being released."

"I am?" I asked, my façade of calm ready to crack. "I'm fired?"

"No, no," Paul said quickly. "I meant released from this room. You're not being fired."

"I'm not?" The quiver in my voice shifted from one of panic to delight, "You're not firing me?"

"We're here to talk with you, Ollie," Craig said in his soft Kentucky drawl. "We need to go over precisely what you can and cannot say to the media."

He called me Ollie.

All of a sudden, I felt a whole lot better.

Craig's directives came as no real surprise. The story, as provided to the American public, would be the absolute truth. I saw the cell phone gun. I called a warning. I threw a fruit plate that changed the shot's trajectory. What I was *not* to say was that I had an indication of the Chameleon's target.

"After all, you don't know for certain that he was trying to kill the prime minister," Craig said. "Keep it simple. You saw the gun. You reacted. That's all you need to say."

"He was targeting the prime minister, wasn't he?"

Craig's eyebrows rose. He repeated, very slowly, "You saw the gun. You reacted. That's all you need to say." His stern look softened. "Wait a few days, Ollie. We'll have more we can share with you then."

"Okay. By then no one's going to remember that I had anything to do with this."

Craig frowned. "Let's hope you're right."

Suddenly remembering to ask, I said, "How is the prince? Will he survive?"

"Too soon to tell," Paul said. "I'll let you know when we find out more."

They went over a few more protocol issues with me, and I practiced answering some of the more difficult questions that might be thrown at me in the coming days. I didn't think anyone actually saw me with the fruit tray. I didn't think anyone saw me being held by Kasim when Tom took his shot. But then again, I'd been focused on survival, not my surroundings. Time would tell.

"I think that about covers everything," Paul said. He stood.

Craig stood up, too. "Is there anything you need from us, Ollie?"

I started to shake my head, then said, "As a matter of fact, there is. Remember that silver skillet that started it all?"

By the time I got back to the kitchen, Jamal and Henry had seen to the feeding of all our captive guests, and once that had been taken care of, the temporary staff had been efficiently questioned by the Secret Service and allowed to go home.

Dusk settled over the White House. As the last remaining "witnesses" were freed, the tension from the long day began to dissipate.

Cyan, Marcel, Henry, and even Bucky welcomed me back with obvious relief. Seems I wasn't the only one who thought my days here were over. After the heartfelt

413

homecoming, the five of us settled in to work, almost silently, cleaning up the final reminders of the state dinner that wasn't. I thought again how this was supposed to have been Henry's final huzzah. His last big event as executive chef. Instead of a magnificent dinner for 140 dignitaries, we'd served a hasty supper to a queue of media folks.

"I'm sorry," I said very quietly when Henry came by.

"For what?" He seemed truly perplexed.

"For . . . everything. Nothing worked out the way it was supposed to — not the dinner, not my efforts to earn the executive chef position, not" — I'd been about to blurt my complaint that I didn't even have his retirement gift in my possession, but I caught myself in time — "not anything. I'm so sorry, Henry. This was supposed to be your big moment."

"Olivia," he said, and the fact that he used my real name made me look up. "Don't you realize all you've done?"

I blinked. I wasn't sure where he was going with this.

"You prevented a man from getting killed today. Your actions thwarted the Chameleon, the *foremost assassin* in the world. Do you think this is some small matter? The finest law enforcement departments in our country and in others — the FBI, the CIA, our Secret Service, Interpol — weren't able to do what you did."

"Well," I said, feeling more than a little embarrassed by his heaping praise, "we don't know that the prince will be okay . . ."

"He will."

"How can you be sure?"

"You don't serve as executive chef for this many years without developing some good contacts. Prince Sameer is out of surgery. The bullet only skimmed his skull and he is expected to make a full recovery. His wife is fine, and the prime minister is back at his hotel."

I let out an enormous sigh of relief.

"All because of you," Henry said.

I shook my head. "It was really Tom Mac-Kenzie who —"

"Ollie." Henry's voice warned me not to argue.

This time, I didn't.

"And as far as the dinner . . . what can I say? Things happen. When your job is on the world's stage, you must be ready for anything. And so we are. How sad it would be, Ollie," he continued, "if my entire career at the White House was dependent on the success of one event." He shook his head, but his eyes sparkled. "I have so many wonderful memories, and so many successes." Glancing around the kitchen at the rest of the staff, finishing up for the night, he placed his hand on my shoulder. "And today I think I have achieved the best success of all."

I didn't expect reporters to be waiting for me at the Northeast Gate. In fact, I didn't even see them at first. They must have been lying in wait across the street at Lafayette Park, because Pennsylvania Avenue was quiet when I slipped out the front to make my way to the Metro. It was dark out, and when a voice shouted, "There she is," I didn't have a clue that they meant me.

I detected a rushing movement from my left and I was suddenly swarmed by at least a dozen microphones, pushed so close that if they'd been ice cream cones, I could've taken twelve bites.

"Ms. Paras, is it true that . . ."

I didn't hear the rest of the question. The street lit up with sudden brightness as cameras honed in on me, white-hot and too close. I blinked, looked away. But I couldn't move. They had me surrounded.

A push from my left.

"The Chameleon. How did you recognize him?"

Nudges from my right. "Is this related to the terrorist's murder by the merry-go-round?"

"Who else was in on the assassination attempt? Was the Chameleon working alone?"

I tried moving forward. They jostled me back.

"Ms. Paras, over here."

I held up a hand to block the light. In the distance I saw trucks. With Pennsylvania Avenue closed to traffic, they'd parked in the distance and come to assault me by foot. Vans and trucks with antennae and satellite dishes protruding from their roofs sat at either end of the street. It looked like an alien invasion.

"I have no comment," I said.

"Come on, Ms. Paras, play fair."

I shot that reporter an angry look. How dare he?

From behind me, a woman asked, "Are you afraid that today's incident has destroyed your chance to be appointed executive chef?"

That hurt. I opened my mouth. Closed it again.

"Ms. Paras," another voice. Male, female, I couldn't tell. Whatever it was, it was testy. "Don't you think the American people deserve to hear the truth?"

I shouted. "The truth is . . ."

They all went immediately silent.

"The truth is . . ." Now I spoke quietly, amazed at the fleeting power I held. "That I have no comment."

They erupted. Yelling, berating, pushing.

"The lady says she has no comment."

I turned.

Tom and a group of Secret Service agents surrounded the group that was surrounding me. It was an impressive sight. I counted seven agents, all male, all tall, all very imposing. They wore no-nonsense expressions and the look of predators ready to pounce. Tom directed his attention to me, "Have you anything more to say to these reporters?"

"No."

"Then," he said, addressing them, "you will all leave the area. Now."

The stalwart agents stepped back enough to allow the media folks to scurry away. And scurry they did. Though not silently. They grumbled and complained that they deserved access to me. That they had every right to be on the public thoroughfare.

I didn't care how much they protested. At this point I was thrilled to be free from their claustrophobic clutches.

Once we were alone, Tom addressed his

418

colleagues. "Thank you, gentlemen. I will see to it that Ms. Paras gets home safely." They nodded and melted away, disappearing through the White House gates like magic. Tom swung his arm toward New York Avenue. A car idled, waiting for us. He handed me into the passenger side and the driver stepped out, nodding to Tom. Tom nodded back, and the other man returned to the White House compound.

I leaned my head against the seat. "Thank you," I said.

Tom grinned at me. "Nothing but the best for our hero."

I smiled back. "You driving me home?"

"Yep."

"You coming up?"

He looked over to me and smiled. "That's the plan."

I felt wonderful again, for the first time in a very long while. "Good," I said, "but on one condition."

"What's that?"

"You are *not* sleeping on the couch."

Chapter 30

"Ollie," Henry whispered, "take a look."

He pulled me in to the old Family Dining Room, where we'd staged all the food prepared for his retirement party. "You're supposed to be in there," I said, pointing toward the State Dining Room, where about fifty people milled, waiting for the party to begin.

"I know, but this is good. You have to see it."

A television stood on a wheeled cart in the far corner. Someone had plugged the TV in. Henry had a remote control in his hand and he perched his tongue between his teeth as he fiddled with the controls. "This'll just take a minute."

"You're not supposed to see this yet," I said, grabbing for the remote.

He avoided my hands. "This isn't my farewell tape," he said.

"You know about that?"

He shot me a look.

The staff had put together a montage of images from pictures taken over the years — from Henry's first day on the job through the last week's disaster. It was a ten-minute retrospective, which we'd planned to show right after lunch. I shouldn't have been surprised to discover Henry knew about that.

"Then what is this?"

The TV's blank blue screen switched to that of an unfamiliar logo.

I started to ask again, but Henry said, "Hang on."

"They're waiting for us in there," I reminded him.

"You think they'll start without us?"

I was spared answering when the logo morphed into action. Henry pressed the fast-forward button three times and the tape whirred into super-high speed. "I should have cued this," he said. I caught a snippet of our kitchen. And people zipping around.

"Laurel Anne's audition tape?" I asked, aghast.

"Yeah," he said with such pleasure I was taken aback.

"But . . ."

"Here it is."

Henry hit "Play" and that horrible day

came back to haunt in full glory.

"I was there, remember?"

He winked at me. "Patience."

The camera zoomed in on Laurel Anne's pretty features. She smiled. "And over here," she said as she moved to stand next to Bucky whose back was to the camera, "is one of the helpers I trained during my original tenure in the White House."

Bucky twisted to look at her, his entire body tense. I winced. She'd referred to him as a "helper." Bucky was an accomplished chef. Not always the most pleasant person to be around, but a sheer genius in the kitchen. I hadn't caught this part of the filming, and I leaned forward to hear better.

"Assistant chef," he said quietly.

"Huh?" she asked.

Bucky repeated himself, barely moving his lips. "I'm an assistant chef, not a 'helper,' " he said. "And *I* helped train *you*."

Laurel Anne's smile didn't fade. She patted him on the shoulder. "Whatever."

Turning her gaze toward the camera, she said, "I'm happy to be back here today to see the fruits of my labors." Affecting surprise, she laid a hand on Bucky's arm. "No," she said with affected clarity. "Not like that. Let me show you."

Bucky stepped back, hands on hips. "Excuse me, Miss Priss, but I'm chopping your asparagus. The goddamn frozen asparagus you insisted on. We don't use *frozen* asparagus in this kitchen, or have you forgotten everything I taught you when you were here for those," he held up his fingers in quote marks, " 'two horrible years' that you always complain about?"

"Oh my God," I said. "I had no idea."

The interchange erupted into a shouting match. All perfectly recorded for posterity by Laurel Anne's camera team. As I watched, I felt a smile spread across my face — I didn't even try to tamp it down.

"Little bit more," Henry said.

I nodded. "This is where I came in."

This was "the meltdown," as I'd seen it. Laurel Anne, in a huff, had picked up Cyan's quince concoction. She held it up for the camera's benefit and began to systematically criticize the dish's preparation. As she poked fun at Cyan's work, Laurel Anne walked through the kitchen, keeping her face toward the camera, making rapid, disparaging remarks.

The kitchen is small. Too bad Laurel Anne didn't remember that.

She didn't see the stool.

Well, not until she fell over it.

The quince mixture went flying. Cyan's

423

recipe had included a fairly generous help-ing of cherry juice. Combined with the honey, the quince, and all the other multi-colored ingredients, it made for a really eye-catching mess. A mess that covered Laurel Anne's last clean apron, and — I laughed out loud — her face as well.

The star of *Cooking for the Best* bellowed as she fell. Fortunately, she wasn't hurt, but as she sat on the floor, she dissolved into tears. Not despondent tears. Tears of frustra-tion, anger, and unadulterated fury.

I remembered that moment. I'd hurried from the kitchen to get some maintenance folks to help with the mess. I also grabbed a few rags from the storage room. The honey-cherry juice combination would be a bear to clean up. The more soaking cloths we brought to the party, the better.

While I was gone, the camera rolled.

And now I watched what had happened in my absence.

"How dare you put me in this position," she screamed. I think she was addressing Carmen. "I told you I hated this stupid kitchen. I told you I hate everyone who works here. Especially that nosy-face Olivia. She left this damn chair here on purpose." Still seated in a mass of muck, Laurel Anne threw a hand out and whacked the stool. It toppled. "She did this. I can beat her any day. Any goddamn day. I did work my butt off at the California Culinary Academy. Marcel is an idiot. He thinks he's so great because he's French. Well, la-di-da. You hear me?"

She wiped at her face.

"Damn it. Shut that damn camera off."

Someone finally did.

"Oh my God," I said again, when Henry hit the power button. "Why didn't you tell me?"

He shook his head. "There's been a lot going on, Ollie."

"You can say that again." I stared at the blank screen. "What do we do if she gets the executive chef position?"

"I borrowed this tape from Paul Vasquez," Henry said. He licked his lips and put an arm around my shoulders. "Let's get to this party, shall we?"

Tom slid into the room and pulled up a chair next to mine. "How was lunch?" he asked just as the waiters brought dessert to our table. Much to Marcel's dismay, Henry had requested a simple treat: rainbow sherbet. His ultimate favorite.

"You missed a good one." I pointed up toward the dais where the screen for the montage was being taken down, in preparation for the speeches. "I'm up after the First Lady."

"You ready?"

I blew out a breath. "Hope so."

Henry sat at the head table with the First Lady, chief usher Vasquez, and a number of other department heads. I shared my table with Cyan, Bucky, Marcel, and some of our favorite waitstaffers.

Cyan tugged at Tom's sport coat. "Is there any more scoop on the shooting?"

He nodded, placing his elbows on the table. "You'll hear more on the news tonight. But . . ."

Everyone leaned forward.

"The Chameleon infiltrated the Alkumstan regime with help from the inside."

"The prince hired him?" I asked.

Tom shook his head. "The faction that supported Prince Sameer's brother hired him. That faction is still very strong. They oppose everything Sameer stands for, but they hope to eventually turn Sameer to their way of thinking. Despite the fact that Mohammed was overthrown, he issued an edict that his brother must not be harmed." Tom shrugged. "So the faction hired the Chameleon. They placed him with the delegates in an underling's position, figuring it would

426

get him close enough to kill the prime minister. We think Labeeb bin-Saleh might've been in on it, too. We're almost sure of it."

"Why did he wait till the signing ceremony? Couldn't he have assassinated the prime minister in a much less public location?"

"It was bad luck and bad timing for the Chameleon. And we had an inkling of what he was up to because of Naveen." Tom addressed an aside to the rest of the table, "Naveen is the man who was caught running across the White House North Lawn a week and a half ago." Tom turned to me. "He knew about the Chameleon's mission, but he didn't know whether the prime minister or the president was the Chameleon's target. Plus, he believed there was a conspiracy in our ranks. He thought Deputy Jack Brewster had been turned. We have since checked him out. Thoroughly. He's clean. It's too bad Naveen didn't trust us. If he had, he'd be alive today."

Jack Brewster. I'd met the assistant deputy of the Secret Service. I sighed. Maybe if I'd had my chance to talk with Naveen, I could've prevented him from being killed.

As though he read my mind, Tom said, "Naveen had good intentions, and we could've used his help. But he brought his death on himself." His mouth tugged down at the corners. "You understand, Ollie, from the time you saw the killing at the merry-go-round, your presence changed all the pre-set plans. Once Kasim — the Chameleon — realized he wouldn't have the opportunity to get near the prime minister before the negotiations began, he decided to get you first. Tactically speaking, it was the perfect strategy. You were the only person alive who could identify him."

I shivered. "Why didn't he do anything at Camp David? That would've provided Kasim plenty of opportunity to get at the prime minister. To get at me, too." Yikes. I'd been alone with the guy. More than once.

"You've seen the place," Tom said. "He'd never have gotten away. And that's what he does best. Camp David is a fortress. It was too much, even for the Chameleon." He smiled. "As were you."

Henry made his way to the dais. I rose.

"Thanks for being such a crack shot," I said to Tom, and kissed him on the tip of his nose.

"And so, Henry," I said, as I wrapped up my farewell speech with a catch in my throat, "we're here to say — in Marcel's words — au revoir. Or maybe *á demain* would be more appropriate. Till tomorrow. Because when we all come back tomorrow, you'll be here in everything we do. In every menu we design. You will *always* be here. Your soul is in the White House kitchen and you're as essential as the pots, the pans, the spices. You are what brings this kitchen to life. I know your legacy will remain part of White House history forever, just as I know you will forever remain in my heart."

The crowd cheered and clapped. Henry stood up to hug me.

When the applause subsided, I reached into the bottom shelf of the lectern. "The staff and I have a little something to give you — something we hope you'll remember us by." I pulled up the heavy yellow gift bag and watched with pleasure as he removed the sparkling silver pan from within the tissue paper. Henry ran his fingers over the lettering: TO HENRY COOLEY, FOR THE JOY YOU BROUGHT TO THE WHITE HOUSE. YOUR COUNTRY THANKS YOU. YOU WILL BE MISSED.

His eyes glistened.

I leaned forward, pointing, as I whispered in his ear. "See that little dent? Remind me. I've got a story to tell you."

I was about to return to my seat when the

First Lady asked me to remain on the small stage for just a moment. She took control of the microphone for a second time. I sidled next to Henry.

"Henry has assured me that my next bit of business would be most welcome, and that he would be delighted to have his retirement party end with an announcement about the future."

She smiled and paused.

My stomach dropped to my knees. I glanced out into the audience and stared wide-eyed at Tom. Next to me, Henry squeezed my elbow.

"Henry Cooley has been the life of the White House kitchen for five administrations. And, as he's often said, he's seen it all and he's done it all. Especially after last week." A titter of nervous laughter ran through the audience. The First Lady took a deep breath, and smiled. "Despite the fact that the White House has benefited from his experience for all these years, and despite the fact that he is retiring today, I have no intention of replacing Henry." She shook her head.

I noticed I was shaking, too. Not quite the same way.

"Today we begin anew. With recent international events happening, literally, on our doorstep, we know that we're at the dawn of a new era. Keeping that in mind, the White House is choosing to welcome a new era in the kitchen as well." She glanced at Henry. "I can never replace this man. Nor would I try. But, I can appoint a woman. It is with enormous pleasure that I announce to you today, the first female White House executive chef . . ." She turned to me and extended her hand. "Ms. Olivia Paras."

Henry wrapped me in a hug. I couldn't breathe, I couldn't move. But when he released me, I somehow managed to cross the stage and shake Mrs. Campbell's hand. "Thank you," I said.

"No one is more deserving than you."

The room, full of staffers, jumped to their feet, applauding. My eyes were on Tom, who grinned with pride and clapped harder than everyone else.

"Thank you," I said into the microphone. I sure hoped they could read lips.

As the applause continued, Henry pulled me aside. "I knew you'd get it."

"How did you know?"

"It's not every chef who can please the president's palate and also save his skin."

I touched Henry's cheek. "I'm going to miss you."

People rushed up to congratulate, tugging

me into their midst, pulling me into a massive group hug.

Henry winked, and stepped aside.

A PRESIDENTIAL MENU

One of the strangest conundrums of being a White House chef is that, perhaps because they spend so much time eating fancy food at official functions, most First Families want simple fare or comfort food when they eat in their private quarters. What the White House chefs are expected to provide for official functions often has nothing to do with the kinds of food that the president likes to eat when he's away from the public eye. A White House chef might spend weeks organizing the hautest of haute cuisine for a single state menu, while in private the president's favorite foods might be cereal for breakfast, a bowl of soup and a sandwich for lunch, and barbeque and corn on the cob for dinner.

These kinds of extremes in the menu keep the White House kitchen on its toes. In addition to the wide range of cooking, there is also the issue of getting a new slate of

"Deciders" in as primary customers every four or eight years. Each president is unique, and that includes what he likes to eat. Early in the presidency, the kitchen staff sits down with the First Family and gets copies of favorite family recipes from them, as well as lists of allergies, food likes and dislikes, and sample menus and wish lists. As time goes on, those menus are updated and refined until tuned to the liking of the primary customers.

Through the years, presidential appetites have varied widely. FDR insisted on serving hot dogs to the king and queen of England and wanted to serve chicken á la king for his inauguration luncheon only to be told that the White House chefs had no way to keep that much food hot. He settled on cold chicken salad instead. Given Washington, D.C.'s weather in January, there was no problem keeping that much food cold. Dwight D. Eisenhower liked to cook; he said he found it relaxing. His beef stew recipe was a staple for White House chefs during his administration. JFK and Jackie had a fondness for upscale Continental cuisine. President Johnson, not surprisingly, loved good Texas beefsteak. Both the Carters and the Clintons liked down-home Southern fare, though both also appreciated voyages into more stylish cuisines. President George W. Bush made simple homestyle food a staple during his White House years, while his father, the First President Bush, had more formal tastes — though, of course, no broccoli.

"Whatever the president wants": That's the ground rule for the job of White House chef. My first duty is to make the president happy. And the First Family, as well. Or, at least, their stomachs. So I listen when the commander in chief speaks about his food. What the inhabitants of the White House do with their political capital is somebody else's problem. I'm concerned with their taste buds — in public and in private.

The commander in chief I work for is a fan of simple meals, which makes my job both easier and harder. In private, he prefers peanut butter and honey sandwiches and chicken pot pies. In public, we both know it's important to fly the flag and impress the sophisticated visitors at state dinners and official functions — but he still wants to enjoy the food. So I get to design menus that work on both levels — impressing the guests, and not being too fancy for the current gourmand in chief.

Here are some representative foods I serve to the First Family in the current White

House in a typical twenty-four-hour rotation. Given the president's taste, all are simple enough for any kitchen:

BREAKFAST
Honey-Almond Scones
Virginia Ham and Spinach Omelet
Henry's Famous Hash Browns
Broiled Grapefruit

LUNCH
Peanut Butter and Banana Sandwich on
   Cinnamon Bread
Matchstick Vegetables with a Kick
Apple Tart

DINNER
Oven-Fried Chicken
Garlic Mashed Potatoes
Ollie's Green Beans
Chocolate Angel Food Cake with Fresh
   Berries

HONEY-ALMOND SCONES

Scones
1/4 cup buttermilk or plain yogurt
3/4 cup honey
2 eggs
1/4 tsp. almond extract

3 cups flour
4 tsp. baking powder
1/2 tsp. baking soda
1/2 tsp. salt
1/2 cup chilled butter
1/4 cup sugar
1/2 cup finely chopped almonds

Glaze
3 tbsp. butter, melted
1 tsp. vanilla extract
2 drops almond extract
1 tbsp. hot water
1 cup confectioner's sugar

Preheat oven to 375°F.

Grease scone pan or place parchment paper on a baking sheet, spray with cooking spray, and set aside. Add honey to buttermilk, stir, then beat in the eggs. Sift together flour, baking powder, soda, and salt. Cut in butter with a pastry cutter. Add sugar and almonds. Toss to coat.

Add the wet mixture to the flour mixture. Stir with a fork just until a ball forms. Turn out dough onto a floured board. Knead 5 to 6 times to make sure it is well mixed.

If using scone pan, spoon dough into the

pan, spreading evenly among the indentations. If using baking sheet, roll dough into a ball and flatten it some. Cut into 8 wedges. Bake for 25 minutes or until medium golden brown. Cool on a wire rack.

In a medium bowl, mix melted butter, vanilla, almond extract, and hot water. Add confectioner's sugar. Stir. If glaze is too thick to pour, add more hot water, 1 teaspoonful at a time, until the glaze has the consistency of thick syrup. Spoon the glaze over the warm scones.

I usually wait at least an hour before serving for the scones to stabilize, absorb the glaze, and develop a fine crumb texture, but the First Family likes them hot from the oven.

VIRGINIA HAM AND SPINACH OMELET

2 tbsp. extra virgin olive oil
4 ounces good Virginia ham, diced
1/2 cup raw spinach leaves, well rinsed in water combined with 2 tbsp. vinegar in it, then rinsed again, drained, and dried (the vinegar rinse should take care of the threat of bacterial contamination)
1 tbsp. minced onion
3 eggs
2 tbsp. plain yogurt

1/2 tsp. tarragon

Couple of dashes Tabasco pepper sauce or other hot sauce

1/3 cup cheese of choice (Asiago, cheddar, Swiss, Monterrey jack, pepper jack, or any mixture of these), grated

Preheat oven to 350°F.

Place 8-inch seasoned cast-iron skillet or good-quality omelet pan on stovetop over medium heat. Add 1 tbsp. of olive oil to pan. Add ham, spinach, and onion to the hot oil.

Stir until ham warms through, spinach wilts, and onion turns translucent. Remove mixture from pan and set aside. In a small mixing bowl, whisk together eggs, yogurt, tarragon, and hot sauce. Place skillet back on stove. Add remaining 1 tbsp. olive oil to skillet and spread to cover entire surface. Pour egg mixture into oiled pan. Cook until bottom is set, then flip egg mixture in pan. (If this isn't something you do regularly and you don't want to destroy your kitchen attempting it, you can also pull the cooked egg to the center of the pan, and rotate the remaining liquid egg in the pan to cover the oiled surface. Either way, the eggs are cooked through, without leaving an overcooked and tough brown layer on the bottom of the omelet.) Top the cooking eggs with the warm ham mixture. Sprinkle grated cheese over top, reduce heat to low, cover, and cook just until the cheese melts. Take off cover. Fold omelet in half.

Serve immediately on warmed plate.

HENRY'S FAMOUS HASH BROWNS
(WITH FRESH CHIVES AND FRESH THYME)

4 tbsp. extra virgin olive oil
3 potatoes, peeled and grated
6 sprigs fresh thyme, rinsed and stems removed (use 1/2 tsp. powdered if fresh is not available)
1/4 cup finely chopped fresh chives (green onions will do in a pinch)
1/3 tsp. salt, or to taste
Fresh chive stalks and thyme sprigs for garnish (optional)

Place olive oil in a large nonstick skillet over medium heat.

Mix remaining ingredients in a large bowl. Place grated potato mixture in a potato ricer and squeeze any excess water out of the potatoes. (This makes them crispy.) If you don't have a ricer, place the grated potatoes between sheets of paper towels and press to remove excess moisture.

When oil is heated to a simmer, pour potato mixture into skillet and mash it down to a thinnish pancake using a spatula. Cook until bottom layer is browned and crispy, about 4 minutes. Turn over and cook other side until browned and crispy, about 3 minutes. Place onto warmed plate or platter and serve garnished with sprigs of fresh thyme and chives tied together with a knotted chive leaf, if desired.

BROILED GRAPEFRUIT

2 ruby red Texas grapefruit
2 drops almond extract
Scant 1/4 cup brown sugar, loosely packed

Turn oven to Broil on high heat.

Cut grapefruit in half across the fruit, exposing halved sections. Place cut sides up in ovenproof pan or on baking sheet.

Mix almond extract into brown sugar. Sprinkle sugar mixture on halved grape-fruits.

Place under broiler until sugar melts and

turns bubbly, about 3 minutes. Since ovens differ greatly, watch carefully.

Serve immediately.

Cinnamon Bread

1 package yeast
1/4 cup warm water
2 cups milk (any kind will do nicely — the richness of the dough will increase as you add fat)
1/2 cup sugar
1/2 cup butter
2 tsp. salt
1 1/2 tbsp. cinnamon
6–7 cups flour
2 eggs, beaten
Cinnamon sugar to garnish (optional)

Preheat oven to 375°. Grease two standard loaf pans and set aside.

Mix the yeast and water in a medium bowl.

Gently heat the milk, sugar, and butter in a saucepan over low to medium heat until the butter melts; do not boil. Remove from heat and set aside.

Sift salt, cinnamon, and 3 cups of flour

together into a large bowl. Add the frothy yeast and milk mixtures and beaten eggs to the dry ingredients. Mix until a soft doughy ball forms. Turn dough out on floured board. Knead until dough is smooth and has the soft and rubbery texture of your earlobe. In the course of this process you may need to add up to 4 more cups of flour to get a nice, springy dough. Knead for 10 minutes.

Cover dough loosely with either a damp towel or greased plastic wrap and leave to rise for 1 hour. Punch down and then divide into two balls of dough. Form into loaves, place into loaf pans, cover, and then leave to rise about 30 minutes, or until doubled in size.

Dust the tops with the cinnamon sugar if desired and bake for 35–40 minutes. If the loaves start to brown too quickly, cover with foil for the remaining cooking time.

Excellent served buttered for breakfast, or as a base for peanut butter and jelly sandwiches.

PEANUT BUTTER AND BANANA SANDWICH ON CINNAMON BREAD

2 tbsp. peanut butter
2 tsp. honey

2 slices Cinnamon Bread (page 311),
  warmed
1 small banana, ripe, sliced into rounds
1 tsp. sunflower seeds (optional, but gives a
  nice crunch)

In a small bowl, mix together peanut butter
and honey. Spread over slices of Cinnamon
Bread. Scatter the peanut butter mixture
with banana slices and sunflower seeds, if
desired. Sandwich can be served open-
faced, or the two slices can be merged into
a traditional sandwich.

*For a lovely fall option, when apples are at
their peak, substitute thinly sliced apple for
the bananas. Honeycrisp apples are fabulous
this way.*

MATCHSTICK VEGETABLES WITH A KICK

3 tbsp. olive oil
2 cloves garlic, peeled and crushed
2 tsp. finely grated fresh ginger
1 tsp. Chinese five-spice powder
1/4 tsp. chili powder
3 large carrots, peeled and cut into matchstick strips
1 cup fresh green beans, ends removed and
  strung, sliced diagonally
3 large ribs celery, cut into matchstick strips

1/2 small head cabbage, roughly chopped as
  for slaw
1 tsp. salt, or to taste

Heat oil in a large pan.

Add garlic, ginger, five-spice powder, and
chili powder, and stir for 1–2 minutes. Add
carrots, green beans, and celery. Stir over
medium heat until vegetables are half
cooked, about 2–4 minutes. Add cabbage
and continue to toss and cook for a further
5 minutes or until all the vegetables are
tender but still crisp. Sprinkle with salt, mix
well, cover and cook for 2 minutes.

Serve immediately.

APPLE TART

1 pie crust (Marcel makes it from scratch at
  the White House, but when I make this at
  home, I cheat and buy the rolled, refriger-
  ated ones)
Roughly 2 pounds (generally about 5 or 6,
  depending on size) of tart, sweet apples;
  Granny Smith or McIntosh, generally
  about 5 or 6, depending on size
Juice of 1 lemon
1/2 cup sugar
2 tbsp. fresh lemon rind, grated

3 tbsp. unsalted sweet butter, cut into small
   pieces
1 tsp. cinnamon
1/2 cup clear apple jelly

Preheat the oven to 400°F.

Place pie crust in a 10-inch pie or tart shell
with a removable bottom and set aside.

Peel the apples and cut them into quarters.
Cut away and discard the cores. Slice thinly.
Place apple slices in a bowl, add lemon juice
and toss until the apple slices are coated
(this will keep them from browning).

Arrange the apple slices on the tart pan in a
tight pattern like fish scales, in overlapping
layers. Continue until all apples are used.
Sprinkle the apple slices with the sugar and
lemon rind. Dot with butter. Sprinkle with
cinnamon.

Place on a baking sheet in the preheated
oven and bake for 15 minutes. Reduce the
oven heat to 375°F. Bake 25 minutes longer.
Keep an eye on the tart for the last 15
minutes of baking. If necessary, cover with
foil to keep from browning too much.

While tart is finishing baking, melt the apple

jelly over low heat, stirring until liquid. Gently brush the top of the hot tart with the melted jelly.

Serve hot or cold, as preferred.

OVEN-FRIED CHICKEN

1/2 cup butter
1 cup flour
2 tbsp. garlic powder
1 tbsp. onion powder
1 tbsp. salt, or to taste
1 tsp. freshly ground pepper, or to taste
1 tbsp. fresh lemon zest, finely diced
1 roasting chicken, rinsed and cut into pieces, giblets (if any) removed (I make stock out of them, but it's perfectly acceptable to just toss them)

Preheat oven to 350°F.

Place butter in ovenproof baking dish large enough to hold chicken pieces in a single layer, or a 9 × 13 cake pan. Put in oven to melt.

Place flour, garlic powder, onion powder, salt, pepper, and lemon zest in a large, sturdy resealable plastic bag. Shake until mixed.

Remove pan with melted butter from oven.

One piece at a time, place chicken pieces into bag with flour mixture, seal, and shake until chicken is coated. Remove from bag, and roll in melted butter in pan. Place in pan, skin side up.

Continue until all pieces are coated in flour and butter, arranged in pan.

Place pan in oven. Cook until chicken is brown and crispy on top and cooked through — about 40 minutes.

Remove chicken from pan. Plate and serve.

Should you desire it, pour off most of the liquid from the baking pan, deglaze the pan, and make gravy. It's fabulous. But the president, though blessed with a good metabolism and a fondness for running, is watching his waistline, so I generally don't serve him gravy with this dish.

GARLIC MASHED POTATOES

2 lbs. peeled and diced potatoes (I like to use traditional Idaho russets, but just about any variety of potato will do)
6 tbsp. butter

1/2–1 head garlic cloves, peeled and mashed
1/2–3/4 cup milk, warmed
1 tbsp. salt, or to taste
1/2 tsp. freshly cracked pepper, or to taste
1/4 cup fresh chives, chopped, for garnish
  (optional)

Place potatoes in a large, heavy-bottomed pan. Add water sufficient to cover them. Put lid on pan and bring to a boil over medium heat, watching to be sure pan doesn't boil over. Once the water is boiling, reduce heat slightly and simmer until potatoes are fork-tender. Approximately fifteen to twenty minutes.

Drain cooked potatoes and set aside. Return empty pan to heat and add butter. When butter melts, add garlic. Cook until tender. Return cooked potatoes to pan. Mash or whip with immersion blender until nearly smooth, gradually adding warm milk until potatoes are the desired consistency. Add salt and pepper. Place in warmed serving dish, top with chives if desired. Serve.

Some people salt the water the potatoes are boiling in, which raises the temperature of the boiling water and lets the potatoes cook faster. I prefer to add salt at the last stage, when I have more control over the amount the dish

449

has — I think it leaves the potatoes more tender, too. But either method works.

OLLIE'S GREEN BEANS

2 tbsp. olive oil
3 cloves garlic, peeled and thinly sliced
1 small onion, finely diced
2 lbs. fresh green beans, rinsed and strings removed
Salt, to taste

Place oil in large, heavy skillet over medium heat.

Add garlic and onion, stirring until softened and onion turns translucent. Add green beans. Stir to coat. Continue cooking until beans are still bright green and slightly crunchy but cooked through. Salt to taste.

Serve immediately.

CHOCOLATE ANGEL FOOD CAKE WITH FRESH BERRIES

1/4 cup boiling water
2 tsp. vanilla extract
4 tbsp. Dutch processed cocoa powder
1 cup cake flour, well sifted or pulsed in a food processor
2 cups sugar

1/2 tsp. salt

12 jumbo egg whites, or egg whites equal to 2 cups (this can be accomplished with 16 large eggs, or even meringue powder, if you don't want to deal with so many leftover egg yolks — but egg yolks make fabulous puddings, a nice Lord Baltimore cake, or custard sauce, so Marcel never minds having leftovers)

2 tsp. cream of tartar

1 pint fresh berries, rinsed, drained, and chilled

Confectioner's sugar and cocoa powder, for garnish

Preheat oven to 350 degrees F.

In a medium bowl, combine boiling water, vanilla, and cocoa powder. Stir until smooth and glossy. Set aside. In another medium bowl, or in food processor bowl, whisk or pulse together cake flour, 1 cup sugar, and salt. Set aside.

In a large, clean bowl (the slightest bit of fat will keep your egg whites from whipping properly), beat the egg whites until foamy. Add cream of tartar. Continue beating until egg whites form soft peaks. Gradually add 1 cup sugar until stiff peaks form.

Remove 1 cup of egg mixture from large

bowl and fold gently into cocoa mixture.

In large bowl, take remaining egg mixture and incorporate flour mixture into it by gently sifting 1/3 cup of the flour onto surface of beaten eggs, and folding them together. Don't overwork this batter or it will lose its incorporated air. Work gently but efficiently and quickly.

Gently fold cocoa mixture into egg batter.

Spoon or pour batter into an ungreased angel food cake pan. Run a knife through the batter in a circular motion to eliminate any large air pockets. Smooth the top of the batter with a spatula.

Place in oven and bake for 45 minutes. Do not open oven door during the first 30 minutes of baking. Top of cake will crack — this is part of its charm. Cake is done when surface springs back when gently touched or toothpick inserted into middle of cake comes out clean. Remove cake from oven and invert pan.

Let cool completely (at least 2 hours) at room temperature.

Remove cake from pan by running a sharp

knife around sides and center of tube pan to release from sides, then remove cake from pan. If cake has removable tube, run knife around bottom of cake pan before removing.

Dust cake and berries with confectioner's sugar. To serve, place cake slice on individual plate dusted with cocoa powder and confectioner's sugar. Heap berries to side of cake. Dust with more confectioner's sugar. Serve.

As a special treat, here are a few more of Olivia's White House favorites.

CRISP TRIPLE CHOCOLATE CHIP COOKIES
2 cups flour
1 tsp. baking powder
1 tsp. salt
1 cup (2 sticks) unsalted butter, room temperature
1 cup brown sugar (light or dark)
3/4 cup white sugar
1 tsp. vanilla
1 egg, beaten until yellow
1 (6-oz.) package milk chocolate chips
1 (3-oz.) bar dark chocolate, diced into chunks

1 (6-oz.) package white chocolate chips
Parchment paper to cover cookie sheets

Preheat oven to 350° F.

In a medium bowl sift together dry ingredients and set aside.

In a large bowl, cream softened butter and sugars. Stir in vanilla until smooth. Stir in egg until smooth. Add dry ingredients 1 cup at a time, stirring to incorporate. Dough will be soft and uniform. Stir in chocolates.

Shape into quarter-sized balls. Place on parchment paper covered cookie sheets, in 3 widely spaced rows — this batter will spread during cooking! Bake until cookies are browned and flat, roughly 15 minutes. Cool on cookie sheets. Remove cooled cookies from parchment paper and store in a tin.

These are excellent crumbled and served over ice cream.

Cucumber Slices Stuffed with Feta and Pine Nuts

1/2 cup feta cheese, crumbled
2 tbsp. mayonnaise

3 drops Worcestershire sauce
1/4 cup toasted pine nuts, chopped
1 clove garlic, crushed and finely chopped
1/2 tsp. dried dill weed
Salt and cracked pepper to taste
3 large chilled cucumbers, sliced thinly
1/4 cup fresh parsley, chopped
Kosher salt, to taste

Combine cheese, mayo, Worcestershire sauce, pine nuts, garlic, dill, salt, and pepper. Spread 2 tablespoons of filling between two slices of cucumber. Place on platter. Repeat with remaining filling and cucumber slices. Garnish with chopped parsley and sprinkle with salt. Serve cold.

BAKLAVA STUFFED WITH ALMONDS, PECANS, AND PINE NUTS

1 package fillo dough (Even chefs buy it
   rather than making it by hand!)
1 lb. (4 sticks) butter, melted
8 ounces almonds, roughly chopped
4 ounces pecans, roughly chopped
3 ounces pine nuts, roughly chopped
3 cups sugar
1 cup water
1/4 tsp. ground cloves
1 tsp. ground cinnamon

Ground cinnamon and powdered sugar, for garnish (optional)

Preheat oven to 350° F.

Mix the chopped nuts with 1 cup of sugar. Set aside.

Remove fillo sheets from package to work surface and unfold. When not handling, keep covered by a damp paper towel or cloth dish towel. Fillo dries out and becomes unworkable fast.

Cut the sheets in half to fit a 9 × 13 baking dish. Cover the fillo with damp towel again. Working quickly using a basting brush, paint the bottom of the 9 × 13 pan with melted butter. Remove a sheet of fillo, place it on the bottom of the buttered pan, brush the fillo sheet well with melted butter. Repeat 6 times. Sprinkle with a thin layer of chopped nut mixture.

Place six more sheets of buttered fillo in the pan and top with chopped nut mixture. Repeat these layers with remaining fillo and chopped nut mixture, ending with 6 layers of buttered fillo.

With the sharpest knife possible, cut the

layers of fillo and nuts into four to six long rows. (Piece size is a personal preference.) Turn pan and slice the fillo into diamonds by cutting diagonally across the long rows.

Bake until golden brown and toasty, about 35 to 45 minutes.

Remove from oven, cool pan on a rack.

While the pan is cooling, place remaining 2 cups sugar, water, cloves, and cinnamon in a large, heavy saucepan over medium to medium-high heat. Bring to a boil. Turn heat down slightly and simmer for 20 minutes.

Pour boiling syrup gently over fillo and nuts in pan.

Cool completely. To serve, place a doily or paper cutout over a dessert plate. Dust with cinnamon. Move the pattern carefully a half inch to the right and lightly dust with powdered sugar. Remove the pattern. Serve the individual diamonds of baklava on cinnamon and sugar-dusted dessert plates.

ABOUT THE AUTHOR

An award-winning author, **Julie Hyzy** also enjoys writing short stories, many of them mysteries and science fiction. Like Ollie in *State of the Onion,* Julie was born in Chicago, but loves the history and grandeur of Washington, D.C.